1/23/00
To Matthew
Happy 22nd Birthday!
Love, Mom & Dad

EX·LIBRIS

Matthew Lemas

Leaving Pico

OTHER BOOKS BY FRANK X. GASPAR

The Holyoke
Mass for the Grace of a Happy Death
A Field Guide to the Heavens

W. D. Wetherell, *The Wisest Man in America*

Edith Wharton (Barbara A. White, ed.), *Wharton's New England: Seven Stories and Ethan Frome*

Thomas Williams, *The Hair of Harold Roux*

A NOVEL

Leaving Pico

BY

FRANK X. GASPAR

University Press of New England

Hanover and London

University Press of New England publishes books under its own imprint

and is the publisher for Brandeis University Press, Dartmouth College,

Middlebury College Press, University of New Hampshire, Tufts

University, and Wesleyan University Press.

Published by University Press of New England, Hanover, NH 03755

© 1999 by Frank X. Gaspar

Printed in the Unites States of America

5 4 3 2

This book is a work of fiction. Names, characters, places, and incidents

either are products of the author's imagination or are used fictitiously.

Library of Congress Cataloging-in-Publication Data

Leaving Pico : a novel / Frank X. Gaspar.

p.   cm. — (Hardscrabble books)

ISBN 0–87451–951–7 (cloth : alk. paper)

I. Title. II. Series.

PS 3557.A8448L43   1999

813'.54–DC21   99–19857

For Georgia and John and for the Old Ones.

We have neither the space nor need to trace, in detail, the place
of the Portuguese in the history of Provincetown.

—Mellen Hatch, *The Log of Provincetown and Truro on Cape Cod*

Saints are traditionally portrayed with halos—blazing circles
of light around or behind their heads. Even when they are not
named, they can often be identified by their symbols. Saint
Michael, for example, holds a pair of scales to weigh the souls
of men and women, and Saint Lucy carries a pair of eyes on a
handle or on a plate.

—Carole Armstrong, *Lives and Legends of the Saints*

"Come away, Hawkins," he would say; "come and have a yarn
with John. Nobody more welcome than yourself, my son.
Sit you down and hear the news."

—R. L. Stevenson, *Treasure Island*

Leaving Pico

1

In 1491 a navigator bearing our family name secretly left a small port on the island of Pico, in the Azores, and sailed east-southeast toward the coast of Africa before he turned abruptly and crossed the Atlantic Ocean, landing someplace on the central coast of what is now Florida, beating Christopher Columbus to the new world by close to a year. He then tracked north as far as the tip of our cape, that raw, hooked finger of sand that would one day become Provincetown, Massachusetts. By the time he got this far north, he understood that he had not found China, and with his head filled with mysteries and ambitious plans, he turned around and sailed back to the Azores again.

My grandfather, a thin, wiry man with a peppery beard, sat on the rotting canvas porch-swing by the back door and pulled wetly on his pipe as he traced that voyage of Francisco Joao Matta de Jesus Carvalho, Navigator, into the black dirt of the dooryard with a long sliver of shingle. It was a map he had sketched many times before, and I could have copied it myself, with my eyes closed. The Old Country—Portugal—was a quick line dashed off somewhere past his right foot, and the Azores, where my grandfather was born, were a series of dots stabbed into the ground a good distance from the coast. The New World was another straight line a few feet to the left. The track of our ancestor's voyage swelled between the islands and America like the bell of a trumpet blowing hopeful news in our general direction.

My grandfather sucked on his pipe again, considered the map, and sighed. We were killing time. He lifted the little stick and pointed it toward the house. "They'll be done soon," he said. He meant my mother and my great aunt and their friends Sheika Nunes and Ernestina the Shoemaker's Wife. My grandfather wanted to hold a clambake in the backyard to celebrate this year's blessing of our fishing fleet, our town's most important holy feast day, and the women were debating among themselves what to do about his plan.

"We'll miss the tide if they don't hurry," I said. I was moping around the yard, waiting to sneak off and go mackerel fishing with him. Mackerel were running out in the harbor, and my grandfather would need pots of them for side dishes at his clambake. My mother and my great aunt didn't like me spending a lot of time with my grandfather because John Joseph Carvalho was a notorious poacher and scavenger, a drunk with no visible means of support except for his over-the-side dory fishing, and the women feared his influence would harm me somehow. My great aunt saw me only as fragile boy-soul somewhere between first communion and confirmation, and she truly feared for my state of grace. I don't think that she understood that John Joseph was less danger to me than I was to myself or that he was liked and even respected by the men in our town. She only looked at things from her side, and she believed that her brother was spreading shame on our family.

I remember back in January of that very same year, when Petey Flores and Johnny Squash found my drunken grandfather wrapped in newspapers and rolled up in an overturned fish barrel behind the packing house on Manny Almaida's wharf. They had lifted him out of his stupor, and maybe even saved his life—there was a big storm and ice was blowing out of the sky. They got Ramao Boia to deliver them all to our door in Ramao's convertible Packard, the town's one wintertime taxi, and even I could read the affection in their gruff faces. But my aunt missed it or ignored it. "Let me tell you, Hettie," Johnny Squash told my great aunt as he sat at our kitchen table, sipping the hot black coffee that she had percolated on the kerosene stove, "John Joseph is a beautiful man."

My mother was in the back room trying to wrestle my grandfather onto his cot, and I sat at the table, wise enough to keep my mouth shut, watching the ice melt and drip from Johnny Squash's red-checkered hunting cap, which he had not removed from his head. The visor cast a shadow over his one eye, glassy and ablaze. The black patch over his other socket had been soaked through in the storm, and beneath it I could see the outline of the empty hole that led back into the darkness of his skull. A snapped hawser during an August squall had knocked Johnny Squash back against the wheelhouse of his brother-in-law's trawler, tearing his left eye from his face. "Beautiful," he said once again, shaking his head, and Petey Flores said, "Christ, Hettie, hey, we love the guy. You know what I mean?"

My Great Aunt Theophila could only see disgrace. She let them drip onto the table and finish their coffee, and then she put them out again into the storm, cursing them in Portuguese as they hunched drunkenly down the narrow walk.

Of course, John Joseph would only let me barely taste his wine and ale. He would never let get drunk or do anything disgraceful. But I knew I would have to lie and skulk to make this fishing trip with him, and I hadn't thought twice about it. I had gotten up early, before anyone could see me, and I had packed a bushel basket with our poles, lines, mackerel jigs, and all the rest of the gear we would need for a day of fishing. I had cached this load of equipment down beneath the North Atlantic Cold Storage wharf, a stone's throw beachward from our house, so that I could leave the yard and go with my grandfather without the women getting suspicious. It was already late morning, and the sun had climbed high enough to wash over the roof of our woodhouse and brighten the small, cluttered yard. My grandfather's dory, the *Caravella*, waited for us, tied to its mooring off the beach, just down the narrow street from where we sat. But the tide was going out, and I was worried that the boat would be left high and dry before we ever got down to it.

"Patience," my grandfather said, but he got up from the swing and walked over to the duckpen and whacked the wire fence with his stick. Our three ducks burst into a fit of quacking and waddled in a circle around their muddy basin of water. Across the side fence I saw our *Lisbon* neighbor Madeleine Sylvia give my grandfather a disdainful look. Her family had come over from the mainland of Portugal, speaking a higher dialect of the old language and schooled in better manners and better notions of prosperity than we Azoreans. My Great Aunt Theophila called all such people *Lisbons*, whether they came from that corrupt city or not. Madeleine Sylvia was a *Lisbon* and ran a respectable boardinghouse—even if it was in the West End of our town—and we were *Picos* and lived in a broken-down house with a shabby yard and garden, and we were her sworn enemies.

If you listened to my great aunt, we were enemies because of the ancient feud between islanders and mainlanders that went back to the old country, to the time before history books. But Madeleine Sylvia leveled real complaints at us. She said that our house and yard were an eyesore. She wanted us to mend stairs, repair fences, paint, clean up clutter, cut back the wild garden, get rid of Elvio the Shoemaker's bedspring from the roof of our house, remove our family of ducks. She claimed that we hurt her rooming-house business. My great aunt could only hiss through her teeth at Madeleine Sylvia. "We do not take orders from *Lisbons*" is what she would say.

Madeleine and my great aunt kept up the war mainly with hard looks and silences. Madeleine was built like a washbucket, with fierce dark eyes and a way of walking that always made her look as though she were marching off to battle. She scared me, but my grandfather never seemed to take her very seriously. He caught her stare and touched the brim of his hat with a little flourish. Madeleine turned abruptly and pretended to sweep something off her neatly painted steps, then took her broom and disappeared into her house, letting the door bang behind her.

My grandfather looked at our own back door.

"You want me to go in and see what's taking them so long?" I said.

"No," said my grandfather, "you might queer it. Anyway, here they come." He swung his leg from left to right, scuffing the dirt with his foot, and the map of our ancestor's voyage disappeared into the earth.

The wooden screen door swung open, chirping on its old hinges, and out walked my mother, followed by Ernestina the Shoemaker's Wife, Sheika Nunes, and my Great Aunt Theophila.

With them came the faint smell of incense and votive candles, and I knew that my great aunt had been praying for guidance to the images of the many saints that covered her bureau-top. Now she walked with the gravity of the Pope himself, ready to give John Joseph her considered answer. My great aunt's full name was Theophila de Jesus Carvalho Dunne, but she was mostly called Hettie, the American name that she had taken as part of her fierce drive to get all that she could from the New World. She had come here from the Azores with her brother, to assimilate and become respectable. For a while, she hadn't done badly. Before I had come along, she had run a fairly successful millinery shop out of the parlor of our little house. The word *milliners*, which for so long had been a mystery to me, still swept across the front window of that room in peeling gold and black decals. Sacks of buckram and veils and a dozen faceless heads were still crammed in dusty boxes out in the woodhouse, and sometimes the old woman would still build hats for her *Pico* lady friends.

My great aunt had also been active in church, a moving force in the Holy Rosary Sodality, and she had been a great fighter for the *Pico* side of things in the Portuguese-American Social Organization, a powerful if *Lisbon*-dominated civic club that conducted all important functions in our town and held whist parties on Friday nights. It was in the PASO Hall that battles raged long and hard between *Picos* and *Lisbons*, fought with wrath and passion, almost exclusively by the women. When the snooty *Lisbons* tried to relegate the *Pico* ladies to mere clean-up duties after a feast, it was my great aunt who would pound the table and spit furious old-county oaths at the likes of Madeleine Sylvia. She was strong and demanded respect. The *Picos* could cook salt fish with tomato sauce as well as anyone, and the damned *Lisbons* could wash the pots!

For a while Great Aunt Theophila seemed bound to take control of the entire organization. This was the great aunt I only knew in stories. It was about this time, late in her life, when she had married Paddy Dunne, a Protestant Yankee, but also an old retired coastguardsman with a pension, and so someone the whole town respected. She and my grandfather and Uncle Paddy and my mother all lived together in the little house. And even though John Joseph liked to drink and poach and tell wild stories with his cronies, my great aunt was still able to demand esteem for our family. Then something happened. It seemed a great mystery to me, for no one would talk about it, but the upshot of it all was that I was born. The fact that I had no father of record proved too much for my great aunt to bear. She saw this as something she could not overcome by force of will, and so, in her eyes, our fragile *Pico* family fell from grace and lost any ground it might have gained against the *Lisbons*. My great aunt was never to realize her ambitions, and she blamed my grandfather, my mother, and—indirectly—me for bringing scandal upon her.

In the end all the shame was too much for her to bear. She fell away from the Church and PASO politics, let her hat shop slowly grow back into a parlor, and brooded on her undoing. By the time I was old enough to remember her, she had already become a dour, thin, gray woman who had set her sights on a place of respect not here on earth, but in the Other World. She devoted most of her days to prayer and rituals, setting up a shrine in her and Uncle Paddy's bedroom. She had arranged her dresser with painted plaster statuettes of Saint Jude, Saint Anthony, Saint Christopher, The Sacred Heart of Jesus, Our Lady of Fatima, The Infant of Prague, and Saint Joseph. She also kept several rosaries, holy water, incense, vigil candles, and a dozen or so book-mark-sized icon cards bearing the pictures of minor saints, one of which was Joachim the Patriarch, a long, thin, dreamy-eyed man in a flowing robe, my own name saint, whom I was said to resemble.

My great aunt's obsession with prayer and the saints and the here-after infected all of us and kept our household in a perpetual spin. But it seemed to pay off for her. It was commonly held among the *Picos* along our end of Commercial Street that Hettie Carvalho had gained the favor of certain of the Blessed, and that these same saints showed themselves to her frequently in minor visions, something which greatly troubled our parish priest but drew a tight circle of devoted lady friends around her.

But now, in the bright sunlight that pressed on her long face and pursed her eyes, I could see the strain that she was under. No matter how much she prayed, my grandfather's clambakes always turned into loud, drunken calamities, and it would be hard to talk my great aunt into going along with one. Yet after what my grandfather had pulled during the festival the year before, he knew his sister would give up almost anything just to keep him close to home, even if it did mean a yard full of his pals drinking ale and generally raising hell.

Great Aunt Theophila gathered her arms about herself and stood grimly. She wore a long black, shapeless dress, and her thin gray hair had been pulled into a pug that sat crookedly on the top of her head. The sunlight seemed painful to her. It blazed on the gold of her eye-glasses as she drew herself up and spoke. "All right, John Joseph, she said, "Have your party.

"No foolishness, Papa," my mother added, over my great aunt's shoulder. "No Summer People. None of your Women." My mother stood tall, full-breasted and pretty, but her face was always creased with some unnamed burden. When she spoke now, she scowled her habitual scowl. Sheika Nunes, my great aunt's most resolute friend, stood beside my mother, shifting her huge bulk from one heavy leg to the other, and Ernestina the Shoemaker's Wife just smiled sweetly from under her flowered kerchief. My grandfather knew a show of force when he saw one. "You don't have a thing to worry about," he said.

My great aunt pointed over the side fence toward Madeleine Sylvia's house. "Don't cause more trouble with the *Lisbon*," she said.

"I'll keep it small," said my grandfather.

"And no going downtown. You stay away from the parade. From the big wharf."

My grandfather's face hardened a bit, but he agreed. He didn't have much choice. I knew he had been planning on this party for a long time.

· · ·

Our Blessing of the Fleet is a ritual that came over from the old country with the crewmen and captains of the old whaling ships and grand-
bank fishing schooners that had once sailed from our harbor. Now the
Blessing was the first feast day of summer in our town, and it signaled
the time when the summer people began to arrive from their far-away
cities to rent shacks and cottages and spare rooms along the water in
those quieter days before all the big motels were built. The summer
people were mysterious to us. They came and walked among us like
ghosts. They dressed in different clothes and spoke a different speech
from ours, from even the *Lisbons* and the Yankees. And they had money.
Of course, my great aunt was wise enough to see this, and though we
did not have a fine boardinghouse like the *Lisbon* Madeleine Sylvia, we
had our own two summer people who came each year to rent the
cramped unfinished rooms under the eaves of our roof.

Each year, on the first Sunday in June, the bishop from the arch-
diocese in New Bedford would travel all the way down to the end of
our cape to say a special prayer over the town's fishing fleet. He petitioned for the safety and prosperity of each boat. It was a time when
captains and crews hauled their boats out of the water to re-fit and repair them and to launch them once again with new paint and bright
pennants and banners. When the bishop arrived he would join the
parade from our church, be driven through the narrow streets of our
town, down to the end of the big wharf where the ocean-going diesel
trawlers would queue up and motor by and each receive its bene-
diction. The men who worked ashore hung our streets with bunting
and colored lights, and even the summer people would celebrate at
the edges of the dancing and drinking, which would last the whole
weekend.

But last summer my grandfather had come up with the disastrous
idea that he should lead the parade of big boats with his jerry-rigged
little sailing dory, and no one, not even my great aunt, could talk him
out of it. She had pleaded with him. "The whole thing is a *Lisbon* oper-
ation," she had said. "Keep your poor *Pico* boat at home. You don't
need the bishop's blessing."

"I don't want the bishop's blessing," he had told her. "I'm going to
bless *him*."

Great Aunt Theophila had demanded that our whole family go to
the wharf, as though our presence might have prevented the mis-
adventure that she had sensed in her thin bones. She had even talked

Great Uncle Paddy into coming, and he usually avoided Catholic cele-
brations.

It had been an overcast, gloomy day to start with, and I remembered how she had woken us all early, not to go the Mass, for our family had stopped attending the church, but to get a good spot at the
end of the long T-shaped main wharf, where a reviewing stand had
been built for the bishop, and where a small crowd had already gathered, sipping sodas from iced bottles and eating hot dogs from Manny
Aruela's steam cart. My great aunt had led us to the outermost edge
of the wharf, just below and to the right of the reviewing stand, and
from there we could hear the parade coming, the wet thump of the
bass drum and the drifting brass of a march from the Portuguese-
American Social Organization Band.

The low cloud-bank had begun to break apart by then, and patches
of sun lay on the broad reaches of the harbor. The air was humid and
warm, and the crowd thickened and pressed. I stepped up on a big iron
cleat and balanced myself there. We could see the parade now, the blue
banners of the Knights of Columbus wheeling in the square back at
the foot of the wharf, and then the throng of fishermen behind them,
all advancing toward us. Four of the men carried a litter with the statue
of Saint Peter, the patron of fishermen, tied atop it, and the body of
the saint was stuck all over with paper money, contributions to the
Church that would bring good fortune to each donor. The bishop followed slowly, riding in the back of Ramao Boia's Packard convertible
with the top rolled down, and at his side sat Father Santos, our parish
priest, his face pale and smiling in the midday light. Behind them we
could see the band, or at least the tall red and green hats and the nodding brass bell of Arthur Enos's Sousaphone.

The band stopped before it reached the crowded end of the wharf,
letting the bishop's car pull into the shade of the packing house, while
the musicians stood in place and played a slow, lush tune. I had been so
taken up with the procession that I had forgotten for a moment why
Great Aunt Theophila had mustered us there. But my mother called
out over the noise. "Look," she said, "there's Papa."

I turned and looked seaward. By then the big motor trawlers were
easing into positions about a half-mile out, getting ready to form a line
for the Blessing. Their decks were crowded with families and guests,
and flags and bright pennants drooped from their rigging. About three
hundred yards inboard of them, my grandfather's dory bobbed and
tacked. There had not been much wind that day, and he was already

making for the wharf, getting a head start over the bigger, faster boats. Someone rode in the dory with him, and after watching for a minute or two, I could tell by the man's movements that it was Johnny Squash. This was not a good sign, for Squash was a partner in most of my grandfather's worst adventures. They sailed slowly in the limp wind, still well inshore of the trawlers. As they drew closer, I saw Squash standing in the bow with his shirt off, singing or shouting and waving a Portuguese flag. My grandfather sat at the tiller, dressed in his black, Holy-Rosary-Sodality-Rummage-Sale, double-breasted suit. Flying awkwardly from the gaff of his sail was the pale gonfalon of Carvalho the Navigator, our family crest, composed of two caravels over a cross of swords against the black volcanic cone of Pico, something my grandfather had invented for us years earlier, and something my great aunt dismissed as complete foolishness. Great Uncle Paddy watched impassively, and my mother scowled with that strange mixture of sorrow and anger that marked her features. But my great aunt openly glared. Her olive face was blanched with rage.

The bishop and Father Santos had climbed up the platform by then, and it was clear that my grandfather was going ahead with his plan to lead the procession in his little *Pico* boat and bless the bishop. He was making slow headway, but he closed on the wharf. The bishop, in his crimson hat and aviator's sunglasses, looked around at the crowd, which had begun hooting and cheering as the *Caravella* bobbed ever closer. But the skipper of one of the big draggers saw what my grandfather was up to and decided to have some fun of his own. The trawler heeled and cut a sharp turn, bearing down on my grandfather and Squash. The people up on deck yelled and shouted, and the *Lisbon* skipper blasted his airhorns. The crowd on the wharf gave up a mixed cheer. But my grandfather knew his rules of the road—sail with right of way over motor vessel—and he held his course. The trawler finally had to come about, heeling again, heading back outside. Again angry shouts mixed with cheers, but my grandfather was now even with the end of the wharf, and my mother said, "He's really going to do it!" John Joseph leaned over the side and dipped an old paint can full of seawater. Then he stood up. The bishop looked confused for a moment, then forced a smile, raised his aspergillum, and made the blessing over the little dory. John Joseph sprinkled water back in his direction and made the sign of the cross. The bishop pushed his sunglasses up on his nose and turned to Father Santos. The priest whispered something into the bishop's ear, and the bishop turned, still holding the smile on his lips, and waved his hand quickly and sharply, motioning to John Joseph that he should move the dory out of the way.

The whole thing should have been over right there, but my grandfather ran into some bad luck. Right at that moment the small wind died completely and he and Johnny Squash were stuck, becalmed right in front of the viewing stand, holding up the entire ceremony. My great aunt swore quietly in the old language. I don't know how long they drifted there. Probably not more than a few minutes, but it seemed like forever. And it must have seemed like forever to my grandfather, too, for the many ales that he had obviously put away during that long morning of drinking with Johnny Squash placed too much of a strain on his bladder, and he was forced to relieve himself right there, over the side, while the bishop, his smile gone, stared fixedly out in the direction of our waiting fleet.

The harbormaster quickly sent a boat over to tow my grandfather away, but the damage had been done. He only made it worse later that night when he had tried to explain to Great Aunt Theophila, "I at least turned my back."

"I know how you think," she had shouted. "You were going to do that all along!" Then she became so choked on her own anger that she could no longer speak. She spat into the kitchen sink, pushed him through the back door and locked him out, retreating to her bedroom where she prayed furiously to the saints on her bureau-top. Smoke from the votive candles and incense bloomed through the house and grew so strong in the bedroom that Great Uncle Paddy, grumbling quietly, moved out to the back room and slept on John Joseph's cot, but only after he had gone out to the backyard and thrown a blanket over John Joseph, who had collapsed quietly into a fetal position on the canvas porch-swing.

Even now, a whole year later, those same troubling memories were hanging over all of us as we stood there in the yard. A breeze crept up from the water carrying with it an ocean smell, fresh brine and the taint of methane, bottom-paint, and net-tar. I could hear the fish-buckets ratcheting and creaking on the trestle at the North Atlantic Cold Storage wharf behind our house. Gulls screamed in the upper air. Finally, my great aunt lifted her hand, the color of an old coffee stain on a napkin, and she shielded her eyes. She looked off in the direction of the beach and not at my grandfather. It seemed that she would have more to say to him after this bargain that they had reached, and she looked for a moment like she was thinking of something. But she finally just shrugged, turned suddenly, and walked back into the house, and the other women followed her. My mother paused on the step just long enough to turn around and cast a gloomy look in my direction. It was almost as if she knew what kind of trouble this summer would bring for us, but of course she had no way of knowing. My mother could often gaze off into some space inside herself and then tell you the whereabouts of some lost thing that you had been searching for, but really she couldn't see the future any better than the rest of us.

2

I had misjudged the tide by a good half-hour. When we got down to the beach, the *Caravella* still floated in four or five feet of water, not far from a scattering of neatly painted rowboats and sleek outboard motorboats that belonged to summer people. My grandfather and I had to bum a ride out to her from one of the men at the Cold Storage wharf, who ran us out in his skiff. The sky was the color of man's workshirt, a rugged, scrubbed blue, with steamy towers of cumulus rising off in its southern edges. Out in the harbor small, angular mackerel gulls crashed the water's surface and fed on minnows that the bigger fish underneath were scaring upward. Closer inshore, nearly above us, fat herring gulls wheeled slowly in the lazy air. The dory dipped easily at its mooring line as we came alongside, and my grandfather grabbed her rail and held us steady while I ferried our gear over.

He put me to work right away. I bailed the dory with one of the rusted coffee cans he kept aboard, and when I had the boat nearly empty, I pulled out the sponge from the gear locker under the bow seat and soaked the floorboards dry and cleaned the gull droppings from the seats and gunwales. While I did this, my grandfather raised the sail, a grimy patchwork triangle of canvas and parachute silk that stretched between a scavenged boom and gaff. The mast was a driftwood pole stepped through the forward seat. The little boat did not have a centerboard, but John Joseph had rigged two lee-boards that dropped like knives over the sides to keep the boat from sliding when we tacked into the wind.

My grandfather had named his boat the *Caravella* because that was the name of a type of ship invented by the Portuguese in the fifteenth century. He liked to think that our great ancestor used caravellas to find America. Back in those days the design of the caravella was a crown secret. "Like new bomber or fighter plane" is how he'd say it. Only specially authorized people could board them or even get near them. "Like you and me," he'd tell me.

John Joseph would sit in the backyard and talk about the old country with Roger and Lew, the two summer boarders who came from New York City each year and rented the cheap little rooms upstairs in our house. Lew was a history teacher and Roger was an artist. Each winter they would send us a carton of books, and each summer when they arrived they brought another carton with them. The books were battered and well used, all stamped with the faint red-ink labels of the New York Public School System. We had atlases, histories, geographies, copies of *Kidnapped, Captains Courageous, Moby Dick*. On long winter nights, when John Joseph would stay home, he'd read to me and his pals from *Captain Blood* or *Treasure Island*, sometimes stopping in the book and going off into his own twists and explanations.

Lew liked to get my grandfather going about the ancestor. He'd sit with him and thumb through history books and look at maps. He was tanned almost as dark as John Joseph but his face was sharp and his eyes flashed when he spoke. Sometimes after he came back from Perreira's Market with the *New York Times*, he would share sections of the paper with me, and I would sit by him on the swing, smelling his perfumed aftershave and his deep, clean perspiration. Roger looked younger than Lew. He was slight, tall, and orange-haired. He drew sketches and painted pictures, sitting quietly behind his easel, his eyes floating behind his thick glasses like strange round fruit.

"What an idea," Lew would say, "when he baited John Joseph. "The Portuguese discovering America."

"It's not a damned *idea*," John Joseph would tell them. "It's an actual fact."

"Then we'll have to find him, my friend," Lew would say. "He'd have to show up somewhere."

They ransacked books looking for some hint of that old captain. One thing Lew agreed on was that America would never have been reached by the older, slower, top-heavy ships. But the caravels and caravellas could slice close to the wind and tack and angle. They were light and agile, getting good speed off much less sail. And they didn't need as many men to sail them, so they didn't have to carry so much weight in supplies.

My grandfather had tried to copy some of the features of a caravel on his dory, but the truth was that it was marvel that it sailed at all.

It wasn't sleek, and it wasn't fast, and we couldn't sail it very close to the wind. But it sailed. And since my grandfather had found the dory washed ashore after a storm, he liked to remind us that this rugged little boat had not cost him a cent.

My grandfather's spirits seemed to lift now that we were on the water. He calculated, "We'll keep two buckets of mackerel for the clambake, and we'll have your ma pickle them in garlic and vinegar. The rest we take up to Juney's Tap and sell them. We'll use the money for supplies." He meant for ale and whisky, but I kept quiet. It was going to be a good day. I was sneaking off, out of sight of my mother and my great aunt for a while. I was fishing with John Joseph, and I wasn't going to do or say anything to put him in a bad mood. He cleated the halyard, and I unhooked the mooring line, and we set off.

Once we were under way, he let me take the tiller and main sheet, and he settled up forward and began to rig our poles. He fastened the mackerel jigs on the light lines and then took his fillet knife and scraped their lead patinas until the jigs shone in the sun. I pointed the bow into the south wind as close as I could come, and the breeze came over the port side and bellied out the sail.

I steered the *Caravella* just to the east of the very tip of Long Point. Sailing in this direction, I could see the last hook of the cape making its final curl west, south, and then east again. I kept the point's deserted beaches on my starboard. Far to the west, where the breakwater met the point, the Wood End light and its abandoned coastguard station rose from dark tangles of poison ivy and beachgrass. It was a good landmark to keep on my quarter, as we headed for the open channel.

As we tracked farther out into the harbor, the wind freshened a bit, and despite the leeboards, the dory began to slide toward one of the harbor's weirs—a sprawling fish trap. The trap's trail of long poles rose like bones from the water, and the broad nets, which formed the two huge chambers called the heart and the bowl, dripped black and wet. I knew this trap. It belonged to Captain Raul Mendes, a *Pico*, one of the regulars at my grandfather's backyard gatherings. The trap worked by leading schools of fish into the first chamber along a straight length of net. Once in the heart, the fish schooled easily through a passage into the trap's bowl, where they stayed, too confounded to find the passages out again. Captain Raul and his crewman Squid Dutra would then motor out in the *Tarquedo*, Raul's trapboat. This was a long, low narrow boat with no masts, and it could float right through a door in the trap, where Raul and Squid would haul the fish aboard. Over the years

Captain Raul had taken boatloads of tuna, herring, and mackerel out of that trap, but he also told us about other things that he found there —pieces of wrecked boats, sharks, arctic seals, cases of goods lost overboard by ocean-going ships, and even two human corpses, ravaged by fish and sea. The trap made me uneasy, and I was probably holding too close to it, for I knew that sometimes small sailboats blew against a trap and caught their rigging in the nets. I might have passed too near the guy lines if John Joseph hadn't suddenly looked up from the tackle on his lap and told me with a quick nod of his head to fall off a few points and slide by the weir.

Once in open water we straightened and beat our way out toward the channel off the tip of Long Point where we could drift in the deep and fish for mackerel. The fish were running in broad, heavy schools, and you could see them darken the water as they came and went, circled and disappeared and came back again. Minnows would frenzy on the top of the water as the feeding schools would pass below us. These were small mackerel, called bullseyes, sleek and strong and perfect for baking in the *moule vina d'ahlos* that John Joseph intended to have my mother make. It's what they would become up at Juney's Tap, too, Juney Costa selling the pickled fish with beer at a dollar a plate. The sea boiled with mackerel. We caught them on our jigs, hand over fist. The jig would snag one through the gills or mouth or eye, and the pole would shiver as the line paid out of the bail, and the fish would zigzag and dive. You couldn't let them play out. They were too strong, so you horsed them in, twisted the hook out, and cast again. We jigged and drifted, not even stopping to drink from the jug of tea that we dragged behind us cooling on a line in the water—-not even eating the sardine sandwiches that I had secretly made that early morning in the dark kitchen.

We filled buckets, each off in our own thoughts, not speaking. I could never guess what might be in my grandfather's mind, but I thought he must at least feel something like the happiness that I felt, a feeling of distance from our bent little world where I was known as only as Rosa's boy because I had no father. Out here what people thought of us didn't matter, and my mother's and my great aunt's sorrows only sat at our feet instead of on our shoulders.

We must have fished like this for a long time before I heard my grandfather swear. I had a silver-and-blue mackerel in my hand, holding it behind the gills as it shimmied in the air and I tried to work the jig loose from under its lip. But as soon as I looked up at John Joseph and saw the sky behind him, I knew why he'd cursed at it. I had been aware of the change in the humidity, and I had sensed the sun ducking in and out of the clouds, but I had been in too much of a trance to pay real attention. The fluffy cumulus that we'd set sail under had become vast, black thunderheads, and now they passed over the sun and swallowed the sky. We were going to catch a squall.

Even while we watched, the sky darkened more, and the air grew still and wet. It was coming fast. John Joseph looked over the side. We had already drifted too far in deep water to reach bottom with our danforth anchor and ride the storm that way. We had blown a good way outside of Long Point and now looked in on its back side. That was our nearest land, and we started to make for it, but the wind suddenly quickened as we sailed, coming right over our beam and leaning us over. Lightning flashed in long chains over the distant shore. The outline of our town, as it curved and hunkered along the shore of the harbor, seemed unreal and dreamlike. Cottages and houses stood out like clumps of paint on a canvas. The spires of the two big Protestant churches and the Town Hall steeple and the granite tower of the Pilgrims' Monument shivered in a lightning flash and then all receded into the dark curves of the coming rain. We both counted until the thunder boomed. "Maybe two miles away," said my grandfather. The wind had come around and was driving us to the south, and in the distance more smudges of rain trailed in dark arches from sky to earth. "Get the sail down," my grandfather yelled, "we're going to get knocked over." He crawled up to the bow and began working on the anchor line. I loosened the halyard and brought down the sail.

"Quick now, empty the basket and those buckets," he told me.

"Over the side, *Avo?*"

He looked at me for a moment, considering. "No, just dump them in the boat."

I emptied the fish onto the floorboards of the *Caravella*, and my grandfather ran the anchor line over his lap, tying three eyes into it, each a few feet back from the danforth anchor. A blotch of rain the size of a nickel grazed my cheek, and the wind whipped back and forth, gusting from several directions now. Thunder cracked again. John Joseph began tying the buckets to the eyes in the line, making a sea anchor to give us some drag and keep our bow pointed into the weather.

I finished securing the boom and gaff just as a jagged sheet of lightning rattled the sky and a wall of rain blew over us. My grandfather slid the array of buckets over the side and paid out the anchor line. Rainwater and spray already sloshed around our ankles, and the mackerel that I had dumped floated belly up and rolled from one side of the *Caravella* to the other as the windswells began to mount and toss us. John Joseph and I furled the sail as best we could, and together we tied the stays around it. It was just in time.

A sea hit us broadside and my grandfather stumbled as the weather gunwale jerked upward, and he saved himself from being vaulted over the side only by going down on his knees. He stayed down. "Get low," he shouted. "Put your weight right on the bottom."

I sat on the floorboards, awash in the three inches of water we now shipped. I knew we couldn't go on like this. We weren't in good shape for this squall. The sea anchor hadn't started dragging yet, and we were still taking waves on our beam. We could capsize easily. I looked at John Joseph for a clue as to what we would do next. He was soaked, sitting in bilge, surrounded by dead mackerel. A wave pitched us again and then another broke over us, knocking his hat off, plastering his hair down on his head. But his expression never changed. He might as well have been sitting in our backyard with a can of ale in his hand. He did grab a can now, one of the old coffee cans, and he started bailing, sliding down on his back and throwing water over the lee side, backhanded. I grabbed another can and began doing the same. Our heads were below the gunwales and we did not watch the sea. We lay there, staring up into the dark rain, heaving and pitching, taking on water from the storm and throwing it back out again in our little canfuls, while scales, blood, and dead fish washed over us.

I don't know how long we slid and tossed in those swells, but for all its violence, the squall couldn't have lasted more than a half-hour. All during the storm, I kept down, as my grandfather did, hanging on and bailing. But my grandfather's face continued to show nothing, except maybe aggravation at being wet. There was no telling what went on inside him. I don't know what I must have looked like, but inside myself I was praying. The women had taught me how to pray. I was praying to Saint Peter, patron of fishermen, to Saint Jude, patron of miracles, and to Saint Christopher, patron of travelers. All the while I prayed, I bailed.

And then I could feel the air changing, the wind softening. I could tell the squall was moving off. We lay there a while longer, and the rain tapered and then stopped altogether, and that odd fresh smell that follows these summer squalls settled over us. The sea anchor had worked, keeping us from breaching and capsizing, and our frantic bailing had kept us from swamping. The sea began to flatten. We stood up.

The harbor looked like a broad pool of oil now. The chop was gone from its surface, and the water heaved slowly, like the chest of a sleeper. It was like I was seeing it for the first time in my life. The yellow land of Long Point stood up for me, looming large, magnified by the clearing air. And the harbor inside glowed with a strange, flat light. Some boats moved inside, back toward land, but mostly there was a sense of stillness over everything. The water moved now with such little force that the boats in the distance didn't appear to float on it at all, but looked as though they had risen through it, like the tops of buildings in air. I felt giddy. I started to laugh. My grandfather shot me a warning look. His clothes were plastered to his body. Fish scales and grime stuck all over him. "I'm not laughing at you, *Avo*," I said.

"I know it." He spit into the ocean. "We beat that storm, and now you feel like there's nothing can touch you."

"That's it," I said. "I feel like I could do anything." I didn't dare say a word about praying.

"Well," said my grandfather, "there's plenty dead sailors felt just like you do."

I didn't answer.

"Look," he said. "The boat's a mess. And see how far we blew? We've got a lot of work here, Carvalho."

So we hauled in the sea anchor and gathered our fish back into the buckets, and we sponged and cleaned and hoisted our sail up again. But through all the work, I thought I might shake right out of my body. I thought my skin might not be able to hold me in anymore.

It took us a couple of hours to get in and cart all our fish up to the yard. As soon as we came up the walk, soaked, loaded down with gear, my mother burst through the screen door. "Where in the hell have you two been!" Her face was swollen and wet from crying.

"Rosa," said John Joseph, "Rosa, calm down." He set some of his gear on the woodhouse steps and caught my eye. His look told me to keep my mouth shut.

"How was I supposed to know the both of you weren't dead out there in that storm?" my mother yelled. "How was I supposed to know?"

"Rosa," my grandfather said, "do you think I'd take the boy out in a storm? We were back on the beach by the time that squall came up."

"You're a liar." My mother arched toward him. "I stood in the rain on that seawall looking for you two. You were not on the beach. What was I supposed to think? Damn it, you go off like that . . ."

"That will do," my grandfather said.

"Damn you, Papa."

"Rosa, we were on the beach down to the East End. That's why you couldn't see us."

My mother wiped her tears with the back of her hand. "Well, how was I supposed to know?" She knew that he was lying, but I could see that she was satisfied wringing the lie out of him. She looked at me, but I looked away, busying myself with the fish buckets, which I moved over to the water spigot, where we would set up a plank over some barrels to scale and gut the mackerel. It seemed like we were going to skate through this one, but then Great Aunt Theophila appeared in the screen door. She eyed us for a moment, and then cursed in Portuguese. My mother took this to be aimed at herself. She spun around and said, "Don't you start on me again."

"You went out and got him," said my great aunt, "and now half the time you don't even know where he is or what he's doing!"

"Will the two of you shut up?" said John Joseph.

"And you," said my great aunt, "you corrupt the boy."

"That's it," said my mother. "Start in on everybody."

"Stop it," said my grandfather.

"Tell *her*," said my mother.

"You are a disgrace," my great aunt hissed.

"That's enough," my grandfather said through his teeth, and he threw his fillet knife against the side of the house. The long blade buried itself in a mossy shingle, and the haft shivered. My mother sucked in a breath, and my great aunt swallowed and crossed herself. My grandfather was silent and watched the knife as if in surprise. He hadn't meant it to stick like that. I knew there was some story about trouble with my grandfather and a knife, but I also knew he wouldn't use that to bully my great aunt or my mother.

No one moved for a second, and then Great Aunt Theophila said, "*Joao Jose*, calm yourself." She spoke quietly and evenly. "Clean your fish and be done with it." She folded her arms on her chest and withdrew into the shadows of the house. I could see the different emotions crossing my mother's face—anger, fear, despair, and then finally defiance. She turned and went inside, and I knew that she would put on lipstick now and smoke Chesterfields at the kitchen table to taunt my great aunt, the way she always did after these fights. At that moment I wanted to think that I considered only her, *her* unhappiness. I was still light-headed from the storm, but now everything became lucid for me. We had been caught in that squall and we did not drown. Maybe that had something to do with it. My head was working so fast that even I couldn't find the connections between my own ideas. But I know it was right then that it came to me to petition the saints for someone to come and marry my mother and become my father and in that way put all the woes of our family to rest.

3

The women taught me how to pray. Religion soaked the house just like the smells of soups and bread dough that hung along the walls. You breathed it. You couldn't escape it. It couldn't have been any other way. Great Aunt Theophila had appointed herself my godmother. In the old church, this meant she was responsible for the state of my soul. She would make me spend hours with her in the bedroom learning the rosary with all its Holy Mysteries, the Stations of the Cross, the various Acts of Faith, Hope, Love, and Contrition, along with the number of years of indulgence—years off from purgatory— you were granted for each recital (three, three, and three). We practiced the Apostle's Creed (five years), the Approved Litanies (an indulgence of seven years, with a plenary indulgence once a month under usual conditions), the Confiteor, the six precepts of the Church, the Holy Days of Obligation, and the fixed and moveable feasts. I learned how to light candles, burn incense, direct certain special prayers and offerings to the Virgin or to the Baby Jesus or to specific saints. My great aunt was the master of prayer. When she had taught me the various prayers in English, we went at them again in Latin. At night the parallel versions of these prayers would roar in my head, but I learned everything. I even learned the lives of the saints and the horrors suffered by the holy martyrs, which gave me bad dreams for a while, but later on became a great source of entertainment for Father Santos.

What my great aunt did not teach me, Sheika Nunes did. I remember once, when I was just small, Sheika Nunes told me that I could have anything I wanted if I prayed for it in the right way. "Try it some time, nice boy," she said, "and see if it doesn't work." She had just finished drilling me on my lessons. She closed the battered blue *Baltimore Catechism* and hoisted herself out of the morris chair in our parlor. "I'll see you tomorrow," she said, and with the speed of a garter snake, she aimed a pinch at my private parts.

Those were the days when I first started praying for things in earnest, and right away I saw a problem. There was no way to tell if anyone heard me. I asked for some mackerel jigs and got them three days later from my grandfather, who showed up with a whole can of them. "Didn't cost me a cent, either," he said. No one asked where he got them. The next thing I asked for was a skiff with an outboard motor, which I wanted to give to my grandfather. It never materialized, but John Joseph did bring home a fine new set of oars right about at that time. I kept praying for things, and sometimes they came and sometimes they didn't. And sometimes things came close, but inexact. This led me to the sin of doubt, for the process of petitioning seemed random and whimsical. Sheika Nunes had something to say about this.

"The saints have better ideas than you do. You can't pester them about foolish things. They have better judgment than to just give you what you want. They only give you what you need. They know."

"Then what's the point of asking for anything at all? Wouldn't they just give you what you need automatically? Because they're good?"

Sheika heaved a sigh at my stupidity and had me say some Hail Mary's. It was how she often ended our talks.

I kept petitioning. It was like talking to heaven on a bad telephone line. I prayed for new shingles for the roof, which had begun to leak that winter, and my grandfather came home with a heavy roll of tarpaper on his shoulder—a roll that looked just like one of the rolls I had seen stacked up against Mister Van Horten's Bluefish Inn just a few days before. It could be that my name saint was just playing games with me. I had wanted a dog. An old outhouse still stood in the south corner of the yard, next to the woodhouse. It would be simple to pull out some of the scrap lumber from under the woodhouse steps and put up a small fence around the outhouse, making it a doghouse. I pictured a big dog, black and heavy, that I would walk on the beach in winter and take to the woods with me in the summer, when he could chase rabbits and squirrels. So I petitioned just like my great aunt and Sheika Nunes showed me, burning incense and candles. Within a week or two my grandfather brought home not a dog but three yellow ducklings that he got from Elvio the Shoemaker's barn up on the hill. He and Uncle Paddy put up the fence around the outhouse just as I had pictured it, and by the time my mother and I finished whitewashing the slats, I had gotten over most of my disappointment.

My grandfather named all three ducklings Dilly, which made my great aunt mutter sullenly in the old speech, but it took care of telling them apart. They grew into identically large, white noisy ducks, and they waddled around their little yard gobbling up spiders and pillbugs. Eventually two of the ducks started laying huge, brown-shelled eggs that carried a strong, pungent taste and reminded me of the smell of the beach at low tide.

Three ducks, of course, did not equal a dog. In the matter of petitioning saints this was troublesome. It didn't seem much different than my grandfather's stories about our ancestor. Both were mysteries. There was no way to tell what was real and what was not. I asked Sheika Nunes about this a few more times, but she would only tell me that I was foolish. "When you ask for something so important that your soul would perish without it, you'll get it," is what she told me. "Your Aunt Hettie knows. The saints come and show themselves to her." I couldn't argue with that.

When I awoke the next morning, John Joseph's cot was empty and a bushel basket of quahogs—the hard-shell clams he loved—sat in the back room sink. Clams were out of season. Small posters on pilings and poles along the waterfront warned that it was illegal to take shellfish in summer, but that only meant that my grandfather had to go out late at night and poach them under the moon. He usually sold his clams to Juney Costa or to the one or two other restaurants in town that had the sense to buy from him at his special prices. But this bushel of quahogs would be ours for the clambake tonight, along with the mackerel and whatever else would turn up.

I saw Uncle Paddy sitting in the swing out in the yard, and my mother and great aunt were off somewhere. I slipped into bedroom and stood at the bureau-top shrine. The plaster saints all seemed to stare at me accusingly. Did they know I was going to petition with serious doubt in my heart? Could they sense my challenge to them to prove themselves to me?

I turned to the icon card of my name saint. I don't think a lot of people petitioned Saint Joachim the Patriarch because, unlike the little icon cards of the other saints, the reverse side of the picture of Saint Joachim showed no special prayer for anyone to recite. There was just the description of who he was and the date of his feast day. But I knew where to turn in my great aunt's worn black missal to find the prayers to the Mass of Saint Joachim, and I did this, beginning with, "O God, who of all Thy saints didst will Blessed Joachim to be father to the Mother of thy Son." It seemed hard to miss.

Yes, maybe Sheika Nunes was right, and maybe proper petitioning could bring about whatever you desired if it was in keeping with a plan for your salvation. And our good priest Father Santos had also told us about prayer being able to move the world. Since we no longer went to church, Father Santos would come to our house, usually after one of my great aunt's visions. He would talk to her about them and ask her questions. His face was heart-shaped and soft, and his eyes were set deeply beneath dark, heavy brows. His skin would have been as tanned as a fisherman's if he had worked out of doors on the water, but his natural color seemed to have faded to a Hostly white from lack of sun and weather. He never gave me quite the same kind of instructions about prayer as my great aunt and Sheika Nunes did, but whenever he visited us, he would keep up a running quiz on the deaths of the Holy Martyrs, which he knew Sheika and my aunt had taught me. So whenever I answered the door and let him in, he would greet me with something like, "Quick, Josie, Saint Jeremy!" and I would say, "Beheaded!"

"Aha, and Juliana?"

"Beheaded!"

"Just beheaded?"

"Tortured and beheaded."

"Exactly, nice boy, exactly. And is your Aunt Hettie in the parlor?"

"Yes, please come in."

"Thank you. And Saint Victor? What about Saint Victor?"

"Basted in hot lead."

"Wonderful, wonderful."

And he would go in and sit with my great aunt, and sometimes Sheika Nunes would join them. Father Santos would talk politely and warn her in a gentle way that apparitions of saints could be the products of deceit. He would talk, say a Rosary, and try to coax her into coming back to church. Then he would tell us all to pray for guidance and clarity. I don't know what he would have said if he knew about my petitions now. I had seen him glance once or twice into the doorway of my great aunt's room and I could tell that he did not like the bureau-top shrine. Real altars were in church. They had bones of the saints hidden in them. This bureau was just a bureau in his eyes.

But that's where I sent up my petitions, along with sweet curls of sandalwood incense smoke. I didn't pray for clarity or guidance, though. I prayed for something real.

I was just finishing when I heard the old car chug up to the yard. I dumped what was left of the burning incense cone into the toilet, replaced my great aunt's mermaid-shaped ashtray on the bureau, and ran out along the walk to help unload the car.

The car belonged to Uncle Paddy, and we all called it the *Pulga*, a name my great aunt had given it because it could creep like a sandflea across the beach if Uncle Paddy let some air out of the big balloon tires. It was an old Model A Ford hardtop, which John Joseph and Uncle Paddy had brushed a flat blue-gray with deck enamel. The trunk of this car had been replaced with the aft five feet of a small skiff that had gone to pieces against the western breakwater in one of our fall hurricanes. So the stern of this little boat stuck out of the rear of the *Pulga* like a truck bed, and I had seen from the bedroom window that it was now full of boxes and bags of groceries.

My mother killed the engine just as I came up to them. The *Pulga* coughed and sputtered and continued to turn over in small spasms until it shuddered and fell silent. My mother and great aunt stepped down from the running boards in tight-lipped détente, and I unloaded what they had brought home for the clambake—sacks of fresh early corn, long loaves of hard-crusted bread from Leona Taves's Portuguese Bakery, and red coils of linguica, the sausage that John Joseph would use to spice everything. Already my mother had pickled and baked the mackerel, and now John Joseph would steam his bushel of clams in a huge pot on the kerosene stove. He and his pals would show up soon with the ale and spirits.

I also knew that my great aunt was up to something when Sheika Nunes showed up a little while later with Fanny Neves, Liliana Mendes, and Ernestina the Shoemaker's Wife. These *Pico* ladies from our neighborhood settled in the parlor, and I could see that they intended to stay for the feast, a sort of private police force, a presence of moderation.

Petey Flores and Johnny Squash were the first men to show up. They both had been drinking already, and they came fumbling through the back door carrying cases of ale and yelling for my grandfather. But when they saw the *Pico* ladies sitting sternly in the parlor, they slunk back outside and left the ale in a galvanized tub underneath the side steps. Squash told me to stand guard over it while they went over to the Cold Storage to bum some ice from Joe Dias, the man in charge of the freezers. I don't know what they thought I would be able to do if any of the women decided to get rid of the ale. And now Magdelena Reis and Lila Roderigues came up the walk, two pillars of the church. They joined the women inside, and I stayed at my post by the ale until my grandfather showed up. Right behind him came Squash and Flores, dragging a big fishbox full of ice. Uncle Paddy slipped out into the yard and opened the first of the ale. It was only about mid-afternoon, but when Uncle Paddy sat on the swing and took a long chug from the golden can, I knew the party had started.

John Joseph quickly surveyed the women in the parlor, then came back out and regarded the men in the yard, as if he were some general measuring troops before a battle and clicking off the odds. He took an ale out of the tub, spit over the fence into Madeleine Sylvia's yard, and went into the back room to start cooking.

When John Joseph cooked for one of his clambakes, he moved about trance-like—quiet, slow, making flourishes with bottles, cans, utensils. He worked for a while in the back room and kitchen, calling on me from time to time to help with filling a pot or with shucking clams, and once he got all the pots boiling and the oven up, he went out to the yard to move among his friends. More men had come by this time—Skinny Henrique and the Avila boys from the boatyard, and Squid Dutra from Captain Raul's trapboat. There was more ale in the big tub now, and empty cans were beginning to pile up in cardboard cases. Captain Raul himself came up the walk after a while, another case of ale under one of this thick arms and a heavy burlap sack over his shoulder. His sunburnt face glowed with importance and good cheer. He greeted the men and called my grandfather over. "John Joseph, Pard, can you do something with these?" He put the burlap sack down on the sidewalk and produced eight hefty lobsters, their claws neatly pegged, bubbles of water at their clicking mouths.

"Go across the street," my grandfather said to me. "Old Man Coelho's big pot. And *invite* him first!"

When I had come back with the big iron pot, Johnny Squash drew me aside and pulled some things out of a bag. His face glistened, and his eye patch was beginning to stain with sweat around its edges. "I found these in the drag, Josie. See what you can do with them." He handed me a long, heavy-bladed knife, not too rusty, with what looked like a bone handle that had been mostly splintered away. "Feel the weight of that."

It felt like a hammer in my hand.

"Got a bad smell to it, though," he said. "Maybe you better soak it in kerosene." The knife did smell like a dead fish or crab that had lain for a long time on the beach.

The other object he pulled from the bag was a heavy ball, the size of a grapefruit, smooth and brown, with light, shell-colored marbling in its surface. "A cannonball?" I said, hefting it.

"Well if it is, I never seen one like that before."

"It's an old candle-pin ball, for Christ sakes." Captain Raul put in, coming over to where we stooped on the walk.

"Maybe," said Johnny Squash, "but look at this." He took the ball from me, stood up, and dropped it on the sidewalk. It bounced like a tennis ball. "What do you think?"

"I don't know," I said.

"Cannon shot," my grandfather said from where he stood near the duckpen. "Stone. Portuguese."

Johnny Squash looked over at him and grunted. Then he said to me, "Here, Josie, Pard, put this stuff away. Especially that knife. That's all I need, Rosa and Hettie giving me hell."

As I gathered up these new pieces of salvage, the women began filing out of the house and setting up chairs around the dooryard, and when I returned from storing my things in the woodhouse, my great aunt was already seated among her her friends. The women looked like a small odd choir watching the rest of the yard, waiting for a signal or cue of some kind.

My grandfather kept his distance from the women, but Johnny Squash scooped up an armful of iced ale cans and walked among them, offering them around. My aunt gave him a withering look, but Squash was well numbed and her stare did nothing. Sheika Nunes took a can, saying "Good for what ails you," and Fanny Neves accepted one also. I could tell my great aunt thought this was treason on their part, but she said nothing. My mother took a can of ale, too, and this caused my aunt to give a short quick oath in Portuguese, but my mother simply looked squarely back at her as Johnny Squash popped the can with his steel opener.

More people arrived. Roger and Lew came quietly down the side steps from their rooms and stood by themselves near the duckpen until my grandfather went over and gave them each an ale. Old Man Coelho finally showed up, too, leaning on his twisted cane, wool cap pulled over his wrinkled forehead. He settled in a chair by the ice-tub and rubbed his old face, a face that had colored and settled with age until it now looked like some kind of root-cellar vegetable. He was the oldest *Pico* in town.

The party swelled. Joe Dias came up the walk, dressed as always in his navy watch cap and army-airforce bomber jacket, despite the season. Joe worked in the freezers all day long and said he never ever got warm, not even in summer. Joe brought a stranger with him, a swarthy, square-shouldered man with a head of rough curls and narrow, sharp eyes. He was wearing a shiny silk jacket with dragons embroidered on the sleeves, the kind men brought back from places they went to during the war.

Then behind them came two women. They were not townspeople, but summer people, wearing long flowery dresses and big, wide-brimmed straw hats. A ripple of distress passed through the *Pico* ladies sitting by the door. I watched my great aunt calculate their arrival. Yes, they were friends of John Joseph, some of those people from away that he invariably ran off with every summer, those women who sat along the wharves and painted bright senseless pictures of the fishing boats —painted pictures of John Joseph, even, in that poor hat of his and with his unshaven face. These were the people from the Other World, and without John Joseph we would never have had any contact with them. Even our own boarders disappeared down into the town each night, off to their bars and their vices, as Sheika Nunes would say. The two worlds of townspeople and summer people existed side by side, like parallel universes, but no one traveled between them except for my grandfather. It marked him somehow. My great aunt saw it as further proof of his ruin. She knew that there was a good chance he would disappear with one of these women. I could read the look in her eyes.

My grandfather walked over and greeted the summer women and then led them fearlessly over to Great Aunt Theophila. "Hettie," he said, "I would like to present my friends Cynthia and Amalia."

Cynthia was tall and heavy, big boned. She wore thick glasses framed in heavy brown horn, and her long hair, the color of my grandfather's, swept back from her plain face and swung down between her shoulderblades in a rope-thick braid. She smiled and said hello. Her friend was shorter, thinner, not quite as gray, her curly hair cropped close to her head, her eyes a blaze of fierce intensity. She carried an umbrella and wore a woven bag slung across her body, and she had decked her hat with clumps of lilac and sweet peas, which shook and nodded when she cocked her head or talked. These blossoms filled the air around her with a saccharine perfume. "I've never been to a religious feast before," she told my great aunt, offering her hand. "Actually, I'm a Bolshevik." My aunt did not shake her hand, and Sheika Nunes shifted her great bulk in her chair and coughed into her lace-trimmed handkerchief.

John Joseph maneuvered his friends away from the *Pico* ladies and over by the ice-tub, where they greeted Captain Raul who gave them each a can of ale. "So you're that wonderful sea captain we've heard so much about," Cynthia said, while Amalia bent gracefully at her knees and slipped three or four cans of ale into her woven bag. I heard Fanny Neves mumble, "*Velha me Deus!*" and I knew that the women expected trouble.

The Eve of the Blessing was being celebrated all over town, and more people kept showing up at our yard, drifting in from the end of one celebration or another. Even Domingo the Beach Cleaner showed up, leaning his pitchfork and shovel against the woodhouse and silently watching everybody. John Joseph and I brought out the lobsters and clams and fish and bread and corn. Their smells spread a lushness in the air, and the women softened and talked and laughed as we all ate. Everyone celebrated my grandfather's cooking, and cartons of ale were now stacked along the duckpen fence. Sometime after the clatter and slosh of eating had subsided, Jaime Costa, Juney's younger brother, pulled his guitar out of its battered case, and in his ragged voice began singing *fados*, those sad, old-country songs of fate. John Joseph was becoming more drunk, and he began entertaining his lady friends from away with stories and pronouncements, and I watched my aunt and my mother shoot worried looks his way, for it was becoming almost certain now that he would go off with one of them before the night was out.

But there were other currents playing through the yard that night, and I might have missed the most important one if it hadn't been for Johnny Squash's strange gifts. I had roamed the yard listening here and there to the men talk as they complained about how the fishing had fallen off from years before and how the town was going to hell with the summer people, and I talked also with Roger and Lew before they politely excused themselves and headed off down the front street at some moderate hour. I had also avoided being caught by my great aunt or my mother or Sheika Nunes and being dragged into that circle of women. I decided to slip out of sight into the woodhouse and have another look at the ball and the knife that had come up out of the drag today, thinking that I might go ahead and take Johnny Squash's suggestion and set the knife to soak in kerosene. I made my way through the people and around the small outer fence and passed quickly into the heavy darkness inside the open woodhouse door.

According to my grandfather, our woodhouse, a small, mossy-shingled two-story outbuilding that crowded the walk opposite the side of our house, had stood completely across the harbor on Long Point at one time. It had been a slightly larger building with only one story then, and it had broken in half while being rafted across the water from the old town that had flourished for a while on that far digit of sand and beachgrass. John Joseph and I had beached the *Caravella* out there many times, and he walked me over its bars and beaches and hills showing me the remnants of that settlement, rows of stones from an old marine railway or shadows of rust from evaporation tanks where salt was taken from Atlantic seawater to preserve the old schooner-loads of flayed codfish. Sometimes we would wind our way between patches of poison ivy to pools where the ocean water leached up through the sand, leaving enough of its salt behind so that we could kneel and drink from our cupped hands. It was hard to grasp that this had been our town once, where gulls now screeched and dived to keep us away from their egg-filled nests in the low beachgrass, and where field mice skittered in the sunshadows at our feet.

On some days, John Joseph brought tins of sardines or tuna for lunch, and we would strip and swim, and then spend the day leaning against the breast of a small hill where he alternately talked and dozed in the sunshine, waking to spend hours looking down the contours of the narrow land, gazing, his mind working on something he never offered to share with me.

I had asked him why the Long Pointers decided to up and move their buildings across the harbor. He told me that the point started eroding, going back into the sea that had spit it up, then he simply said, "railroad," as though that one word explained everything.

After those long-dead men had floated our woodhouse over, a second floor had been added and then a chimney with a stove-hole on each floor. No one had lived in the little shed for years past remembering. The steps to the upper floor had all but rotted away against the east side of the building, and they sagged toward the ducks' house, clinging erect by who knows what inertia. Beneath them, my grandfather and great uncle kept a woodpile, which this stair threatened to collapse upon, and which I was told to stay away from. This eyesore

was one of the things that the *Lisbon* Madeleine Sylvia so often complained about. We never went upstairs in the woodhouse, but we used
the downstairs for various kinds of storage. This was where John
Joseph kept his gear, his oars, lines, buoys, paint, caulking, nets, fids,
marlinespikes, buckets, and clamrakes. There were also two coal bins
on the east end of the little room, and in a corner near the gate of one
of the coal bins, we kept a fifty-gallon kerosene dispenser from which
we pumped our daily fuel for the cookstove. A huge table took up most
of the space in the center of the woodhouse—a heavy oaken, ornately
carved and scarred relic of furniture on which sat a glass case from
Great Aunt Theophila's hat shop, an array of the painted heads on
sticks where she once displayed her wares, also bucksaws, axes with
great, heavy rusting heads, shovels, cans, coalhods, objects I couldn't
name.

Everything in this room was covered with a fine black dust from the
coal. Not much light found its way in here, even during the daytime. As
I stood now inside the door, I had to wait for my eyes to adjust to the
darkness, and then I felt my way back into the corner where I kept my
own things. It took me some time to feel my way around and get my
hands on the ball and the knife, and when I did, I found that it was
really too dark to do anything with them. I turned around and started
to come back toward the door where the dim electric bulb from the
yard cast a quiet rectangle of light, and when I did I saw that while
I had been in the shed, Joe Dias and his curly-haired friend had come
over and settled on the woodhouse steps. Between them they had laid
their jackets and some plates of food. I stood behind them now,
blocked, and before I could say anything or do anything to make them
notice me, Joe Dias said, "Carmine, you don't know enough about how
things work around here. If you ask me, you are looking for all kinds
of trouble."

"Ah, well, Joe, you probably know what you're talking about."

"Sometimes I do," said Joe Dias. "I'm going to get out of here now.
Why don't we go up to Juney's and have a whiskey before we go
home?"

"No thanks," said Carmine. "I'm drinking this ale. I don't want to
mix. You go on, hey."

"Suit yourself," Joe said. He stood up and finished his can of ale, giving me an opening to step out of the woodhouse. But before I moved
again, I looked at this man Carmine, and I followed his line of sight
out into the yard, into the heart of the group of *Pico* ladies as they sat

now, most of them in animated conversation. From his vantage on the step, Carmine was quietly and seriously contemplating my mother, and as I looked at her, I could see that she was aware of his gaze and that something as palpable as speech traveled between them. Of course, I thought about my petitions earlier that day. I had just a few terrified minutes there in the semidarkness behind the doorway to wonder at how directly and suddenly the saints might be able to intervene in our lives if they really wanted to, and then the clambake's small catastrophe fell.

My grandfather tried to keep his word to Great Aunt Theophila. He did get drunk at the clambake, but that was to be expected. He did not keep the party small, as he had agreed to do, but that hadn't caused the trouble. It was the people from away. Not Lew and Roger, of course, for they were something like neighbors, even if they did pay rent. And Cynthia only drank a bit too much and made the mistake of flirting with Captain Raul in front of his wife, Liliana, who responded by threatening Cynthia with a good dose of the evil eye because Ernestina the Shoemaker's Wife was sitting right there and had the power. Ernestina just smiled, though, and refused to be drawn in. Finally, it was only Amalia who started the ruckus. Several hands hoisted her atop the moldy fence along Madeleine Sylvia's yard. She had somehow stripped down to her brassiere and pantaloons, and she held her umbrella over her head, attempting to walk the fence as though it were a tightrope. A small gasp went through the *Pico* ladies, and Sheika Nunes, who had drunk a few ales, stood up and shook her flesh-dimpled arm at her, yelling, "If I were ten years younger, I'd tear her hair out, the *canailla!*" My aunt looked at her in shock. Sheika remembered herself and made the sign of the cross, saying *"Velha me Deus."* The gesture had its effect on Amalia. She made some sort of connection, then turned to Sheika and the women and shouted, "Eisenhower is the Antichrist!"

The fence crunched once, lurched beneath her, crunched again, and gave altogether, crashing down in pieces and dumping Amalia into the duckpen. She tried to right herself, but she kicked a portion of the duckpen fence down, and Dilly, Dilly, and Dilly tried to take to the air and hopped and flopped around the yard. "Put some clothes on that woman this minute!" my great aunt called out. Her voice shook. At the same time, Liliana Mendes shouted, "Don't touch that crazy *puta rafada!*" She was yelling at her husband Raul, but her voice carried to all the men, and they stopped uncertainly while Amalia thrashed around in the ducks' pen and fell once into the buried washtub that was their pond. It was my mother who acted, running into the back room and coming out with one of my grandfather's checked wool workshirts. She pulled Amalia from the duckpen and got her to put her arms through the sleeves of the shirt and then buttoned it for her. "Damn it, Papa, I knew this was going to happen," she said when my grandfather came over to help.

"We're clearing out," my grandfather said. He pulled Cynthia by the arm, and she grabbed at Amalia, and although my great aunt jumped to her feet and stood by the gate to block him, she was undone by me and by Petey Flores who knocked her down as we both dove for one of the ducks, trying to stop it before it ran up the walk and out into the street. So my grandfather left that night not with one of the Women From Away, but with both of them, and two days later, when he had not yet returned, Great Aunt Theophila lapsed into her special state of grace and received a visitation from one of the saints.

4

Father Santos knocked on the screen door, and I let him in. He was dressed in black pants and a black shirt, his crisp, white collar biting his pale neck. "Josie," he said, touching the side of my face with his soft hand, "tell me, quickly, Saint Florian?"

"Flayed and drowned," I said.

"Excellent. And Saint Lawrence?"

"Grilled on hot coals."

"And Hettie is in the parlor?"

I showed him in. Sheika Nunes was already there. She had called Father Santos. That morning, peering down the trapdoor that opened in the back room's floor, Great Aunt Theophila had seen water rising through the earthen floor of the circular cellar. "It's a spring," she proclaimed. "Holy water is rising from a spring." She cajoled Uncle Paddy into putting on a pair of hip boots and going down into the cellar, which by then held about two feet of dark water, and we all hovered over him in the trapdoor's opening. "Seawater," he said when he climbed back up the ladder, cobwebs in his hair. "There's a full moon and there's high course tides running. You know it happens in all these old houses along the water."

My great aunt wasn't disappointed for long. Later that morning she stepped outside to dump a basin of dishwater onto the spearmint—a treatment for especially potent herbs that she had learned from Ernestina the Shoemaker's Wife—when a small dark woman appeared to her under the clothesline. The woman was young and beautiful and dressed in a rag of a brown cloak, and she was surrounded by the unmistakable nimbus of pale light—the color of lemons and snow, as my aunt described it—that bathed the Blessed in their earthly manifestations. My aunt was shaken after the appearance, and she had sent me for Sheika Nunes, who tended to her while they had waited for Father

Santos, making pots of tea, and serving her *sopas* made from Royal Lunch crackers.

"Maybe it was Monica, patron of mothers," Sheika suggested. "Wasn't she dark and small? I can check my books."

"By-and-by, by-and-by," my great aunt said, wearily.

Sheika had waited, as she always did, for my great aunt to complete all the details of her vision. She sat and listened with complete devotion, her pretty green eyes fixed on my aunt. Sheika could be bossy and meddlesome, and she was as militant a *Pico* as my aunt was, but she had a softer side, too. She was a widow and lived alone in the upstairs of her big house just behind Old Man Coelho's place. Her only daughter was grown and gone to live in Harpswell, Maine, with her lobsterman husband, but Sheika did not miss her so much as she missed her own departed husband, whom she herself had nursed during his final hours. In the right mood, the mention of his name could melt her to sorrowful weeping, and Manny Nunes had been dead as long as I could remember. But Manny was why Sheika was so interested in Great Aunt Theophila's visions. Sheika was fearful about Manny's well-being in the Other World.

In the last days of his illness, Manny had spoken aloud to figures at the foot of his bed. The figures had come to carry him over to the Other World, and Sheika, who could not see these beings herself, nonetheless tried to shoo them away with a broom. "Oh, Hettie," she would cry to my great aunt, "they came and showed themselves to him, just like they show themselves to you. He was such a *good* man." And Sheika would go on to tell about Manny's goodness, and then she would ask my great aunt if, in the course of her visions, she had learned anything about Manny's whereabouts in the Other World. Sheika was afraid for Manny because when those invisible figures from the Other World made their last visit to her husband, carrying him off with them, he sat up and pointed into the space past the bed and said, "Dark wings! Fire! Tell Captain Raul to get the paint!" Then he lay back and expired. The neighbors could hear Sheika's wail all the way up and down the street, and they came running to find her sobbing. "The devil stole him, the devil stole him," she cried. "He wasn't supposed to go with him, but the devil stole him, that son of a bitch."

Father Santos had tried to calm her later. Dark wings and fire, after all, didn't have to mean the devil. Manny could just as easily have been describing the blazing glory of an angel. John Joseph pointed out that Sheika had heard Manny cry out in English, and everybody knew that

Manny's English was not that good. He might not have been accurate in describing what he saw. As for what he meant by shouting for Captain Raul to get the paint, that was anybody's guess, and everyone still gave their opinions about it when the story came around again in our parlor or dooryard.

But Sheika still feared for Manny's afterlife. She made her First Friday Masses without ever a miss, regardless of weather or circumstances, and she dedicated the indulgences she received to his soul. When she and my great aunt sat saying rosaries together, Sheika's prayers were for Manny. And she always kept one of the large votary candles—the ones that stood in the cast iron stand to the right of the main altar of our church—burning for him every week. There was an offering box for these candles, and you dropped as much as a folded dollar bill into the slot, but Sheika paid nothing. She always said that the poor were never meant to pay for candles, and that God the Father, Jesus, and the Holy Virgin understood this. Sheika hoped that she would receive just a word or two about Manny from my great aunt—about how he was doing and where he might have ended up. But my great aunt never got any information about him from any of her saints, and it wasn't any different this time.

Father Santos had settled on the sofa and sipped tea with the women. "Hettie," he said, "why do you think this woman who appeared to you had a message for *you* in particular?"

"I can't think why, Father." My great aunt was humble now and physically transformed. The flesh on her cheeks relaxed, and fullness and color came to her. I could look at her face and see the young woman she once had been, proud and dagger-eyed.

"What do you think this visit means for you?"

"That I should perform a cleansing."

The Father pressed on with careful politeness. "Do you feel she meant anything else?"

"Perhaps a sign will come."

"What manner of sign?"

"I don't know. I'd be guessing."

"Concerning the church?"

"I couldn't say."

"Hettie, such visits are rare." My aunt was silent at this, and Father Santos pushed on. "The saints are best regarded as forces, Hettie. Thinking of them in human shapes is just a device to help us consider their nature more easily."

"But they were people once," Sheika said. I poured her more tea and sat back down at the far end of the sofa from the priest. "It makes sense that they would present themselves to us in the way they used to look."

Father Santos paused a minute, and I couldn't hold myself back. "How do you know if the saints are really doing things in your life?" I asked. "How do you know if you're getting what you asked for?"

Great Aunt Theophila didn't like the interruption. "Josie," she said, "go outside and play." I didn't want to leave just then, but Father Santos was there, and I didn't want to make a fuss in front of him. I slid off the sofa and went down to the *Caravella*, where it sat beached on its sandbar, and I bailed and sponged her. John Joseph hadn't been around to do it, and I didn't know when I would see him next.

I don't know what the priest and my great aunt and Sheika finally came around to talking about, but the cleansing that my aunt had mentioned came down on us literally. Sheika showed up the following day covered in a great blue sail of an apron, her thick hair tied up in white cloth, and my mother emerged from her room also aproned and with her hair bound in a similar way. When Fanny Neves stopped by on her way to work at the Bluefish Inn and dropped off an armload of hand towels, all with the blue stripe and name of Mister Van Horten's hotel down the center, I knew we were in for a serious overhaul. "Stick around, Josie," Sheika said. "We're going to tackle that back room of your grandfather's." This was something that my great aunt had wanted to do for a long time, and now that John Joseph wasn't around to stop her, she'd have her way.

"That room is just how he likes it," I said, but no one paid any attention. This little room was a small space behind the kitchen, and it must have been a kitchen itself once in another time, for a narrow brick chimney ran up the center of one wall, and in the corner by the backyard window there was the small black sink that smelled sharply of hammered copper and a faucet that spit dun-colored water. A walk-in pantry took up most of the other end, and in between lay my grandfather's folding iron cot. The room was cluttered with boxes of old clothes, washtubs, cooking pots, foul-weather gear, two big mantle clocks that didn't work, and several peach boxes of the books that Roger and Lew always brought me and my grandfather. My great aunt put me to work on the books right away. She was suspicious of them. She told me to take them out in the yard and dust them off, but I knew she just wanted them out in the light in convenient piles, so she could go through them and censor them from me. She felt there was something citified and dirty about these books, even though Lew had told her they were important for me to have. But the big box of history and geography books belonged to my grandfather, and I knew that she would not touch those. This was where my grandfather searched for some clue about the mysterious disappearance of Carvalho the Navigator, who discovered America, only to be forgotten. Lew would say, "John Joseph, the implications are all here. You might be right, my friend. But there's nothing. Nothing at all." And my grandfather would whack the duckpen fence with a stick and growl, "Of course not! The damn _Lisbons_ swindled him out of everything!" My great aunt sniffed at these books as I lugged them past her. "Foolishness," is what she said. "It's where he gets all those foolish ideas. He makes things up because he knows he's a failure himself."

I worked at the books, and Uncle Paddy dragged out some boxes of his old coastguard things, items of dark clothing, smaller boxes with insignias and brass buttons in them, brown-tinted photographs of stiff, uniformed men against backgrounds of watchtowers, the dunes, the ocean. Uncle Paddy had been part of the old Beach Patrol. He got a disability check every month because he had been hurt during a rescue in a winter northeaster. He had pictures of the wreck, a big schooner lying on its side in the heavy surf. He had another picture showing five bodies covered in blankets in the snow on the beach, beside a horse-cart. He collected the pictures and sat on the swing, kicking it lazily back and forth. He whistled to himself and looked far away. The light smell of the sea and the heavier, sweet smell of off-loading fishing boats blew in from the Cold Storage wharf and drifted over the yard. Every once in a while one of the women would call and I would go over and help. They went at the floors and walls and shelves with galvanized buckets of water and yellow bricks of naptha soap. The dingy curtains came down from the windows, and Sheika Nunes boiled them in one of our big copper tubs. My mother ran from steps to clothesline, the dripping curtains and bedding soaking her apron front, and all this commotion had the ducks quacking in endless circles around their little pen.

Then the noon-break whistle up on the Cold Storage freon tank blew, and almost before its wail died away, Joe Dias clumped up our walk, coming directly from his job in the big freezers, bomber jacket open at the collar, watch cap pulled down over his knobby head, his open galoshes jingling at the buckles. He had a basket of strawberries under his arm, and his friend from the party, Carmine, marched behind him. Sheika spotted him from the doorway and stepped outside. "Hey, what's the news, Joe Dias?" She heaved her bosom as though she was weary of something.

"Well, let me see," said Joe. "Heard there was a big car crash out the New Road last night."

"Anybody hurt?"

"No," said Joe, "just some summer people." He looked around at the clothesline and at all the boxes in the yard. "Oh, boy," he said.

"That back room," said Sheika. "John Joseph's run off again, you know."

Before Joe could answer, Great Aunt Theophila came to the doorway. "Hello, Joe." She looked at Carmine and pursed her lips.

"I got this big mess of strawberries, Hettie," Joe said. "I wanted to give you people some. They'd go bad before I ever got to use them all."

My great aunt kept her eyes on Carmine. He grinned deep creases around his eyes and fiddled with a button on his shirt front. "I came along with Joe to get my jacket. The one I left here the night of the clambake."

"I'll get it," I said. "I know the one you mean." I hopped into the woodhouse and brought out his silk jacket and handed it to him.

"Thanks, Pard," he said. He shook the blue silk a few times and hooked it over his shoulder. Then he smiled at my mother.

"Those strawberries are beautiful," she said. "Here, I'll take them inside and wash them. Joe, do want to stay a minute and eat some with us?" She walked out to Joe and took the strawberries, and I saw her glance down at her soaked apron-front. Her hand went automatically to her rag-tied hair. She didn't look at Carmine at all but turned quickly and went into the house. My aunt followed her. I could imagine them hissing at each other through clenched teeth, but I didn't hear any arguing.

Sheika Nunes had sat in one of the chairs by our spool table, and now she crossed her chest with one arm, leaned her head a little into her hand and stared at Joe and Carmine, who still stood in the middle of the walk. "Take a load off your feet, Joe," she said. Then, she looked straight at Carmine and smiled. "What's your story, mister?"

Carmine rubbed his nose and smiled back at her. "No story."

"Well, I heard about you at the PASO Hall the other night. You come from New Bedford?"

"Yes, ma'am," Carmine said. "Who might that be that was talking about me?"

"Oh, I don't know," Sheika said, waving her hand.

"What else did you hear?"

"Nothing else," Sheika said. "You're just a mystery."

"No mystery," said Carmine. He smiled and pointed. "I'm going to start fishing with Alfie DeCosta this week. I'm going to be around for a while."

Joe Dias jumped in. "I knew Alfie needed somebody on the *Fortuna* real quick, so I put him on to Carmine here. My cousin in New Bedford knows him."

"My poor husband, God rest his soul, was a trapper with Captain Raul Mendes," Sheika started, but then Great Uncle Paddy got up from the swing and walked over to the door. He seemed to notice Joe and Carmine for the first time. "How do," he said, nodding his shaggy white head and disappearing into the house.

"Afternoon, sir," Carmine said to his back. I took a careful look at Carmine in the bright noon light. He sat squarely now in one of our chairs, and he leaned forward when he spoke, his elbows on his thighs, and his hands clasped loosely between his knees. The sleeves of his khaki workshirt were rolled up to his elbows, showing his forearms, thick and heavy-veined, tanned and weathered. On his right arm the faded blue outline of a tattooed dagger showed through his tan, a snake twisting up its blade and along its haft. Beneath this emblem there was a small banner with words in it, and I was trying to read them from where I sat, but then my mother stepped out into the sunlight again, and Carmine snapped to his feet. "Can I help you with those?" he said. He pointed to the pot of cleaned and sliced strawberries she held in her hand.

"Sure," my mother said. "You can help." She handed him the pot and pointed to the spool top. "Over there." She had taken her hair out of the tie-cloth, and over her dress she wore a fresh apron of deep blue, covered with white and yellow cornflowers. She went back into the house and returned with saucers, coffee mugs, and the percolator pot. "I know you take evaporated, Joe," she said, "but I'm not sure about your friend here."

Carmine turned to Joe, and Joe jumped slightly. "Oh," he said, "this is Carmine Raposa. He was sorry not to get to talk to you on the night of the clambake."

"Good to meet you, " said my mother.

"That was a wonderful party your papa threw," Carmine said. "Too bad about that fence and all." My mother glanced over at the ruined fence, then dropped her eyes to the coffee. "Evaporated?"

"Black," said Carmine, smiling.

Sheika Nunes pulled out her handkerchief and blew her nose. "So where are your people from?" she asked.

Carmine brushed his hand across his mouth and looked over at Joe. "Montijo," he said.

"Isn't that right near Lisbon?" Sheika asked.

"No, no," said Carmine, "not that close at all."

"Ah, well." She let her voice trail off and looked at the pot of strawberries. "Rosa, let's have some of those."

Great Aunt Theophila came out of the house to sit and eat berries with us. She kept her face empty of expression. It grew uncomfortably quiet for a moment, and then Sheika Nunes said, "Hettie had a vision."

Joe Dias nodded energetically, and I saw my mother shrink a bit in her chair. She did not want the attention to shift to Aunt Theophila, but she also might have been worried that Joe Dias would go off on one of his stories about the White Rat In Oilclothes, something he always brought up whenever Aunt Theophila talked about her visitations. The North Atlantic Cold Storage was one of the three remaining big fisheries in our town. Its main building rose four stories above the waterfront, but it was old and weather-beaten, and the walls and roof sagged. Joe Dias was in charge of the labyrinth of freezers that wound through the building, and it was his opinion that if they ever thawed, the whole structure would crumble. One night, on his rounds to close the plant, he somehow got locked in a freezer, and after wandering the ice-hung corridors and rooms and not finding an unlocked door, he sat down on a fish box, knowing that he might freeze to death right there among all those stiff flounder and haddock and ling cod. He was sitting with his watch cap pulled down over his ears and his bomber jacket zipped up around his neck, shivering, when around the corner came a white rat, about the size of a big dog, walking on its hind legs and dressed in yellow oilclothes and a black sou'wester. The rat sat down on a fishbox next to Joe and talked with him all night, telling him over and over again not to fall asleep. "Saved my goddamn life," Joe would say. "And I still hear him all the time, walking around the freezers, whistling." He seemed to think that this visit somehow put him on a level with Great Aunt Theophila, but she always bristled when he brought it up. "He's got rats in his *head*, that guy," is what she would say.

But my mother wasn't going to let Joe cut in. She looked at Carmine. "Do you plan to stay here in town after the summer?"

My great aunt looked darkly across the table, but my mother ignored her.

"You bet I plan to stay," Carmine said. "This place is paradise."

"It gets cold in winter."

"Well, I guess it does that just about everywhere."

"Not in Florida," my mother said.

"You're right there."

"Of course, I've never been to Florida," my mother said. "But that's what I've heard."

"I've been there," Carmine said. "Got a brother-in-law there. Hot as blazes and full of snakes. Alligators, too."

"Oh," said my mother, "now I don't think I'd like alligators."

"I wouldn't mind having an alligator," I said, but no one seemed to hear me.

"Well," Carmine said to my mother, "they got them on farms down there. You can buy them and take them home."

"What for?"

"Darned if *I* know."

The rest of us ate strawberries while the two of them talked. I couldn't tell if my great aunt was listening or just thinking hard. She watched this stranger without giving him the smallest bit of encouragement. She might have been figuring how to get rid of him. We were finishing the berries when the five-minute whistle sounded from the Cold Storage, and Carmine and Joe rose to leave. Carmine offered to help my mother carry the dishes inside. She accepted. And as Carmine walked out the gate, he turned and promised to bring us a big haddock from the boat, first day out. "Oh, good," my mother said, but Great Aunt Theophila just stared after him, stiff as a statue. Was all this evidence of the power of prayer? I had to wonder if my petitions to my saint had brought Carmine into the yard for my grandfather's clambake. I didn't have to wonder whether my saint brought him back for his jacket. I didn't have to wonder who had pulled it quietly into the woodhouse the night of the party, or who told Joe Dias we had it at the house and that Carmine should come over and get it.

It was me. I did all that.

5

Elvio the Shoemaker and Uncle Paddy hunched over the radio set on the stained wooden table. The table sat against the house in a little ell in the backyard, and above it a dim-watted outdoor light shined down on the men. They had been eating cold whiting fillets and boiled potatoes, and Uncle Paddy had brought a bottle of Fleischman's whiskey outside and set it between them, along with two small glasses. Elvio wore a pair of thick black headphones, the size of teacups, over his ears, and he slowly turned the dials of the big radio back and forth. My Great Uncle had salvaged the short-wave set from a wreck on the back beach, and Elvio had repaired it. It sat in the dim light without any covering on its tubes and coils, and its insides glowed orange and yellow in the warm night air. The radio was connected to the bedspring on our roof by a long black insulated wire. Elvio and Uncle Paddy had turned the bedspring in the general direction of the Azores, and Elvio had wired it to receive signals. Elvio believed he would be able to listen to broadcasts from the old country using this setup. He knew a lot about radios because along with his shoe-repair shop in his barn up at the edge of the woods, he also kept a fix-it shop, where he repaired irons, telephones, radios, heaters—almost anything. Half of the barn was hung with pegs and shelves of heels and soles, coils of wire and spare parts. The other half held the pens where he raised his ducks and chickens. Uncle Paddy didn't really care about listening to broadcasts from the Azores because he didn't understand a word of Portuguese, but he liked to fiddle with the radio set, and he wanted to see how far away it could reach. He also liked to sit in the yard and drink whiskey with Elvio, even though Great Aunt Theophila nagged him about the whiskey and his blood pressure.

The women had gone to bed already, and they probably thought that I had gone to bed also, but I sat in the shadows on the canvas swing and watched the men until they finally gave up for the night, having tuned in to voices speaking in several strange tongues, but none of them that Elvio could recognize as Portuguese. After Elvio shuffled off up the walk, Uncle Paddy laid a piece of heavy oilcloth over the old radio and picked up his whiskey bottle and went inside. I followed after a while, but there was too much on my mind for me to go to sleep. I had, after all, ruined my own experiment in talking to the saints. I hadn't trusted my saint enough to bring the stranger Carmine on board by himself, and so I had taken steps. This might even be some kind of sin, though I didn't seem to care about that very much. But I could tell that my mother had liked him. And if a saint really did send him up the walk and into my grandfather's party, who could doubt that this was for the best? But it was the petitioning that puzzled me. Had I been answered or not? Suddenly nothing seemed real—or else everything did. Didn't it follow that if you believed in one thing, you had crossed a line and therefore believed in everything? It was too much for me.

I went into the back room and sat on my grandfather's cot, newly made up with fresh blankets. My great aunt had scrubbed and organized the room, as if by putting all his clutter in place, she might rearrange John Joseph's life to conform to her ideas of what he should be. I reached into one of the now-alphabetized crates of books and pulled out a couple of volumes of Portuguese history, the books that Lew and my grandfather scoured for hints of the great ancestor. There were maps and familiar names, and I wandered through the pages, stopping to look over passages that my grandfather or maybe Lew had underlined. I wasn't paying attention to the time or much of anything else, but I jumped suddenly when I sensed someone standing outside the screen door. It was my grandfather. He pressed his face to the screen, his hands cupping his eyes, looking in at me.

"*Avô*," I said, "you're back."

He slipped inside the door and held a finger up to his lips. "Keep it quiet," he said.

I saw the unsteadiness in his hand—the barest trembling. He moved noiselessly across the little room and sat next to me on the cot. We were close enough to talk in whispers now. "What are you doing up?" he asked.

"Couldn't sleep," I said. There was no way I'd tell *him* about this stuff with the saints.

He looked around at the room. "What the hell happened here?"

"Ma, *Tia*, and Sheika Nunes."

"A formidable gang."

"*Tia* had another vision."

"That makes sense," he said. "She always seems to have them when I'm not around."

"When you *take off*," I said. "I'm glad you're back," I added quickly.

He cleared his throat. "Actually, I just came to pick up some things. I'm going to stay down the other end of town for a while."

"With that woman?"

"Her name's Amalia, Carvalho."

"Listen," I said, "something's going on here. Some man came calling for Ma. Carmine. He was at the clambake."

"Hettie'll chase him off."

"Maybe," I said. "Maybe he's different. He's from away. He's a *Lisbon*."

John Joseph gave a little snort. "Hettie must have loved that."

"Well, it's not like he's from here. It's not like he's in PASO or anything like that. We heard from Madeleine Sylvia, by the way. About the clambake. About the fence."

"Which way does the wind blow?" He had his hat off and was leaning back against the wall now.

"She said she's going to the Town Hall to file a paper."

John Joseph snorted again. "Just talk," he said.

"*Tia* was pretty upset."

"It'll blow over. Who propped the fence back up?"

"Uncle Paddy and Elvio. They had the radio going tonight."

"Well, I owe them both a favor. Fact is we need a whole new fence, one that isn't rotten."

"Why don't you stick around for a while?" I asked. "It's late."

"Late is correct," he said. We were quiet for a while, and then his breathing fell into a deep regular rhythm, his exhalations sweetening the room with tobacco and malt. He had tumbled into sleep there beside me on his cot.

Carmine showed up at our house again on the very next day. It was late afternoon, and I had just come home from the beach where I walked out to the sandbar and bailed and cleaned the *Caravella*. It was the *Fortuna*'s first day back out fishing, and Carmine had made good on his promise. When I walked into the house a big haddock already lay dressed and garnished and ready for baking in my mother's black speckled roasting pan. John Joseph had awakened late and walked a small seabag of his things down to Amalia's, but he had come back to talk with my great aunt and Uncle Paddy about Madeleine Sylvia's latest threats, and he sat at the kitchen table now with a can of ale in his hand. Joe Dias, Carmine, and Uncle Paddy sat with him, talking. I was surprised to see Carmine back so soon even though I had kept up steady petitions to my saint. This time I had done nothing to get him to visit, though. My hands were clean.

"Well here's the guy," Carmine said, winking at me. "I was waiting for you. I brought some things for everybody, but I wanted you all here."

"Carmine just wants to pay you back for the hospitality you all have showed him," put in Joe Dias.

"You his lawyer?" said my grandfather.

"No, hey, really," said Carmine, "Joe's right. I just believe in returning the good feelings. It's just the way I am."

He asked my mother and Great Aunt Theophila to come in from the parlor, and for a moment I thought my great aunt might refuse. But she came, silently following my mother to the big table, and Carmine laid out his gifts from a brown shopping bag at his feet. For Great Uncle Paddy he brought a bottle of Fleischman's. In the same way he had observed my uncle's brand of whiskey, he had noticed my grandfather's brand of pipe tobacco, for he produced next a large red can of Prince Albert. For Aunt Theophila he pulled out a small velvet box and withdrew a string of blue glass rosary beads. My aunt took them in her hand—so dark and brown by contrast—and stared at them with a look of I know not what on her face. "And here's one for the kid," Carmine said to me, reaching for another small box. It was a fountain pen and mechanical pencil with a small tube of extra leads. "Do we have any ink?" I asked.

"Don't be rude," my mother snapped, but Carmine smiled again and pulled out a bottle of Carter's blue-black and pushed it across the table to me. I opened the ink and started to fill the fountain pen, but my great aunt took the pen—and the pencil, which was still in the box—and said, "Don't play with that now."

I glanced at Carmine, as if he could help me out with this, but he raised his hand and said to me, "No, no, don't worry. Plenty of time for that later."

I watched him as he felt around for the last gift. "This is for you, Rosa."

My mother could not hide the delight on her face. Carmine gave her a long narrow box which she opened to reveal six egg-shaped bars of yellow soap that smelled like freshly cut lemons. "Oh," was all she could manage to say, but she said it with an inflection that made the muscle of Great Aunt Theophila's jaw ripple.

We sat at the table. Uncle Paddy opened his whiskey bottle and poured shots for all the men, and John Joseph opened his new can of sweet Prince Albert and filled the bowl of his pipe. My great aunt took the rosary beads into the bedroom and closed the door. I doubt if she prayed on them. I never saw them again. But while she was in the bedroom, there came drifting among the smells of pipe smoke and Fleischman's the unmistakable odor of devotional incense.

My mother got up to tend supper, and Uncle Paddy passed more whiskey. Carmine pulled a half-dollar out of his pocket and made it walk across the backs of his fingers, which were short and thick, with knotted knuckles that did not look as quick and agile as they were. My grandfather then got up and wiped the table with a damp cloth and puffed elaborately on his pipe, blowing out a perfect ball of smoke that rolled away from him over the wet tabletop. As it neared the opposite end, he called to it and waved his hands in a gesture of command, and the ball of smoke reversed its direction and rolled back toward him. "Some magic," Carmine said.

"Learned it from Houdini," said John Joseph.

Carmine nodded. "Yes, sir."

"You still in the army?" John Joseph asked.

"Ha," said Carmine. "Say, Joe, you do a trick now."

"Don't know any," Joe Dias said. "I could tell you the story about that white rat I saw."

"Save it," said my grandfather.

"Last call," said Uncle Paddy, and he poured another round of shots.

Carmine's presence altered something in the house. I could judge it in small behaviors, like the way John Joseph remained at the table and did not fuss after my mother as she cooked the big fish. Now he paid no attention at all to her doings in the other end of the kitchen and the back room. And aside from telling Carmine that our family was descended from the great ancestor—Carvalho the Navigator—he did not break into any of his long stories. He sat and watched Carmine and let him do most of the talking. In between her husking corn ears and slicing onions, basting the fish and rolling dough for a blueberry pie, my mother kept coming over to the table, circling it, asking if anyone needed another can of ale. "Some people like to bake their potatoes right with the haddock, but I don't know if they do that in New Bedford," she said, putting a can of Ballentine's in front of Carmine. "Do you like sugar in your corn water?"

"For Christ's sake, Rosa," John Joseph said.

"For Christ's sake, yourself, Papa," said my mother, turning flatly away from him. An old shadow fleeted across her face but vanished quickly as she returned with a clean ashtray and took up the old one from the center of the table.

When supper was finally ready, Great Aunt Theophila refused to come out of her bedroom, and Great Uncle Paddy had to go and fetch her. Joe Dias was drunk by then, but he confined his conversation to saying, "Wonderful, finest kind," about everything that was passed to him. Carmine's face was flushed, and his eyes, black as anthracite, narrowed into a self-pleased smile. He spoke to Great Aunt Theophila about the famous apparition of Our Lady of Fatima, back in the old country in 1917. I watched my mother regard him with a flat, calculating look, taking him in slowly. She watched the effect he was having on Great Aunt Theophila. My great aunt had left her angry sulk and seemed to listen civilly as Carmine went on about the three children and the trial that they had in convincing the authorities of their vision. "Of course, ma'am, you can understand that kind of thing yourself, from everything that I hear." He went on to talk about the miracle of the dancing lights that was witnessed by thousands near the grove of Fatima.

"Well," said my grandfather, washing down a mouthful of haddock with a can of ale that he had got up and fetched for himself, "you seem to know a lot about it."

"Saw it in the pictures," Carmine said. He turned to my mother. "You like the pictures, don't you, Rosa?"

"Oh, sure," my mother said.

Carmine spoke to my aunt again. "I don't go to Mass anymore, ma'am. Ever since the war. Don't ask me why. I just don't."

My mother watched him carefully, and now so did I. He had commandeered the table and managed to keep everyone under a charm as he talked about everything from rigging an otter trawl to harvesting cork in the old country. He filled the room. I started to feel dizzy, and yet I never wanted him to stop. But he did stop, finally, as my mother gathered up the empty pie dishes and carried a pot of tea to the parlor. John Joseph used this small interruption to slip quietly out the back door, but the rest of us followed the teapot. My mother came around and poured for everybody, and when she went back to the kitchen to clean up, Carmine excused himself and went in to help her. "Well, I never saw such a thing," my aunt said, but no one was paying her much mind, for Joe Dias had settled back into the morris chair and was recounting his tale of the white rat in oilclothes.

"*Irra! Cagao! Charlatao!* The man walked into our house to supper without even asking—without giving us a chance to say 'ah, yes or no'!" my aunt said later, after Joe and Carmine had left. "*Putanheiro!*" And she marched to the back room sink and spit into it, turning to me to say, "I don't want you taking presents from that man!"

"It's not any of your business," my mother said to her.

"It's my business all right," said my aunt. "If it's not my business now, it'll be my business later. Isn't that how *he* got to be my business?" She nodded furiously in my direction.

"That has nothing to do with it," my mother said. "Carmine just wants to make some friends."

"I know what he's after."

"Yes," said my mother, "you know everything."

"I like Carmine," I said.

"You are *not* to like him," said Great Aunt Theophila. "You don't know any better."

"Hettie! Come to bed now," said Uncle Paddy. All three of us turned in surprise to see him standing in the bedroom doorway. He usually let these skirmishes die out on their own, but he stood now, heavily filling the doorway. "Enough," he said. "Come to bed."

Aunt Theophila looked confused for a second. She stared at him, and he looked back at her with his pale, flat eyes and then he stepped to one side so she could move through the doorway. She passed him, muttering something in the old speech, too softly for me to hear.

The next day, after the *Fortuna* had come back from fishing and had taken out its catch at the Cold Storage wharf, Carmine returned, scrubbed and pressed, with a lacquered box for my mother. It was a deep plum color with shiny brass hinges and a tiny catch that unlocked the top. When she opened it, it played a lilting tune. "That's the *Blue Danube*," Carmine explained, while Great Aunt Theophila looked on with folded arms.

He came again to help Uncle Paddy fix an electric socket that did not work, lying on the floor beside my great uncle with an array of pliers and amber-handled screwdrivers while Great Aunt Theophila, my mother, and I stood behind them in silence. "Here's the ticket, here's the bugger right here," Carmine said, pulling out a stiff, foul-looking piece of wire in ratty insulation. "Now don't touch that, hey, or you'll get the juice right through you."

Sometimes in the afternoon when the house was quiet, I would steal into my great aunt's bedroom and sit on the white ruffled bed-spread and look at the collection of images and icons on the bureau. Sometimes they seemed to accuse me of something, and sometimes they appeared to cast their eyes from me, as though I had injured them. How could anyone tell what he was getting into when he prayed for something?

One evening Carmine came to the door, dressed in a shiny, dark brown shirt and khaki pants, both pressed with knife-edged creases and starched to formal stiffness. My mother informed me that he had come to take her and me to the movies, and I could tell from the clipped conversations among Carmine and my mother and great aunt that this had been somehow discussed and worked out in advance. He gave Great Aunt Theophila a box of chocolates, bid her good bye, and walked the two of us out the door and down the front street.

Once we were past the hill to the east of Juney's Tap, Carmine took my mother's hand, and I walked along slightly behind them. Summer people crowded our little ribbon of sidewalk and walked in groups right down the middle of the street, so that cars had to creep along and edge by them. We did not usually go downtown much in the summer and almost never in the evening. The color and commotion among these people from away seemed like a carnival to me, or rather it seemed like swimming under water, holding my breath and moving in a world that was not fully my own. And these strange people swam past us. It was hard to understand how we all breathed the same air. Surely one of our worlds would have to perish. But Carmine walked us steadily past the candy shops and souvenir shops, making people step off the narrow sidewalk and give way to him and my mother. We passed the green benches in front of the Town Hall and walked down into the town square where there was a small space for parking cars at the head of the main wharf. Carmine ordered us all orangeades from Manny Aruela's steam cart and then took us through some of the sum-mer shops. He bought my mother a bag of cashew nuts and for me a paper cone of pink cotton candy. In another shop he bought my mother a glass ball filled with water and a red rose. He let me pick out a small silver flashlight that could shine in three colors. When we finally got to the movies, I sat in the dark with a box of popcorn on my lap, and I could only think of Carmine. His presence seemed to use up air in the theater. The movie unwound in its cascade of images and I made sense out of none of it.

Great Aunt Theophila and Sheika Nunes were sitting in the parlor when we got home. "Hello, ladies," Carmine said.

"It's after eleven o'clock," said my aunt, looking at me and then my mother. If there was going to be trouble between them I wanted nothing to do with it. I slipped out of sight and went to bed right away, and I played disks of color on the ceiling with my new flashlight, not listening to any of the low-voiced conversation that came after I heard Carmine leave through the back door.

The next morning I left the house as soon as I could, gathered up a bucket, my spyglass, and a few other things, and went down to the seawall and waited for the receding tide to beach John Joseph's dory so I could bail and scrub it. The day was bright and hot, and the harbor smelled its deep, warm smell of summer. The water shimmered pale and flat, yellow and green along the shore, but going to a long, even blue farther out. Other boats dipped at their lines near the dory, and beyond this small anchorage a flat, gray scow brooded on a rusting chain. Already an early trapboat had come in to the end of the Cold Storage wharf and was taking out. The trolley—another old Model A, this one stripped and running on bare wheels—chugged up and down the wharf along its rusty tracks, pulling the hoppers of fish up to the tramhouse at the wharf's head. I could see Manny Buckets and another man at the tramhouse. They were working the sluicegate that emptied the fish from the tramhouse tank into the big wooden bucket that ratcheted empty down the trestles, was filled when the men opened the gate, and ratcheted heavily back up to the top story of the Cold Storage building, where the processing would begin. I could not tell from where I sat whose boat was taking out. It could have been Captain Raul's or it could have been Old Man Prada's—there were not many others. As Captain Raul lamented regularly in our yard, the ranks of the real trappers were thinning out along with the fish.

I sat for a long while lost in a kind of fog, when a figure walked out from under the wharf just as one of the fish-buckets was being winched up the tramway. A fine mist of fishy saltwater fell over him, and he turned and shook his fist at the men operating the bucket winch. It was Domingo the Beach Cleaner. He limped slightly as he walked toward me in his hip boots, his left foot dragging just noticeably. He carried on his shoulder his shovel and pitchfork, and he wore one of Captain Raul's old skipper's hats on the back of his head. He walked along the edge of the receding water, and when he came opposite me, he stopped and gestured. "Abaa," he said.

"I'm waiting for the tide, Domingo," I called back to him.

He took off the old hat and motioned down to the east with it. "Baaa. Abaa abaa."

"What? The town wharf?"

"Baaa aba." He waved the hat again, annoyed with me for not being able to understand him better.

"John Joseph?" I asked.

"Ba," he nodded.

"He's staying with someone down the East End."

"Ba."

"He'll be back soon," I said. "I'll take care of the *Caravella* for him."

Domingo pointed to the dory and made a hooking motion with his fist.

"Okay," I said.

He shook his head.

"I don't know what you mean, then."

He stood between me and the *Caravella* now, and looked out at the old dory and then back at me and shook his head in disgust. Domingo had no patience with me nor with himself when I could not understand him. He had chased me with his pitchfork once when I had laughed at him because of some wild gestures he was using to get a point across. But John Joseph always understood him perfectly, and the two of them carried on long conversations, John Joseph using any words he pleased from his big vocabularies in both languages.

Domingo was as old as my grandfather, and they had been boys together on the Island of Pico before coming ahead of their families to the new country on American fishing boats. But only a few years after he began fishing out of our town, Domingo had died and come back from the dead, and this had left him afflicted with his limp and other infirmities, and so he did not work out on the water anymore but worked for the town as the cleaner of its beaches. He walked them from the eastern rockpile to the western breakwater, burying the occasional goosefish that washed ashore to rot in its death's head grin, clearing away the broken bottles, the horseshoe crabs, the skates and skate egg cases, the dead gulls, and anything else that might foul the sands for the summer people.

There was nothing wonderful or miraculous about Domingo's journey to the Other Side and back, not the way my grandfather told it. Domingo was young and strong and worked on the *Amor de Deus*, a small dragger still in our fishing fleet. The *Amor de Deus* was side-to in a choppy swell just after a tow with the otter trawl, and as the big wooden drag doors that hold the net open were being winched up, the boat lurched and Domingo was struck in the side of the head with a quarter of a ton of oak and iron. He was knocked sprawling on the deck, unconscious, blood streaming from his mouth and ears. Papa Deke Boia, then the captain of the *Amor de Deus*, let the catch go and had Domingo taken down below, and then turned the boat back to the harbor. By the time they got back to the wharf Papa Deke was certain that Domingo had stopped breathing, but when the town's doctor, Doctor Hermann, a very young man then, examined him, he found that Domingo *was* breathing but that he was in very grave condition and so had him taken by car to the hospital, some fifty miles of narrow curving road back down our peninsula. But the drive was too long, and the doctors there found him dead when he arrived, and they had his body taken away. He stayed dead for several hours until he awoke on a gurney in the corner of a basement long enough to groan and get the attention of an orderly. He stayed in the hospital for weeks before coming back to our town, but he would never be the same. He came back from the dead with nothing. He not only had no news of that place that he had visited for those long hours, but almost as if to be sure nothing would be said about that Other Side, Domingo's speech, some of his sense, and much of his physical ability had been taken from him.

Father Santos and Sheika Nunes both said that Domingo had been touched by God and was therefore the better for it in some way, but I did not think Domingo felt that way about it. He wore around his neck a *taleiga*, a small cloth bag containing a charm that Ernestina the Shoemaker's Wife had put together for him to help make him whole again. My grandfather had told me just how many years ago Ernestina had given him that *taleiga*. As far as anyone knew, he had never taken it off. And as far as anyone knew, no sign had passed from him about anything he had seen on the Other Side. As I sat there on the bulkhead and watched Domingo limp on down to the westward, it seemed that only in a dream could you carry a message across that void, and then, what good could it possibly do you? And yet before I had even finished with this thought, a boat began rounding the point. It was smaller than a toy from where I watched, and I could make out just enough of it under its cloud of feeding gulls to guess which boat it was. I took my spyglass out of the bucket. It was not a spyglass at all really, though I called it that, but one-half of a pair of fieldglasses that my grandfather had found and given to me. The left lenses and prism had been broken, but the right side was intact, so John Joseph had sawed the glasses in half with a hacksaw blade. "Virtually a telescope," he told me. The glass worked fine. The boat was the *Fortuna*, coming back with a good catch. On deck aft I could make out the figure of Carmine throwing something over the side. It was Carmine and not a dream of him, and that had to count for something.

6

"Vasco da Gama," Lew said emphatically. "If you refuse to count Columbus, then without a doubt, Vasco da Gama."

"In a pig's ass," said my grandfather. It was early evening, and he and Lew sat at the spool table, while Carmine and my mother sat in the swing. Roger sat on the steps, quietly drawing something in one of his big pads. I tossed cracked corn, a corn at a time, into the duckpen.

"I know, I know," Lew said. "You say that your old Captain Carvalho was the greatest, and maybe he was, but until there's evidence . . ."

"Evidence?" said John Joseph. "It was all destroyed."

"But why?" Lew reached two more Ballentines out of the sack at his feet and slid one over to my grandfather.

John Joseph took the ale and opened it. "He vanished," he said. "And then history forgot him."

"Ha," said Carmine. "Maybe he sunk in a big storm."

My grandfather ignored him.

"What was he up to?"

"He had big ideas," said my grandfather.

"Me, too," said Carmine. "I got big ideas, too. That's how a man gets ahead." He would not drink any of Lew's ales but kept a bag of his own by the swing. He tossed off the can he had been drinking, stooped, fetched another, and turned to wink at my mother. She smiled.

"That old navigator could have had the world in the palm of his hand." John Joseph made a clutching motion and looked at us solemnly.

"He was here," I said to Carmine.

"John Joseph told me."

"Of course he was here," my grandfather said. "No good sailor could have missed this harbor."

"True," said Carmine.

"Even the Pilgrims wound up here, and they were headed for Virginia," I said.

All the history books talked about the Pilgrims settling in Plymouth, but they had landed here first, before pushing on. "That's why we have the monument," I said.

"Why that pathetic bunch gets a monument is beyond me," said my grandfather. "A bunch of farmers. What, about a thousand miles off course?"

"Because they were the first *Yankees*," Carmine said.

"Well," said Lew, "and they kept records. Generally speaking, no records, no history."

"That a fact?" Carmine said, kicking the swing a little.

"Farmers," said my grandfather, disdainfully. "Name me one goddamned farmer that ever did anything worth talking about."

"Don't swear so much, Papa," my mother said.

"Old MacDonald," said Carmine. My mother laughed a little.

"You're ignorant," John Joseph said.

"Well, I try," said Carmine. "I never been up in that monument of yours, though. I ought to do that some day. Don't you think so, Josie?" He gave me one of his winks.

"You know," said Lew, after a quiet space of a few minutes, "I have to agree that your Captain Carvalho vanished all right." He gestured vaguely into the air with his ale can.

"All she wrote," said Carmine.

John Joseph spit at the woodpile. "Yes, all you heard of after that was Cabral and that gang."

"And the Corte Real brothers," I said.

Lew grinned at me. "Right-o, Joachim," he said. "And don't forget you-know-who."

"Don't mention him to me," my grandfather said. "If you ask me, it was *him* and those other damn *Lisbons* did the old captain in."

"Who?" said Carmine.

"Are you dense, man?" said John Joseph.

Lew laughed into his ale, but Carmine caught him. "Nobody's talking to *you*," he said. He turned to my grandfather. "Hey, it was just *fado*, John Joseph." He shook his head. "It wasn't meant to be."

"*Vay cagar!*" my grandfather said.

"Papa!" My mother stamped her foot, but Carmine only laughed. How quickly he had blended into our little household. He was with us nearly every day now, showing up usually after his boat had off-loaded and he had washed and changed into a set of his finely pressed shore clothes. When he was in time for supper, my mother would set out a plate for him, and if he showed up later in the evening, she would sit with him in the dooryard, sometimes along with John Joseph and the rest of us as we did on this night. But often, too, he would take my mother and me on walks down through the center of town, threading our way through the alien crowds and stopping in all the summer shops as we had done on that first trip to the movies.

I don't know why Great Aunt Theophila didn't drive him off. Maybe it was the power of my saint. Maybe it was because there was some small particle of hope hidden away in her heart. Carmine always paid her a special respect. He brought her vials of holy water and boxes of votive candles and small red packages of incense cones in fragrances of orange and sandalwood and pine. On the nights that he arrived at suppertime, he always came with sacks from Perreira's Market, full of yams and potatoes and carrots and corn, bottles of Pepsi Cola, and of course cans of Ballentine's. The icebox and pantry swelled from his visits, and he was always sure to bring something of a favorite of my aunt's—the yams, or sometimes fava beans or turnip tops, which Great Aunt Theophila never acknowledged aloud, but which she had my mother prepare for her nonetheless. And still, Great Aunt Theophila clung to a sense of foreboding about him. "He talks like he's going to stay the winter," she would say with disgust.

"What are you afraid of?" my mother would ask.

"*You* know," my aunt would say.

But still Carmine remained with us, and none of us could seem to figure out where that would lead.

Now Carmine stood up from the swing, and the seat squeaked back and forth as the balance shifted. My mother wrapped her hand around the rusted chain that suspended the canvas seat and steadied herself. She looked up at Carmine. He ran his fingers through his hair and walked over to the fence to stare off toward Madeleine Sylvia's house. When he turned around, he said, "Rosa, should I tell John Joseph my plan?"

"I don't know," my mother said. "Suit yourself, I guess."

"What's this?" my grandfather asked. He looked from my mother to Carmine and back again.

Lew got up from the table. "Roger and I are late already," he said quietly.

"Big ideas," Carmine said.

My grandfather said nothing.

"Good night, all," Roger said. He and Lew disappeared upstairs.

"You're a man who respects big ideas," Carmine said to my grandfather. "You have to have big ideas to get ahead. You have to be ambitious."

"Like you?" said John Joseph.

Carmine cleared his throat. "Just listen. You know fishing's a good living, but it's not going to last. Think of this town and where the money is. I ask you that one question is all, hey. Who is the richest man in town?"

"Mr. Van Horten," I said, when my grandfather did not answer.

"Keerect," said Carmine. "And does he go fishing?"

Again my grandfather only looked at him. "No," I answered. "He runs the big hotel."

"Exactly. He makes his money off the summer boarders. That's how it's done. It's the future."

"He's a god-damned summer boarder himself," my grandfather said.

"Carmine wants to start a restaurant some day," my mother said.

"Clams," said Carmine. "Seafood. A seafood restaurant. You can't beat this idea."

"Don't count on it," said my grandfather.

"You'd be part of it," said Carmine. "You'd be the supplier of all the shellfish."

"I could help with the cooking," my mother said.

"Hell, we'd be in Florida every winter. We could have a restaurant in Florida, too."

"When's all this going to happen?" my grandfather asked.

"Couple of years."

"Count me in," said my grandfather.

"You mean it?"

"You're ignorant," my grandfather said.

"Papa . . ." my mother started, but before she could finish, we all heard the stretch of spring on the screen door, and Great Aunt Theophila, wearing a light kerchief and a long, dark dress, stepped out and took a chair.

"A nice evening for sitting, ma'am," Carmine said.

"What kind of foolishness are you all talking about out here?" she asked.

"The Pilgrims," said my grandfather.

"In a pig's eye," she said.

John Joseph pursed his mouth to one side, looked at Great Aunt Theophila and then looked over at Carmine. "Our friend Carmine here was saying how he'd never been up in our great monument to the Pilgrims," John Joseph said.

"Neither have I, nor anyone else with any sense," said Great Aunt Theophila. "What are all these beer cans doing all over the yard?"

"The boys upstairs," my grandfather said.

"I'll take care of it," Carmine said, but he didn't move.

"We could all go sometime," my mother said.

"Go where?" said Great Aunt Theophila.

Carmine looked at my mother and then spoke to my aunt. "Up in that big stone tower, ma'am. It would be educational."

"I see," she said. She looked over at me. "Josie, the kerosene bottle needs filling."

"Okay, *Tia*," I said.

"It's late," she said. She got up and walked toward the door.

"Good night, ma'am," Carmine said.

I couldn't tell if she answered him or not. Carmine stretched. "Josie, you'd better get that kerosene for your aunt. I've got to go, myself. Captain Alfie will be banging on my door to go fishing at three o'clock in the morning."

"You're not going to leave?" my mother said.

"Best thing," Carmine said. "Right, John Joseph?"

"Leave me out of it," said my grandfather.

"We'll all go up in that thing tomorrow if I get ashore in time, though."

Carmine walked off and my grandfather ambled down the walk, heading toward the East End. My mother went into the house, and I pumped a bottle of kerosene from the dispenser in the near-dark corner of the woodhouse. My mother and Great Aunt Theophila were already arguing by the time I carried the bottle back indoors.

"You simply cannot continue to go walking with that man all over town," Great Aunt Theophila said. She let her brown fist drop into her lap. "People will talk."

"And what are they going to talk about?" my mother snapped.

"He's a *Lisbon*. What else about him, we don't know."

"Why don't you leave us alone?"

"Leave you alone?" said my great aunt. "God help us. I left you alone once, and look what happened!"

. . .

The next day, when Carmine appeared in the late afternoon, dressed up and ready to take us on our walk, I understood that my mother had scored a small victory. "Up the monument!" said Carmine, and my mother and I left the house without a word from Great Aunt Theophila.

Carmine was expansive on our walk toward the center of town. "You'll get a thrill out of this, Josie, I guarantee it. "I've been up in the Empire State Building, you know, and that's the tallest in the world. You can't compare your monument with that, but I can tell you, you'll get a thrill all the same."

I didn't say a word to Carmine, but I had already been up in our monument a few years before. John Joseph had taken me, and we had gotten in for free simply because he had refused to pay the man in the cramped little ticket booth at the bottom of the tower. My grandfather and I had kept this trip to ourselves because he told me Great Aunt Theophila would give him trouble about it. She saw the monument as something for the summer people, something our people had no business visiting. But Carmine was here now, and he was taking us up to the tower, and my aunt said nothing to stop him. His way with her made me dizzy.

We walked along the front street and down past the center of town, then doubled back leisurely, taking a quiet walk along some back lanes and sidestreets, making our way to the monument's grand hill. Along our way we passed Captain Small's Home, what we all called the *poor house*, the place where our town provided for the infirm and indigent. It was a two-story clapboard house near the edge of the old Yankee cemetery, and it was where Domingo the Beach Cleaner lived. My grandfather would bring me along with him when he visited Domingo in the winter months, and we would take him boxes of Royal Lunch crackers and jars of cheese spread, or when such things were not easily come by, simply pockets full of Lipton tea bags, which John Joseph lifted from Great Aunt Theophila's pantry. I pointed out Domingo's window to Carmine, but he was holding my mother's hand now, and paying me no attention.

We rounded the big hill and made our way up the walk, Carmine stopping at the booth and paying our entrance. I leaned back and looked up. The tower stood two hundred and fifty feet high, with ornately-capped arched openings at the top where people could look out in the four cardinal directions. Sometimes the wind would howl through these openings, and in the dark, on a winter's night, coming back from a visit to Domingo, my grandfather used to spook me by telling me the thing was alive. He also told me that this hill was where our great ancestor would have buried a stone marker to claim this land for Portugal, since all the old navigators carried these stones to make such claims. "This thing," he would say, "is built right overtop that stone. It's the highest hill overlooking the harbor, so that's where the old captain would plant it. You'd have a hell of a time finding it now, though."

I didn't say anything to Carmine about John Joseph's stories now. I just watched him take my mother's hand again and walk her like a queen among the summer people entering the tower. There were people all around us in their bright clothes, and they laughed and screamed to hear their voices echo up the long shaft. We ascended the series of long ramps that ran along the walls, up and up. The walls and the sides of the ramps were covered with the bright graffiti of strangers—names and dates and drawings in lipstick, pen, and pencil. Carmine and my mother walked, swinging their hands like they were summer people themselves, and I saw Carmine say something to her that I couldn't hear, but it made her laugh. Then they stopped, and Carmine asked my mother for her lipstick. He took it from her and on a clear space on the inside wall of a ramp, he drew a lopsided heart with both their names in it. "*Now* look what you did," my mother said. "What if somebody sees that?"

"Well, so what?"

"They'll talk," said my mother.

"Who?" said Carmine.

"I don't know."

"Well I don't either," he said.

"You ruined my tube of lipstick."

"Hell, I'll buy you two more afterward." Carmine tossed the little gold tube to me. "Go ahead, write your name."

I looked at my mother.

"Go ahead," she said.

I printed J-O-A-C-H-I-M in thick letters.

"It's a long way up," my mother said.

"Josie, you can run up ahead. I'll walk with your ma. She's not as strong-legged as we are." He winked, and I took off jogging up the long entrail. When I finally reached the top I had time to lean against the iron rail and breathe hard and let myself shiver with the height. There was a mild wind coming out of the west. Tiny scrolls of white crawled along the surface of the harbor, and the summer people around me held onto their hats as they peered down at the town.

When my mother and Carmine finally emerged from the stairwell, they stopped and blinked in the late afternoon sun. They didn't come over to the rail right away. Carmine's silk dragon jacket luffed in the breeze. He pulled out a Chesterfield and lit it, cupping the match, then lighting one more with the tip of that one for my mother. Backed by the gray stone of the tower and flushed by the climb, she seemed to glow in that high, rare light. She took the cigarette in her lips and drew on it deeply. Her long hair was pulled back in the tortoise combs that Carmine had given her, and behind her ear she had pinned a red flower that she had plucked from the cemetery fence on our way to the hill. The wind whipped her dress around her long legs, and the line of her stockings showed darkly in the sun. "That's one tough-looking cookie, your ma," Carmine said. He took his Brownie camera from around his neck and snapped a picture and then took one of me, and he shot several others from each side of the platform.

"See if you can find our roof," my mother said. She would not come near the fencing at the edge until Carmine put his arm around her waist and walked her there.

"Ha," said Carmine. "Look, hey. The summer boarders look like ants down there."

I stood with them a while and watched the crawl of summer people along the wharf. The Boston steamer, tied up at the wharf's end, looked like a toy with precise, intricate detail. It blasted on its airhorns now, and the sound soaked the town below us. A few of the bright knots of people broke up as some began to run for the wharf. The boat would leave in ten minutes. I left my mother's side and walked around to the back, the north-facing platform, and I looked out over the scrub woods and dunes and ocean. The sea was darker there than on the harbor side. From there you got a real sense of what the town grew from: naked land, beachgrass, dune, swamp. The wind picked up. It snapped at me now and drew the skin of my face pleasantly back. When I looked out on the bare and empty parts of our town like this, I felt lonely and afraid. It was easy to tell that there was a wildness here that nothing— no powers in heaven—presided over. Great Aunt Theophila wouldn't think so, but maybe she was wrong. Did something preside over the fortunes of the faithful, only? I thought of Carmine, his arm around my mother's waist. I heard the Boston boat blow its final warning blast. The breeze freshened off the water, and the chambers of the monument whistled deeply. I was aware that I stood in the cavernous hollow of one of its mouths.

On the way home we roamed the summer shops and Carmine bought us an early supper of *salchicas* at Antone Lema's Hot Dog stand. We stopped in Parson's Pharmacy and Carmine bought my mother two tubes of lipstick. The heights of the monument had filled him with talk. He spoke of taking my mother flying in an airplane. I walked behind them and watched them again. They held hands, fingers entwined. My mother did this easily, carelessly. They stepped slowly and every few steps their shoulders would touch. I let myself fall farther behind, and then they did not notice me until they approached Juney's Tap. As though they had crossed an imaginary line, Carmine dropped her hand, and they both stopped and turned, waiting for me to catch up with them. A few steps later, my mother pulled the flower from the pin in her hair and tossed it over a hedge.

It was just dark when we got back to the house. Great Aunt Theophila, Sheika Nunes, and Ernestina the Shoemaker's Wife sat in the parlor. "Well, here they are now," Sheika said quickly as we came through the kitchen. She aimed a quick pinch at my ass as I passed her chair, and she gave Carmine a thin smile. He produced a bag of saltwater taffy that he had bought in one of the shops and gave it to her. "Sweets for the sweet," he said. He turned to Ernestina and my great aunt. "Good evening, ladies."

Sheika took the bag of candies from Carmine. "I surely don't need *these*," she said, shrugging the heft of her body.

"Run them through your cat and sprinkle them on your roses, then." He smiled deeply at her and then he shifted his attention to Great Aunt Theophila. He read something in her face. "What's wrong, Hettie?"

"We're not late," my mother said sullenly.

"Oh, it's the one across the fence," Ernestina said. She smiled as though she knew of some joke that no one else could get ahold of.

"The *Lisbon*," my great aunt said. She looked at Carmine then looked away.

"Don't start *that* stuff," said my mother.

"It's Madeleine," Sheika said. "She got ahold of Arthur Enos down to the Town Hall, and he just came by to say that she can get a paper."

"An order," said Great Aunt Theophila.

"What are you talking about?" my mother said.

"Ask John Joseph," said my aunt. "He had to have those *canailla* at his cursed clambake. Now the *Lisbon* is causing trouble. She can get an order to make us build the fence new and tear the side stairs on the woodhouse down. The outhouse, too. And the ducks will have to go."

"Go where?" said my mother.

"How should I know?" Great Aunt Theophila said.

"They could all come up to Elvio's barn," Ernestina said.

"Like hell," my mother said. "They're sweet little things. They never hurt anybody."

"That's not the worry," said my aunt. "Who has the money to build a fence? Who's going to fix those stairs?"

"Nobody's taking those ducks," my mother said.

"We were waiting for her to come out while Ernestina was here," Sheika said. "She would fix her good." Ernestina smiled. Even though the *Pico* ladies all said she was a *bruxa*, someone who could give the evil eye, mostly Ernestina just smiled and listened, although she often made special teas and herb pouches which were known for their effectiveness against grippe, gout, and other ailments.

"She's afraid to show her face," said Great Aunt Theophila. "Imagine, going to the Town Hall!"

Carmine cleared his throat. "Maybe it doesn't mean anything," he said. "Maybe all you need to do is talk to that fellow . . ."

"Arthur Enos," said my mother.

"Yes," said Carmine. "Tell him you'll do those things. I could put a new fence up easy."

"We are being bossed," said my aunt. "I won't have it. Where John Joseph is, I'd just like to know."

Carmine sniffed, and my mother shot him a look. If he had been going to speak, he changed his mind.

"He's never here when we need him," said Great Aunt Theophila. "He causes all this trouble, and then try and find him! All he's good for is to drink with those bum friends of his and tell those ridiculous stories. He thinks he's the Prince of America. He came over on a damn fishing boat just like all the other men. Then because he couldn't get anything to go right, he gets drunk and tells us we're descended from the King of Portugal or whatever else."

"The Navigator," I said.

My great aunt glared at me.

"Go make us all some tea, Josie," Sheika said.

Carmine looked at me then spoke to my mother, but for all to hear. "I'd best be going. Early fishing in the morning."

"I'll walk you to the door," my mother said.

My great aunt shook her head but she didn't say anything, so I went to the kitchen and put the *chaleira* full of tea water over the kerosene burner and then slunk away from the parlor. I wanted to go the bureau shrine and talk with my saint, but Uncle Paddy was lying on the bed awake, staring at the ceiling and whistling some old tune softly to himself. I went off to my own bedroom, angry at my grandfather now, and thinking of the power—maybe the power—of Saint Joachim the Patriarch, for it was true that John Joseph was not here to help us with our troubles, but now Carmine was. He even said he'd help with the fence. I lay in bed until the *Pico* ladies left and the house grew quiet. Perhaps it was a sign of something from my saint, because I drifted off into sleep saying a string of *Pater Nosters* and then at some hour John Joseph woke the house up when he came home. I jumped from sleep when I heard him swear, "Jesus Christ Almighty," and then I heard a frenzied quacking coming from the back room. A light went on in the kitchen. "Papa, you're drunk," my mother shouted.

"There's a god-damned duck in my bed," John Joseph moaned.

"I put the ducks in the back room," my mother said. "You think I don't know how to respond to a threat? What if someone tries to take them?"

"Rosa, you're crazy," my great aunt called out. "You can't keep those dirty things in the house."

"Get the hell outdoors where you belong," my grandfather yelled at a duck.

"Papa, you can't!"

It was too late for my mother to stop John Joseph. I came out of my room just in time to see him hurl one duck and then another out the back room door. "What a humiliation," he said.

"Put them back in the pen then," cried my mother. "They'll run away. If anything happens to them, *you're* responsible!

I ran out in my shorts and put the ducks in the pen, cutting off the fracas that I saw developing. My grandfather, looking very tired, muttered something in Portuguese about the Pope, and as if the entire house were a quilt that he could somehow pull over his head and shut out the world, he lay back on his rumpled cot and passed out with all his clothes on.

7

According to Sheika Nunes and my great aunt, it was important to remember that the saints were once real people who had talked and breathed, just like anyone else. This is why we kept images of them in plaster and plastic and stone and wood. It helped us to keep from confusing them with, say, angels, which we could never become —unless we died as an infant right after baptism while we were still in the most pure state of grace available. But this was something that was beyond our reach once we were old enough to even think about it. The images were only there to remind us of the saints, but the images didn't have any special properties—unless there was a miracle, like when a wooden statue would weep real tears for whole crowds of people to see, but this usually only happened in one of the old countries. The statues and cards on Great Aunt Theophila's bureau had no miraculous properties themselves. We had to pray beyond them. Once my grandfather choked the image of Saint Anthony, patron of lost objects, when he couldn't find his good handline. This was a wooden rack of heavy gauge line that he used for fishing in the deep channels for monster halibut. He had been about to miss a good tide and came in from the woodhouse cursing in Portuguese and thumping around the house in his hip boots. Finally he stomped into Aunt Theophila's room and grabbed that mild-faced statue around the neck and throttled it. "Give it up," he grunted, his thick knuckles turning gray with force, as though he might pop the head off the plaster body. He had his handline back within minutes, which must have puzzled him, for I had slipped out and put it back into his gear basket, right where he had just looked for it. I had taken the line earlier that morning to show to Roger and Lew, and I had forgotten it on their upstairs kitchen table. It was just another one of those situations that clarified nothing, like when I pinched Carmine's wonderful silk jacket. You could say a saint was behind it, acting through me. Or you could say otherwise. Cases like this didn't prove much. They just kept you thinking.

What to make of the next day, late afternoon when the boats were in, and Carmine showed up with Freddie Pessoa from the boatyard, planks and two-by-fours over their shoulders? "Some scrap from down at the boatyard," Carmine said. "Freddie wasn't going to do nothing with it."

"Just sitting there in a pile," Freddie said. He was a skinny man who always wore a Red Sox baseball cap and a mess of brass keys on his belt. This was wood for the fence we had to repair. It wasn't enough, but it was a start, and the men laid the boards down alongside the old mossy ruined fence while Madeleine Sylvia watched from her back porch. What more sign could I wish for? Here was Carmine, strong and direct, changing the course of our fortunes. I saw now how Great Aunt Theophila must view John Joseph, for *he* should have done this. Instead he had done nothing but drift back and forth from the back room to his woman friend down at the East End. He drifted and we all drifted with him, except for Carmine.

Carmine started eating supper with us regularly that week, and it was a gloomy, drizzly Friday when he showed up with a bucket of squid, which my mother fixed in a stew and served with hot bread. It was nearly dark when we finished eating. Carmine opened two new cans of ale for himself and Uncle Paddy, and just then there came a knock at the back door. It was Joe Dias. My mother got up and let him in, and Carmine leaned back in his chair and called out to him, "Joe, hey, come in, come in." Great Aunt Theophila drew up and gave Carmine a look that struck him like a stick. I could see he caught her meaning. *What are you doing, inviting people in as if this were your house?* Of course, she said nothing aloud with Joe Dias standing there, but Carmine settled the front legs of his chair back to the floor and dropped his eyes. My mother led Joe into the kitchen. "Oh, jeeze, you're still eating supper," he said.

When neither Carmine nor my aunt would say anything, Uncle Paddy motioned to the table. "Sit down," he said. "Have something."

"Oh, no," said Joe. "I just ate, thanks. Maybe an ale."

"John Joseph isn't home, if you've come looking for him," Aunt Theophila said in a flat voice.

"No, Hettie, I came to see Carmine."

My mother eyed Joe Dias coldly. "What are you up to?" she said.

Joe waved his hand and turned to Carmine. "Mooney Prada is tied up down to the Cold Storage Wharf, and he can't get his engine started. Tide's going down you know, and he might get stuck."

"Somebody could just tow him out past low water," Uncle Paddy observed.

"Be the best thing, Paddy, no doubt about it," Joe Dias said, "but you know what Old Man Prada is like."

"Who is this guy?" Carmine asked. "Do I know him?"

"You know. He's got that old trapboat, the *Nossa Senhora*."

Carmine nodded.

"Well," Joe said, "I come down the steps of the plant, and I saw a gang down there at the wharf, so I went and looked. Mooney says there's something balled up with his wiring. I thought maybe you'd go take a look at it. Wouldn't hurt it none, I figure."

"I don't know all that much, Joe."

"You know more than those guys down there."

Carmine looked at my mother. "Maybe I'd better go and see if I can help."

"Suit yourself," my mother said, shrugging and looking away from him.

"It won't take but a few minutes, Rosa," Carmine said. She didn't answer him. He ran a knuckle over his lips. "Hettie," he said, turning to my great aunt, "would you mind if I went along? I hate to run from your table."

"Don't fall overboard," my great aunt said dryly.

"I'll go, too," I said.

"It's started raining," said Great Aunt Theophila. She used a tone that meant I should stay home. But my mother said, "Take your slicker jacket," and I got up from the table.

The rain that Great Aunt Theophila had seen beading on the glass of the kitchen window was hardly more than the drizzle that had fallen all day—just a heavy, drifting mist that sparkled in the backyard's outdoor light and darkened the shoulders of Joe Dias's bomber jacket with a slow stain. Carmine and I wore yellow slickers—he had borrowed John Joseph's from the peg in the back room. He also took the long, black flashlight we kept there.

Old Man Prada's trapboat was tied up at the first ladder, and I could make out several figures down on the boat, holding heavy lights and standing in the drizzle under other lanterns that had been fastened on the wheelhouse. I followed Carmine and Joe down the wharf's slippery ladder. The *Nossa Senhora* rode low with the outgoing tide, and the water that she floated in was black and slick, the surface textured only by the misty rain which clung to the old boat's planking and lay in a film over the lenses of the battery lanterns. The *Nossa Senhora* was one of the oldest trapboats in the town fleet, and she was always giving Old Man Prada troubles—leaky seams, broken steering chains, bent propeller shafts—and he often tied up to the wharf and tried to fix things himself rather than taking her into Ferreira's Boatyard, where the cradle fees, as he told it, took the food right from his mouth.

Old Man Prada stood in the aft hatch of the wheelhouse, chewing the stub of a rain-soaked cigar, his wool skipper's cap pulled down over his brow. Although I could not see them clearly, I could tell from their low voices and silhouettes that Freddie Pessoa and Louis Avila were down below him, bent over a part of the engine, and crowded next to them was Manny Buckets holding a big square battery lantern. "This is Carmine," Joe Dias said. "You seen him around. He's fishing on his cousin Alfie's boat."

"The guy from the Guinea boats in New Bedford," said Manny Buckets.

"That's me," Carmine said.

"There's juice at the battery, but it don't seem to go nowhere," said Louis Avila. He was bareheaded and wore a paint-stained sweatshirt. His face was tight and serious in the mealy light of the lanterns.

"You couldn't get anybody else from the boatyard?" Carmine asked.

"Clement Cabral is the man to see, but he's off somewhere by this time," Louis said.

"I went by his house," said Freddie Pessoa, speaking from the shadow where he huddled. "They were gone already. Probably took Lucia to the show."

"They don't have trapboats in New Bedford, do they?" Manny Buckets asked Carmine. There was an edge in his voice. I moved my small light just a bit and shined it on part of the engine's manifold in a way that I could see Manny better. He wore a dark fatigue cap with the brim turned up. I knew the look in his droopy eyes. He had been drinking.

Carmine straightened up and smiled at Manny the way he so often smiled at Great Aunt Theophila. "No trapboats there to speak of," he said.

"Try, try," said Old Man Prada, putting a hand on Carmine's shoulder and pointing to the engine. It sat there like a hole in the darkness smelling of fuel and old metal. Carmine bent down and touched some things, followed some wires with his fingers, tapped here and there with his screwdriver, asked for more light. "Did you smell anything?"

he asked. "Was there any smoke or sparks?"

"Nothing like that," said Louis Avila.

"Well," said Carmine, "better tow this thing out farther on the wharf while there's still water under the keel."

"Nobody had to come from New Bedford to tell us that," Manny Buckets said.

Freddie Pessoa laughed a nervous little laugh. "Manny's a kidder," he said to Carmine. "It don't mean nothing."

Carmine smiled. "Well, he might hurt my feelings."

Old Man Prada chewed his cigar in resignation. "I'll stay with the boat. You boys can get me a tow?"

"Sure," said Louis Avila. We all moved back up the ladder to the wharf, the men first and me scrambling up after. The drizzle still floated down in a soft curtain past the wharf's single yellow light, and I edged toward the small shelter of the net shed.

"Sorry, Mooney," Joe Dias called down to Old Man Prada.

"Yeah," said Carmine. "I'm okay on the easy stuff, but this engine is over my head."

In the space of a few more heartbeats we all would have walked from the wharf and gone on our ways, and nothing would have happened, but Manny Buckets opened his wide mouth once more. "Rosa Carvalho must be some of the easy stuff, then," he said quietly, almost as though he spoke to an imaginary person at his elbow, a trace of contempt in his voice. This caught me like a hook in my flesh. Manny Buckets had once—only once—come calling on my mother with a heart-shaped box of candy under his arm, but he had been drunk, and my mother had sent him away.

Carmine stopped at this, and I heard him sigh. He walked over to Manny Buckets. "Do you and me have to go someplace and talk privately?"

"Well," said Manny, "I just meant that the woman has a history."

The sound came first, before I saw any movement at all. Just a quick splat. And then I realized that Carmine had hit Manny Buckets.

Manny just looked at him.

"Apologize!" Carmine said. Manny did nothing. He was half a head taller than Carmine, and much heavier.

Then I saw Carmine's yellow slicker flash again, and there was another splat as Carmine's hand struck the side of Manny's face.

"So you are getting the best part of her," Manny said.

And Carmine, almost too fast to see, hit him again. Manny started swinging now, his big right hand looping from somewhere in back of his hip. Carmine saw it coming only at the last moment, but he had time to throw up a block. It didn't do him any good. Manny's fist crashed through Carmine's upthrown arm, hit him on the forehead, and knocked him over backward where he skidded several inches on the wet planks.

"All right," said Manny. "That's enough."

No one moved except Carmine, who scrambled to his feet and tore John Joseph's slicker off and tossed it aside.

"That's enough!" Manny said again. "Be still!"

Carmine didn't listen to any of that. He edged in on Manny with his hands up, his left foot forward, his head weaving from side to side. He hit Manny three or four times, faster than I had ever seen anyone throw punches before, but Manny held his ground and hit Carmine again, this time in the chest. Carmine's feet went out from under him again, and I heard him wheeze to get his breath as he lay there in a heap. He didn't stay down long, but he got to his feet slowly this time, and this time Manny watched him and waited for him to come, his big hands balled up by his sides.

No one moved to break up the fight. Then I saw something flash in Carmine's hand. And then, as if I were dreaming, I saw another hand, black and shiny, holding a pitchfork, rising over the side of the wharf. It was not the Arch Fiend but Old Man Mooney Prada rushing up the ladder, in his rubber-gloved hand one of the pitchforks he carried on the *Nossa Senhora* to offload the herring and mackerel and whiting into the wire lift baskets. "What the hell are you doing, you two ignorant sons of bitches!" he yelled. "Who the hell is going after my tow?" Everyone on the wharf stopped as Mooney Prada, pitchfork in hand, rose up the ladder, stepped to the wharf, and advanced on Manny and Carmine.

"Go easy, Mooney," said Louis Avila.

Old Man Prada turned on Louis and unleashed a string of curses in the old tongue, and this gave Carmine a chance to ease away from him. Manny Buckets backed against the net shed and leaned there catching his breath. "I'm running the god-damned hell aground, and you are all up here beating each other's brains out, which you ain't even got any," Mooney said.

"I'll go get your tow, hey," Carmine said, and he moved between Mooney Prada and the wharf's edge just as Mooney swung around again with the pitchfork and started to swear some more in Portuguese. The old man's sudden movement caused Carmine to overreact and he jumped back, slipped, and caught the backs of his heels on the log that ran along edge of the wharf. He beat the air with his arms and managed to hang out over the water at an odd angle long enough to say "Aay" before he fell off into the dark.

If we had been under a dread spell ever since we came to the old trap-boat, Carmine's falling overboard seemed to break it. Joe Dias and Old Man Prada helped Carmine back up the ladder to the wharf. His clothes were plastered to the solid form of his body. He sputtered and shook water from himself. Freddie and Louis already had Manny Buckets in hand and were leading him off in the direction of the boat-yard. "I never seen such a bunch of damn foolishness," said Mooney. "Carmine, you shouldn't pay Manny any mind. He's ignorant."

"Ah, well," said Carmine uncertainly. He took his shirt off, wrung it out and put it back on, then did the same with his pants. He picked up my grandfather's slicker and pulled it over his shoulders.

"Jesus, I've gone and done it now," Joe Dias said. "Rosa and Hettie will blame this all on me for sure. We'd better go up to Juney's for a while. You can clean up in his toilet."

I followed the men along the back of the Cold Storage loading docks and around the brick outbuildings until we came out on the front street, a few houses down from Juney's Tap. It felt like everybody in that smoky room stopped what they were doing when we walked in. I was too young to be there, and Carmine was soaked, but we made our way back to a corner booth and sat down anyway. The men drank wine to warm them up, and Carmine bought me a bottle of Coke. A knot about the size of walnut sat above Carmine's left eye, and even as we sat there it got bigger. From time to time he'd reach over to my cold Coke bottle and roll it over the swelling. "He made me see lights," Carmine said, "but I've been hit harder."

I was quiet.

Carmine lifted his wine glass and drank off the rest. "I was lucky not to hit the deck of that boat on the way down. Would have broken my back," he said.

Again I was quiet.

"It was a matter of honor, Josie," Carmine told me. "It's what had to be done. You understand?"

"Sure, I understand," I said. "But right at the end. What were you going to do?"

"What's that?"

"I saw something in your hand. A little knife."

"Not a chance," Carmine said.

"Just when Mooney came up the ladder."

"It was dark, Josie. You didn't see anything. There wasn't anything."

"I just thought . . ."

"Look," said Carmine, "it's nothing. You think I'd use a knife in a fight like that? With that guy Manny Buckets? Never happen. I'm not saying I don't have one. I'm not saying I wouldn't carry one. It's just good sense. You can ask old John Joseph about that from what I hear. But tonight you didn't see anything."

"Well okay," I said.

"You want to search me?" Carmine looked at Joe Dias and back at me. He gave a little laugh.

"Hettie is going to throw a fit," Joe said.

"It was dark," Carmine said.

"You just slipped," I said. "That's what we'll say."

"You've got it right, Joachim," Carmine said. "Good man." He ordered two more wines and another Coke. "You're with the men, now," Carmine said and winked. "You know, I don't mean any disrespect— Paddy and John Joseph are two tough guys. I've heard stories—but they're old. They're old men, and that's where they live. They live in those stories. You need to be around someone younger. Show you some things. Show you how to be strong."

I didn't know what he wanted me to say, so I took a long swallow of my Coke.

Joe Dias looked at the clock over the bar. "You'd best be getting back, Carmine. They'll have a fit."

"Well, how do I look?" Carmine asked.

"Not so hot," Joe said.

Joe Dias left us at the corner of Commercial Street, and Carmine and I walked quietly through the back room door. We took off our slickers and hung them on their pegs, and we dripped for a while on the floor. "What the hell happened to *you*?" my mother asked Carmine when she came and saw his soaked clothes and his bruise.

"I slipped and bumped my head."

I expected that my mother would see through this, and I braced myself. But she only turned back to the kitchen and shrugged. "Well," she said, "you could have done *that* right here."

I was worried that Great Aunt Theophila or my mother would find out about the fight. It seemed impossible that news of it wouldn't travel along the fences and hedges of the West End and find its way into our household. But days passed and nothing happened. Joe Dias stayed away, but Carmine kept coming for supper, the bump on his forehead shrinking and darkening each successive day that he came knocking with his bags of vegetables and buckets of fish. He kept bringing gifts, too. Good beeswax candles for Great Aunt Theophila, and spices and perfume for my mother. He and Freddy Pessoa brought in another load of planks and laid them with others by the fence, and he cleaned up the duckpen and painted the stairs to Roger and Lew's with gray deck enamel. It wasn't everything that Madeleine Sylvia wanted, but she must have eyed this as some progress, because she was quiet and our household had calmed some since we received her *Lisbon* orders. One late afternoon when Carmine was sitting on the swing with an ale and Uncle Paddy and Elvio the Shoemaker sat at the big radio, Johnny Squash and my grandfather showed up, hauling a big round rusted piece of metal in a kid's Radio Flyer wagon. They pulled the wagon into the center of the little yard and sat around it, prying ale cans. The thing sat in the wagon, crusted with barnacles and oxidation and smelling of the sea.

"Come from the *Coracao*?" Paddy asked.

"Hung the drag on her this morning," Johnny Squash said, his eye already gleaming from the afternoon's drinking.

"Old steamship gauge," Elvio said.

I went to the woodhouse and got a screwdriver and began chipping some of the crud away while the men talked. In a short time I was able to uncover some lettering: *White Iron Works—Brooklyn, New York.*

"I heard of the Bath Iron Works down to Maine," Johnny Squash said. "You know. Finish every ship ahead of schedule and under budget. Never heard of the White Iron Works, though."

"There's a lot you haven't heard of," said my grandfather. He fished an ale can out of the carton by his feet and looked at Carmine. "What do *you* say?" he said. I watched my grandfather watching Carmine.

There was a moment when something passed between them. My grandfather's look was hard and even. Carmine met him with the same sort of look, but then he pursed his lips, sniffed, smiled, and said, "I've been to Brooklyn. It's a big place. Might be an iron works there."

Uncle Paddy leaned back from the radio, folded his hands over his stomach, and spoke slowly. "It's not a steam gauge, I can tell you that. Oil gauge off a big motor vessel, more than likely."

"You'd know better than anybody," Elvio said, lifting one of the phones off his ear.

"Imagine I would," said Uncle Paddy quietly.

"What will you do with it?" Carmine asked. He leaned forward and rested his elbows on his knees and looked from Johnny Squash to my grandfather and back again. "It's not worth anything, is it?"

"Ha," said my grandfather. "Is it not?"

"Worth something to Juney Costa," said Squash.

"He'll widen the tab," said John Joseph.

Carmine nodded. I knew from the start that this piece of salvage would find its way to Juney's Tap, and Juney would place it in one of the small windows that faced the front street. It would sit there next to the corrosion-green hard-hat diving helmet, the several harpoons, four cannonballs, rusted kedge anchor, brass ship's bells, four-wheel block and tackle, and various other objects hauled out of the drag of the *Coracao de Jesus* because of Johnny Squash's luck at hanging the trawl on submerged objects. Juney Costa liked to have this stuff around, and he would pay in drinks for good items. His walls were hung with figureheads, lobster claws, whaling darts, nameplates of wrecked ships. And now this thing that sat in our yard would be hauled up the street and traded for some number of wines and ales. This is where John Joseph would come in. He would negotiate for Squash and get a piece of the take.

The men were gathering themselves to leave for Juney's when my mother came out the door, drying her hands on her blue apron. "Where are you all going off to?" she asked. "Papa, I'm cooking. It's almost supper."

"Just as far as Juney's," my grandfather said.

"And I suppose you're going off with them, too?" she said to Carmine. All the men hesitated an instant. My grandfather drew on his pipe, puffed some smoke out of the corner of his mouth, and stared off at Madeleine Sylvia's backyard.

"I'll be right back," Carmine said to my mother. She turned her mouth down in disgust and went back inside, forgetting for the moment that I was with the men.

I considered the risk that Manny Buckets might be in Juney's and that some kind of trouble might start up again, but when we arrived he wasn't there. John Joseph and Squash hefted the wagon and the gauge up the front steps of the bar, causing a commotion among the men inside when they deposited the thing in the middle of Juney Costa's worn and stained floor. Juney liked it at once. He came out from behind the bar and pulled his glasses out from a case in his shirt pocket. When he bent above the gauge, his belly sagged over the waist of his baggy green pants. He scratched at the rust here and there with a fingernail and said, "Oh, she's a beauty all right. Finest kind." Immediately, he and my grandfather started haggling over its value. I don't know what they settled on, but by the time we all sat down in a booth, Juney was already pouring wine and ale. I didn't ask for anything so I wouldn't draw attention to myself, but John Joseph looked at me anyway. "Carvalho," he said. "You'd better get on out of here."

"Why?" I said.

"Because Hettie'll have a cat if she thinks I took you in here."

I felt myself color. "You're never around," I said, "and then you send me away."

He stood up. "Come over here," he said and walked to the door. I walked after him. He opened the door a crack and held it. "Look," he said, "I'll sleep in the back room tonight, and then tomorrow we'll sail. You been looking after the *Caravella*?"

"Of course," I said.

"Look, no trouble now. Go on back or we'll *all* be in the soup. We'll sail tomorrow. Let that be the end of it."

I said nothing and walked out of Juney's. I was glad to be going sailing tomorrow, but I didn't tell my grandfather that I had wanted to hang around just as much because of Carmine as of him. Maybe even more so.

The next morning was bright, cloudless, sunshine spilling in the windows and the smells of blossoms and ocean sifting through the screens. I woke early. I didn't see John Joseph anywhere in the house. My mother had taken the *Pulga* off on some errand, and Uncle Paddy sat in the yard reading the Boston paper. I walked around quietly so I wouldn't get snagged into some chore that would make me miss going off with

John Joseph, but just before I could make my way from the house, I heard my aunt say from her bedroom, "What's this? What's this? I smell perfume!"

I stood at an angle so I could peek through the open door of her room, and I saw her rise from the made-up bed where she had been sitting and move to the bureau altar. She drew a wooden kitchen match across the brass handle of the top drawer and lit a taper, then she lit all the votive candles and three cones of incense. She did all this with such complete absorption that she would not have caught me spying even if she looked right at me. When all the candles and incense cones were burning, she blew out the taper, made the sign of the cross over herself, and began to pray in soft murmur, Latin prayers, prayers of petition for I knew not what, but I sensed that one of her visions might be coming, and if one came, it meant Father Santos and Sheika Nunes, and I didn't want anything like that to spoil my day. I repeated some prayer of my own, to my own saint, mechanically, and I got out of there fast.

John Joseph was already down at the seawall watching the harbor. The *Caravella* was beached high and dry on its brown lump of sandbar, the tide still out beyond it but already on its way in so the dory would be afloat soon. This gave us time to walk out and load our supplies aboard, cart down the oars and baskets, bail and sponge her. I also stowed some new supplies that I had bought with my own money, for I had been sneaking down to the town's main wharf over the past two weeks and diving for money when the big excursion boats off-loaded their tourists from the distant cities. I told my mother and Great Aunt Theophila that I was swimming off in the other direction, near our West End breakwater because Great Aunt Theophila had forbidden me to dive for money. She did this pretty much for the same reasons that she had forbid my mother to go to work as chambermaid for Mr. Van Horten, down at the Bluefish Inn. She saw such things as demeaning and not worthy of a Carvalho. She believed diving for coins was the next thing to begging, something no *Pico* should ever do, especially down in the middle of town in front of everybody, including all the *Lisbon* captains who took their catches out at the packing houses on the big wharf. My mother didn't feel the same way—after all, Great Aunt Theophila had used the same argument to keep her from working outside the house, but I knew I'd start a row if I told anybody about what I had been doing.

Diving for money was simple. You just had to tread water by the side of the wharf and yell up to the summer people as they thronged off the cruiseboats and made their way ashore to eat hot dogs, climb the Pilgrims' tower, and buy cotton candy and nuts and souvenirs in all the shops. You yelled "Heave a nickel over," and down came nickels, dimes, quarters, even a half-dollar every now and then. There were the cheap ones in the crowd, who watched you for nothing, never reaching into their own pockets, and there were the penny-throwers, too. We kept the change in our cheeks until we rested and then moved it to the pockets of our cutoff pants. Sometimes to show our contempt we tossed the pennies back up to the wharf. I kept my money stashed in a baking soda can in my corner of the woodhouse, and I had drawn from it to buy some of the things I on-loaded this morning.

As soon as we had enough water under us, we got under way. "We'll go along the back side today," my grandfather said. That meant that we would cruise the south, outer shore of Long Point. The sea was flat and easy. I watched the way John Joseph maneuvered the dory. He was a great sailor, even in that ramshackle little boat. He held his wake behind him as straight as a length of stretched cable. We passed the weirs to starboard and tacked long, way off to the southeast and then beat back westward along the outside of the point. The long tacks gave me time to haul out some gear. I hung a net bag over the side with bottles of soda in it. I had packed a lunch of tuna and a fresh, long loaf of bread. From the marine hardware I had bought several chrome mackerel jigs—much better than the old lead jigs we used, which we had to continually burnish with the back of a knife in order to get them to shine. I had bought also a plastic box with small compartments for holding hooks and sinkers, a one-hundred-yard spool of braided nylon fifty-pound test line, and a new plastic handle for my reel.

"Where'd you get all the loot?" my grandfather asked suspiciously.

I told him about the diving.

"You're rich," he said.

"There's money left if we need anything."

"Keep it stashed. Don't tell anybody about it." He spit over the side. "If somebody sees you down at the big wharf and it gets back to Hettie, you'll be in the soup, you know."

"I'll wear these." I pulled out a pair of goggles.

My grandfather shook his head. "A thin disguise."

We were silent for a while as we sailed up the back shore of Long Point, and when we reached some shoal water off the second knuckle of that long finger, off the lighthouse at Wood End, I went over the side to look for sea clam beds with my goggles. John Joseph rigged a line, and I went into the clear water, brisk in the main currents of the bay. He made a few slow tacks, pulling me along behind the boat as I held onto the line and searched the sandy bottom, rolling over on my back when I needed to breathe. We found a fair bed, shallow enough for me to get down to, and filled a bucket, and wet a towel and covered the big shells from the sun. We anchored there in the shallows, and I lay back against my life preserver and let the sun warm me while John Joseph pulled in the net bag of soda that had been cooling. He opened a bottle for me and one for himself, and then the can of tuna. We ate the tuna from the can with our jackknives, and we washed the bread down with our sodas as the *Caravella* rocked easily on her line.

The sun was high and pressed on me, a gentle weight pushing the water's chill out of my bones. My grandfather leaned back, pillowing his head on his rolled-up shirt. Maybe this was *Grace*, what Sheika Nunes and Great Aunt Theophila always talked about attaining. It seemed we floated outside the world of trouble, beyond where anything could harm us. We lay like that, in a false peace, until I broke it. Off to the west several of the town's draggers were raising their hulls, careful miniatures in the bright distance. "I think I see Alfie DeCosta's boat, the *Fortuna*."

John Joseph turned lazily, looked over the gunwale, and when he couldn't see well enough, sat up. "No, it's the *Stella Maris*."

"Not the right color," I said. "See the dory on the wheelhouse? It's dark. It's not orange. It's Alfie and Carmine."

"Carmine the *Raposo*."

I don't know why John Joseph startled me with this. He didn't say it with rancor. But it did describe Carmine. He was a fox, smart and patient enough not to get discouraged or sent away by Great Aunt Theophila. There was no way I could even bring up the idea of my summoning Carmine with petitions to my saint. John Joseph would never stand to hear anything like that. But it seemed at least possible that there was a charm around him, a protection. Already he had altered our fortune.

"He's not a *Pico*," I said aloud.

"Ha," said my grandfather. "He's a *Lisbon* that never made it!"

I took a breath. "He's going to marry ma," I said.

He looked at me with surprise. "He said this?"

"No."

He spit over the side. On the shore, not far from the hulk of the old coastguard station, something or someone had stirred up a circle of gulls whose cries carried out to where we were anchored. I followed their flight for a moment and then tried to say what was on my mind.

"He'd be my father, then. Things would be better."

"Your father?" John Joseph said. "I think not. Not your father. What are you saying?"

"Well, I mean my stepfather, then. But it would make a difference."

"Maybe," said my grandfather. "But maybe not."

"Maybe not to you," I said. "But it would to me. It would to Ma."

"Don't feel so sorry for yourself. Or for the rest of us. You're not the king of the world yet."

His voice was taking an edge. Maybe he was just jealous or afraid of Carmine. But I could tell that this was going in a bad direction.

"*Avo*," I said, "there's so much that goes on that nobody talks about. You. Whatever happened to ... to grandma?"

"Back to the old country," said my grandfather quickly. "That's that. It doesn't have anything to do with you."

"And what about you? *Tia* makes it out like there was some big trouble."

"What do you care about those things? You have a roof over your head. You have plenty to eat."

"Our family," I started to say. Then I didn't know where I was going with it. I stopped. I couldn't get any more words to come out. John Joseph was quiet, too, and we sat in a gloomy silence until the gulls on shore rose up again, crying and circling above the clumps of beach-grass where they made their nests. Then I spotted two figures who walked from behind a hillock. I could tell by how they were proceeding that they had walked over to the point along the West End breakwater. They approached the water's edge, two women dressed in shorts, wearing nothing above their waists and carrying small, brightly colored shoulder bags. Even in that distance I recognized them from the night of the clambake. They were my grandfather's friends Amalia and Cynthia. I watched them in a kind of trance, their slow amble, their long breasts looking so strange and wonderful to me because they made no attempt to hide or cover them. When they saw the dory sitting off-shore, they waved and called, and then they did a little dance, waving their arms over their heads like tree branches and shuffling in a circle around one another. They sang a little song and laughed, those sounds coming out to us across the water like small bells tinkling.

My grandfather stood up and waved his hat. Then he turned to me. "Time to go," he said.

Even at that distance I liked watching this strange sight, the unfamiliar bare flesh of the women. But something drew me down, also. It was my grandfather. He had known that the women would be out here all along. So his coming sailing hadn't been for me, really. He just wanted to be laying off the point so Cynthia and Amalia would see him. I burned inside.

"Carvalho," he said, "up anchor. Hettie will say I've been corrupting you."

I did what he said, but I was quiet and sullen. We came around on a reach and pointed east for a while, making our way back into the harbor. I was still brooding when I saw a motorboat coming our way, speeding out from the east. I watched it close in on us, as though it had some business with us. It was a fancy Penn Yann lapstrake, with a windshield and a big red and white Johnson 35 on the transom. It met us quickly and cut across our bow, leaving us bobbing like a cork in its wake. "Sons of bitches," my grandfather growled. He held our course as we rode their wake. I watched the sleek boat slow up and come around again. There were four people in it, two young men and two girls. The were delighted with our dory and its ratty sail. They came our way laughing and pointing. My grandfather stood up and waved them off. "Right of way," he yelled. "You are in my right of way!"

The man driving the Penn Yann circled us once, watching and waving.

"You god-damned ignorant summer boarder!" my grandfather yelled.

They couldn't have heard my grandfather over the noise of their motor, but they sensed his anger and this amused them even more. They circled us again, and then the man in the back seat stood up and gave us an elaborate phony salute. The girls were pretty, in bright bathing suits, and they threw their heads back and laughed. Suddenly I was filled with hatred. It wasn't for them. It was for my grandfather and the pathetic little dory we sailed in. I hated him for being old and selfish and a failure and full of stories that were as ridiculous as this boat that these people were laughing at. My aunt was right. Carmine was right. I felt sick.

The man driving the boat—just a college kid with a crewcut and dark sunglasses—goosed his engine and swung the stern around, pulled off from us, and really gunned it. He cut one more broad circle around us. The sharp curves of his hull slapped the water. Once again we pitched helplessly, but they had tired of us, and they drew away to the west.

My grandfather was pale. He stood up, took off his hat, and mopped his forehead. I slid around him. I said nothing. I took the tiller in my two hands.

"Take in the sheet and come to port a bit."

I followed his direction, still too angry to speak.

He sat up in the bow, his hat off, his pipe in his teeth, and he said nothing to me except to give me orders. More rudder, more sheet, putting me through paces, rounding buoys and moored boats. I did everything he said. I concentrated on keeping the wake straight. We must have sailed like this for more than three hours. The tide had come all the way in and was now ebbing, and he led us east, picking our way through some of the outermost anchorages of the East End section of the harbor. There were signs of the first inner bars breaking, but we were well offshore and had plenty of water under us. John Joseph stood up and looked around, shading his eyes, and then he called for me to swap places with him. He took the tiller and sat erect, watching over the bow. He came around and then upwind sharply, and there before us was the Penn Yann. It lay quietly at its mooring, its Johnson trussed up, a blue canvas cover stretched over its cockpit.

John Joseph brought us alongside smoothly and told me to fender us off. I took hold of her gunwale. He reached over and pulled our sterns even. "Give me the gear can," he said. He had been waiting for them to moor all the time he had me sailing. He pulled his pliers out of the can, leaned over, and snapped the shearpin from their propeller. He tussled with a small fixture and then pulled the prop clear off. "Shove off," he told me.

We set a course back to the West End. "Are you going to throw it overboard?" I asked.

"No," said my grandfather. "I'm going to personally give it back to them." He spit forcefully to lee. "Right after they go out and buy themselves a new one."

8

My grandfather spent the next two nights with us, sleeping on his back room cot and gathering with his pals in the dooryard. I know he stayed around because the tab that he had negotiated over the ship's gauge at Juney's had not run out, and he wanted to stay close at hand. For me, the world had become too complicated. On the third day, my grandfather wandered off, whistling to himself, heading for the East End. Uncle Paddy had just taken my mother and Great Aunt Theophila off shopping in the *Pulga*, so I found myself alone in the house. I went into my aunt's bedroom and lit a votive candle and petitioned to St. Joachim the Patriarch. I used a considerable number of prayers in English and Latin, but I spoke to the saint in my own words, too. Something was not going right. When I finished petitioning, I flopped backward on the big bed where Uncle Paddy and Great Aunt Theophila slept. The afternoon light angled in the window panes and sparkled on the amber bottle of Fleischman's that sat on Paddy's table. The summer air was thick outside, and bees and hornets buzzed over the blossoming hydrangea and hollyhock under the windows. I closed my eyes. I smelled perfume.

I smelled perfume.

It was same perfume that my great aunt had smelled days before. It was the perfume that Carmine had given my mother, and its smell on the bed was so faint that at first I doubted whether it was really there at all. But it was. And unlike my great aunt, I knew exactly how it got there.

The day before, I had come back from an afternoon of diving at the main wharf. I made my way home by beach, going along the bulkheads and seawalls, crossing the boatyard railways and cutting underneath the Cold Storage Wharf. Then I walked up the small beach to our bend in the front street. By coming home this way it looked as though I just had been swimming here in our West End. I was happy to see that the *Pulga* was gone. I slipped into the woodhouse to stash my goggles and deposit my take of four dollars and eighty-five cents into the baking soda can. I knelt in the half-darkness of that corner of the shed and pulled out the basket where I hid my things, where I still kept the big knife and the strange ball that Johnny Squash had given me. Then I heard the sounds.

At first they were almost nothing, but then they rose above the gabbling of the ducks, the distant racheting of the fish buckets on the wharf's trestle, and the almost silent hum of the freezer engines from the deep heart of the Cold Storage plant. I listened for several minutes before I recognized that they were the voices—something like the voices—of Carmine and my mother. They sounded as though they were weeping. Yes, it was a soft sobbing or whimpering that rose and fell and floated like a breeze in and out of the window screens across the narrow walk. I froze where I was, squatting on the coal-dust covered floor.

I could have retraced my steps and gone back to the beach, but I didn't. I stayed there and listened until I understood what I listened to. It was sex, and it was not hurried or rough or wild but some slow continuing thing that kept rolling their different voices together and apart and together again. Then it struck me that *this* was the center of that strange and exclusive happiness of my mother's and Carmine's, the thing that closed a world around them. Wouldn't there be swift and utter retribution for this? I couldn't think of what to do or what calamity might fall on them now.

But the only thing that happened was that *Pulga* chugged around the corner and crunched to a stop against the side yard. Then I understood the wisdom, the craft of Carmine and my mother in choosing my great aunt's bedroom. There on the big bed, with the room's windows facing the walk, they could not be surprised by Uncle Paddy and Great Aunt Theophila coming home. They could hear everything well in advance. They hadn't counted on someone like me coming from the direction of the beach in bare feet, sneaking around in my own right. I pulled myself farther back in the shadows while Paddy and my great aunt shut down the motor, shuffled around a bit, and finally came up the walk carrying some small sacks. For a second I was sick with idea that Carmine and my mother would not have time enough to compose themselves. I strained at the air to hear the back-room conversation. I heard Carmine's voice. "Paddy, look here, hey. We came in early with a pile of crabs. Rosa has them boiling on the stove." And in that moment the sharp, sweet smell of crabs boiling on the kerosene burner reached me in the gloom of my dark corner.

If Joachim, Patron of Fathers, was offering me moral instruction by battering my spirit, I didn't like it, and I told him so to his beatific face while I burned my great aunt's incense in her mermaid ashtray. I petitioned often in the next few days. Great Aunt Theophila prayed, too, standing at the little altar with all its candles blazing. It seemed she might be working herself up to another vision, but nothing came of it. She praised me for praying so much. She could never have guessed what was on my mind. Even Sheika Nunes came and patted my buttocks and pinched my cheeks and told me how good it was to see me taking my devotions so seriously. She carried her own sweet smell of perfume and dabbed at her florid cheeks with a lace-trimmed handkerchief. "Oh, Josie," she'd say mysteriously, "if only my Manny were here." And then she'd take up a prayer with me or just murmur something to herself, her eyes closed, her pale head swaying.

When Lew and Roger knocked on the back door screen one morning, I was distant and preoccupied. My mother held the door for them to come in, but they called me out into the yard. They had set a corrugated carton on the ground. Lew was obviously excited. "Here," he said, his dark eyes shining, "is the thing itself." He pulled a scuffed volume out of the box and laid it by the radio equipment on the ell table. I touched the book, drawing my fingers over its scarred cloth cover, but I didn't open it. "It's a great book," Lew said. "One of the greatest. It's about Portugal and all the great sea voyages. It's all a big poem."

"It's by a guy named Camoens," Roger said. "It's really pretty good. Lewie read some of it to me last night. It's not like your *Captain Blood* or *Treasure Island*, though."

"There's more, too," Lew said. He pulled out another book and then another. "John Joseph will like all this stuff. Explorers."

John Joseph of course was not around to look these books over. "No Carvalho the Navigator?" I said, but I couldn't come up to their level of excitement.

"There's a Carvalho that went to Brazil," said Roger.

"Well, *something* like that," Lew said. "He was blown there in a storm, I think. He wouldn't be your man, though."

I took the books, and I'm not sure I even said thank you, but I carted them back to my room and looked at them late each night in a deep escape while I listened to the boards of the old house settle and creak. Sometimes, I'd hear old Paddy get up and urinate in the toilet and slough back to bed, the springs creaking as he lowered himself by Great Aunt Theophila's side. Sometimes I'd smell incense wafting on the currents of summer air, and then I knew that Great Aunt Theophila was burning some petition, perhaps lying in bed, but I pictured her wild-eyed, rocking before the altar. I was afraid she might figure out how the perfume ever got on her bed, and then sometimes I was afraid that she already knew.

And then, on a blazing clear afternoon, I came home from diving at the wharf, and I walked in on a terrible row. As I crept up the walk and into the woodhouse, I thought that they might be arguing about *me*. It was late. I should have been home an hour earlier, but the water was clear and warm and the diving good, and I had over four dollars to stash, but when I heard the angry voices I thought maybe my ruse had been discovered. I opened the back door and slipped into the house. No one noticed me. My mother was smoking a Chesterfield, her lipstick a bright vermilion, and she scowled at Great Aunt Theophila. Sheika Nunes and Uncle Paddy stood by, looking distressed. My aunt had dropped her curious reserve of the past weeks and was spitting words through her teeth. "I knew there was something wrong with that *canailla* the minute that damn fool Joe Dias brought him up the walk."

"You don't know anything," my mother said.

"Are you saying it's not true?"

"Consider the source," said my mother. She drew deeply on her cigarette and blew a funnel of smoke in my great aunt's direction. "That Manny Buckets is nothing but a drunk."

"He's got a job. He works. You're just too high above him, so you think."

I retreated to the back room and sat on John Joseph's cot.

"I heard it from somewhere else, too, and not two hours apart," my aunt went on.

"Hettie," chimed Sheika's low sweet voice, "go easy. It might not matter at all. These things can be worked out."

"Sheika's right," I heard Uncle Paddy say. "I was married before. I was divorced."

"Divorced is divorced," my great aunt countered. "This, this *Lisbon* is only separated, and it was a Catholic marriage, too."

"For god's sake, Hettie, *we* weren't married in the Catholic church."

"And don't think I'm not sorry!" spat my aunt.

I'd never heard her take this tone with Uncle Paddy. I buried my head in my hands.

"It didn't stop you though, did it," said Uncle Paddy.

"Well," said my aunt, "you were a respectable man."

"Don't you go saying that Carmine isn't respectable," my mother broke in. "You don't know anything about him."

"That's right. I don't know anything about him."

"Sure," said my mother. "You don't know anything about him, but you go listening to that PASO gossip and to Manny Buckets, who's got holes in his head."

"At least he's from the Islands," my great aunt said, as if that settled it. By now I had enough to piece things together. Great Aunt Theophila had not discovered the secret of the perfume on the bed—at least they didn't seem to be fighting about *that*. But I could see that Manny Buckets had taken revenge on Carmine for the fight, and now his gossip was a battleground in our kitchen. I rolled over and put my face in John Joseph's pillow. It was soft and smelled of his hair. Even if he weren't off to the East End with his women, he could do us no good here. Uncle Paddy tried to placate Great Aunt Theophila, but she was raging, swearing in the old tongue. "Ah," she said finally, "they'll all blame me in the end. I should have watched harder. I shouldn't have let my guard down."

"No one's going to blame *you*, Hettie," Sheika told her.

"Blame her for what?" my mother shouted. "What's the crime?"

"Well," Sheika said, "I suppose just because the man didn't tell us everything about himself, doesn't make him bad."

"You can bet he told *that* one," my great aunt said. "I can see them laughing in their sleeves over all their little secrets."

"Hettie," I heard my great uncle start, but Great Aunt Theophila cut him off.

"That man is a coward," she said. "Here I am with *Lisbons* across the fence trying to run my life, and *Lisbons* in my own house. This is what I get for all my troubles."

"Who cares where he comes from?" my mother yelled.

"We don't even know *that*," my great aunt yelled back. "New Bedford, Fall River, Mystic, Fairhaven—the man's lived everywhere from what I hear. Does he even have a home?"

"Hettie!" It was my great uncle, his voice booming, but Great Aunt Theophila was too caught up in her rage to stop.

"I don't care," she said. "He comes here no more. No more of his damn fishes and yams. No more walking down the middle of the street to God knows where, parading in front of everybody."

"You can't stop me!" my mother cried.

"I can't stop you? I raised you up when John Joseph didn't know which way to turn. I'm the one who keeps this house from falling apart. Don't tell me what I can stop and what I can't stop. As long as you live under this roof . . ."

"We're *engaged*," my mother said. "Stop *that!*"

My great aunt started cursing again, but Paddy shouted, "Stop it! I want this all to stop this minute!"

The room fell silent and I heard a nervous coughing, and then, in a completely different tone from anything that had gone before, I heard my great aunt's puzzled voice: "What . . .?"

There was no answer to this right away, but the next thing I heard was Sheika saying, "*Velha me Deus!*"

"He's having some kind of spell!" my great aunt cried.

I heard a series of sounds, shuffling of feet, furniture moving, and then a melding of distressed voices. I jumped off the cot and rounded the door to the kitchen. The first thing I saw was Sheika's face, blanched, her lips trembling. She stood blocking my view of the morris chair so that I had to slide around her and in between my mother and great aunt. Uncle Paddy was slumped in the chair, his white head lolling to one side, his eyes staring off into the distance. His chest heaved as if he were laboring at something, and his skin shone like a drunk's. Sheika began to wail. "He's going to die, just like my Manny did."

"Shut up!" My mother said. "You say things like that and they come true!"

Great Aunt Theophila had fallen into kind of trance and only repeated, "You did this, you did this, *Oh Madre de Jesus*," while she kissed the crucifix of the rosary that she wore around her neck.

"Josie," my mother said, suddenly becoming aware of me next to her, "go across the street to Old Man Coelho's and use his telephone. Call Doctor Hermann. Tell him your Uncle Paddy's having a spell, and tell him to hurry up."

She began loosening Paddy's shirt, and when I didn't move right away, she yelled, "And *you* hurry up!" She put her hand on my great uncle's forehead and seemed struck by a thought. She looked at me and said, "Go get Ernestina the Shoemaker's Wife, too!"

I ran in a blur to Mister Coelho's and made the phone call, and then

I ran out into the street again, this time up the long hill to Shoemaker's Way to fetch Ernestina. The sun was flattening the shadows of the houses, and an oddly peaceful light hung over the little street between the rows of hedges and pickets, rosebushes and hydrangeas. Fanny Neves stood on her front step with a length of black garden hose, playing a spray of water over her hedgerow, and I did not even wave to her as I ran past.

I was nearly out of breath when I reached Ernestina's house. This was the end of Shoemaker's Way, where the hill's little paved street relaxed into a dirt lane that passed the stark white house and Elvio's barns and ran into the woods where it turned into trail. It was the edge of the town, and here Elvio could run his shop and raise his ducks and chickens without being harassed by any *Lisbons*. The yard itself was crowded by the woods, bayberry and briar and trash alder leaning up against the unpainted pickets. Blueberries and wild raspberries tangled along the fence also, but inside the yard, Ernestina kept a strict garden for growing kale and corn and all the herbs she used in her different teas and cures. In the center of the garden stood a creature made of twigs and sticks, fashioned in almost a human shape. This was a garden spirit, which she used to keep watch over the garden, putting a charm over the herbs and keeping out the rabbits and moles. There was a spookiness to the place. It was easy to see how Ernestina had come to be known as *bruxa*, one who could charm for good or ill.

I knocked on the door of the main house and Elvio answered. "I need to speak to Ernestina," I said.

He nodded. "Any news on the radio?"

"No," I said. "It's Uncle Paddy. He's sick."

Elvio called over his shoulder to Ernestina. "Rosa's boy is here," he said in the old speech.

"*Velha me Deus*," Ernestina said when I told her about Paddy. "Go sit over there," she said, pointing to the table by window. She went out into her yard and came back with a handful of blossoms.

"Are you going to make him some medicine?" I asked.

"Yes, but these are for us. If the doctor's coming like you say, there's no sense in us getting in his way. Some nice *cha hervas* will make you feel better."

I drank a mug of the tea that she made by steeping the blossoms in a pot of hot water.

"Don't worry," Ernestina said. "I'll make your uncle a *taleiga*. The trick will be to get that old Yankee to wear it."

Dusk had begun by the time we walked back down the hill. I was afraid to think of what we might find. Maybe the big ambulance from the hospital up the Cape, or worse, the long black hearse from Barbosa's Funeral Parlor. I took it as a good sign when the only car I saw there was Doctor Hermann's shiny old Plymouth.

But there was one surprise.

In the kitchen, talking to Sheika Nunes, stood Carmine. When he saw me he came over and put his heavy arm around my shoulders. "Don't worry, Josie," he said softly in my ear, "I saw a lot of things in the war and all, and your old uncle doesn't look like a dying man."

But later that night, after Ernestina and the doctor had left, and while Sheika and my great aunt set up a vigil of prayer in the parlor, Carmine sat outside in the swing with my mother. They talked in low, flat tones about our family's situation.

"It's all his pension that keeps us going," my mother told Carmine.

"He might pull through, hey," Carmine said.

"Even so," my mother said. "I've fought with the old lady about letting me work down at the Bluefish—chambermaiding, like Fanny does. But she won't hear of it. She's got rocks in her head. If anything happens to old Paddy we'll wind up in the poorhouse. She's going to blame me for that damn spell, too."

"How?"

"We had a row. Not about anything much, but Paddy might have got his blood pressure up. He's never had this before."

"He's not getting any younger."

"All the more reason why I should be doing something." She paused. "Before the restaurant thing, I mean."

I sat in a shadow by Uncle Paddy's big radio and listened. It was true that the Bluefish Inn provided a good living. There was work from May to September and unemployment money all winter. And Fanny Neves always brought things from work, and she distributed them up and down our neighborhood. Because of her we all got free soap, towels, sheets, blankets, laundry detergent, which she brought us in big, brown paper shopping bags, paper towels, and even sometimes big cans of peach halves or stewed tomatoes. Work at the Bluefish would be good for our household. But I hated to hear my mother talking in these practical terms while Uncle Paddy lay stricken. And I hadn't forgotten the fight, the perfume, the engagement.

I didn't have time to think about what my hand in all this might be, for just then a noisy galumphing of hip boots came from the darkened walk, and into the yard strode Petey Flores, Johnny Squash, and my grandfather. "I just heard the news," John Joseph said. The lush sweetness of muscatel floated in the air.

"You're too late, Papa," said my mother.

"He's dead?"

"No, he's inside in the bedroom."

He removed his hat and scratched his head. "Well, how is he?"

"Blood pressure," my mother said. "It gave him a spell. And where the hell have *you* been?"

Great Aunt Theophila must have heard my grandfather's voice through the screen door. She came to the back steps and looked out at us. Her face looked crumpled, ancient in the bad light. When she looked at Carmine and my mother on the swing, I shuddered, and I saw my mother shrink a bit. But it was my grandfather who spoke first. "Hettie, I came as soon as I heard."

"*Si, si,*" she said, "Go in and see him. Go by yourself."

Johnny Squash and Petey Flores moved over to the chairs by the spool table and sat down, and my grandfather went into the house. He came out a few minutes later, and he seemed in good spirits. "He looks damn good for a man who just had a spell," John Joseph said. "He tells me that the women are trying to kill him."

"He talked? He spoke to you?" Great Aunt Theophila asked.

"Most definitely," said John Joseph.

"*Gracas a Deus.*" She went inside and my mother followed her.

My grandfather looked at his pals. "Let's go raid the flats for some quahogs. We'll steam a pot of clams for old Paddy, and in the morning he'll be like new. It's a full moon, a low tide. Domingo's on patrol somewhere, but you know he'll look the other way for us. We'll have to wait a few more hours for the tide is all."

"I can't make it, hey," Carmine said suddenly. I was startled for a second to hear his voice. I had forgotten he was even there. The men all looked at him sitting on the swing, his smile a small crescent of reflected light. "I can't make the clamming. I have to work. We go down the boat at three in the morning."

"You're up late for a fisherman," my grandfather said. Of course, his friends Squash and Flores were fishermen, too. But even I could tell that Carmine had not been invited. He got up and started down the walk. "I'll bring you some potatoes for your clams, hey," he said as he left.

· · ·

I listened to the indistinct voices coming from inside the house, and after a while Sheika Nunes left to go home. She told us that Uncle Paddy was responding to their prayers. I watched a light go out and then another. John Joseph got up from where he had settled on the swing and reached inside the door and switched the outdoor bulb off, and now we sat in starshine. One light lingered in the house. It was not the light from Great Uncle Paddy's room, which would have shone directly on the walk from the side window—it was farther in, on the other side, and I could make out its indirect glow through the screen of the back door. It was the light from my mother's bedroom, and I sat and wondered what it was that kept her up now and how she set about recovering from this day that I had not recovered from yet myself.

When her light went out it was with suddenness and finality, and John Joseph began talking, the line of his beard coming up at us from time to time in the glow of his pipe. "Paddy Dunne was a barrel of a man in his day," he said. "He won't ever talk much about how he got banged up in that breeches buoy years ago. Christ, he was a kid then, out there on the back side by Peaked Hill Bar. The coastguard had things to do in those days."

"Uncle Paddy doesn't like us talking about any of that," I whispered.

"Certainly," said John Joseph. "That's Paddy for you. These Yankees have no sense of the heroic. They never had a heroic age like we Portuguese did. The truth is he saved a boatload of Portagees. It was the *Maria*, a big old-time trawler that went aground on those banks out there in a big blow in February. She was beam-to and heeling over, and the surf was pounding the hell out of her. Nobody would have got off without those coastguard boys. It was Paddy and his watch partner found her.

"Now in those days the guard walked the beaches from half-way hut to half-way hut, and they'd signal a disaster by shining their Coston lights up to the nearest hut. That's what old Paddy did. It was freezing, mind you, and a gale blowing down out of the northeast, and black as net-tar on that beach. You couldn't hear a damn thing either because of the way the surf boomed up and down the shore.

"They got their signals along, though, and the boys up at the station came down with the breeches buoy cart and rigged the cannon and fired the shot line out to the wreck. Now usually the crew on the grounded ship would rig up the buoy, but when they sent the whip over—the heavy line that would pulley the men back and forth on the breeches buoy—nothing happened. They signaled back and forth best they could, but the gang on the beach knew they were going to lose that crew if they didn't get them off. There were already pieces of that old trawler getting thrown up on the beach. They could see them in the white foam.

"So Paddy says, 'I'm going out boys,' and he took a dory and rowed himself out through the surf. You see, on the block and tackle that the life-savers sent out, there were instructions on how to rig her up. Trouble was the directions were in English and French, and none of those Portagees could read them. So Paddy got it all rigged up right for them, and he lifted one of those men up and tied him on the saddle. This man had a broken leg. All the while the wind was freezing ice on all the boards and rigging, and the waves were pounding in the hull. Your uncle stayed until every man was off."

"How did he get hurt, then?"

"Wave knocked him back down into the hold and he hit his back. He was lucky he fell where he did, though, or else he would have gone overboard, and that would have been that. As it was, he had to hitch himself back up to the buoy all by himself, hurt like that, and get back to the beach. The storm pounded that old Portagee boat into splinters."

John Joseph drew on the pipe and sighed.

To my right, I heard Johnny Squash stir in his chair, and then I heard the clink of glass against shirt buttons and then the cap of a wine bottle unscrewing. His arm moved in silhouette as he swigged, and the sharp, sweet smell of port crept into the night sea air. He passed the bottle to Petey and then to John Joseph who took it up and held it in the starlight before him. "To the health of Paddy Dunne," my grandfather said, "hero, spouse of my sister, the one-day-to-be-sainted Theophila of Pico."

9

Going through the various liturgical calendars, prayer books, and books on the lives and deeds of the Blessed, you can arrive at up to seven Saint Joachims, depending on how you count. Some of the Saint Joachims are without a doubt among the Blessed and have been canonized without any dispute, like Joachim Saccachibaru, a native of Japan and a convert who became a doctor of the Franciscan Order and was later martyred by crucifixion. Other Joachims, like Joachim of Fiore, are generally conceded to be among the Blessed, but their credentials are not so clear. Joachim of Fiore was acclaimed during his lifetime for his fervor at the Mass, his eloquence in preaching, his love for all creatures, and his life of poverty. But in spite of all his virtues he had the bad judgment to be a writer of books, and these books were used later for evil purposes. So he never achieved full sainthood, which I thought was completely unfair when Sheika Nunes first read to me about it.

Sainthood was complicated. Sometimes two sources would disagree on the sanctification of a particular candidate. Joachim Royo, a Dominican Martyr strangled in jail, one of Father Santos's favorites, fell into roughly the same category as Joachim of Fiore—definitely Blessed but uncertainly canonized. But if you made a list of all the Saint Joachims and started with the most documented and ended with the most doubtful, Saint Joachim the Patriarch, *my* Saint Joachim, would come in last. Almost nothing is known about him except for one obscure reference in the often-discredited apocryphal Gospel of James, yet he's considered to have been the father of the Blessed Virgin Mary, and he is therefore celebrated—sometimes—as the patron saint of fathers. You could argue that he was the patron saint of *absent* fathers, since throughout the overwhelming bulk of Scripture, he is never around when anything important happens.

So in picking out Joachim for my name, my mother maybe showed something about how her mind worked, for this guy was as shadowy a figure as my real father, or even my grandfather's old navigator. Yet this was the saint that I had petitioned, and now after one thing leading to another, my Great Uncle Paddy lay in his iron bed with the shadow of death upon him.

Great Aunt Theophila prayed to saints of her own, to Saint Jude, patron of the impossible, and to Our Lady of Lourdes, patron of bodily ills. Sheika Nunes helped her with these prayers, but I steered clear of the two women so they wouldn't drag me into their intense devotions in the parlor.

Pico neighbors pitched in to help us while Uncle Paddy was down. Captain Raul Mendes showed up after taking out at the wharf, and he brought us a huge tuna steak. He dressed it out himself. He had taken seven of the big horse mackerel out of his trap that morning, and Ernestina the Shoemaker's Wife saw that as a certain sign that Paddy would get better in seven day's time. She kept brewing her pots of tea —her *cha hervas*, which always left us feeling soothed and well-cared-for. Sheika showed up with a dishpan full of bread pudding, and Fanny Neves brought us ten pounds of hot dogs from the Bluefish Inn's big kitchen. Roger and Lew peeked in on Uncle Paddy each morning and left the city newspapers for him to read, and Liliana Mendes and Fanny joined Sheika and my great aunt, and the four of them pounded through an afternoon of rosaries in the parlor. Fanny also offered to pay Father Santos to say a Mass for Paddy's health, but this set off an argument among the women about whether or not you could offer a Mass for a Protestant. I sneaked away to the wharf at this point, and I don't know what they ever decided.

On the third day after the spell, Doctor Hermann arrived for his scheduled visit. He went in and sat on the edge of the bed and chuffed the rubber squeeze-bulb of the blood pressure sleeve and announced the good news. "The pressure's come down," he said. Uncle Paddy said nothing. He sat propped up on his pillows and scowled into a corner of the room. After Doctor Hermann had left, Uncle Paddy called me over and asked me to pour him some of Ernestina's *cha hervas*, which I did. He sipped at it a bit while he watched the women in the other room. After a minute or two he whistled to me, very low, and raising his eyebrows he nodded at the Fleischman's bottle over on his night table. I checked for the women myself, and I dashed over and tossed a finger's width of whiskey into the tea. My great uncle took it down in two broad swallows. Later that day, just before supper, he got up, pulled on his pants, slipped his leather braces over his shoulders, and called to Great Aunt Theophila. "You can make the bed, Hettie," he told her. "I'm all better now."

Great Aunt Theophila started to protest. Her lips puckered and she began to speak, but I watched the quick blink of her eyes as she thought the better of it. She went into the bedroom and cleaned up the room while Uncle Paddy put on his straw Panama hat and went out in the yard and sat by the big radio. Captain Raul came up the walk a short time later and sang out a loud greeting. "Paddy Dunne," he said, "Pard, you look brand new."

Paddy leaned back in the chair and folded his hand over his stomach. "Can't complain," is all he said.

I didn't know what to think. Paddy's spell seemed to change everything, but only on the surface, like a glass calm offshore that hid a three-knot current underneath. Uncle Paddy had risen from his sickbed in fine spirits, but he still didn't look right to me. The doctor had left two squat tins of pills for him, and Ernestina had made him a *taleiga*, filling a small pouch with camphor and herbs from her garden, and laying a charm over it. What struck me was that Paddy wore the *taleiga* and he took the pills. He had a look of surrender about him, and maybe I imagined it, but he seemed to walk slower, and his barrel chest rose and fell more heavily with each breath. I know Great Aunt Theophila sensed something, too. She was more eager to wait on him now, and she kept her prayer vigils going with a special force.

My mother and Carmine kept having their talks about our dismal finances. I stayed away from them. Even though the big fight about Carmine and my mother was never resolved, it disappeared, ducked below sight. He continued to come to our house, but he didn't come for supper anymore. He started showing up later, when the dishes were already washed and stacked in the cupboard and the sun was down on the west side of the woodhouse. He spoke politely to Great Aunt Theophila, but mostly they avoided each other's eyes. Carmine brought magazines for Paddy and a large box of Muriel Coronellas, which my great aunt refused to have lit in the house. Paddy and Carmine would smoke them in the yard while Carmine waited for my mother to come out to him.

Sheika Nunes beamed over Uncle Paddy's recovery. She caught me in the kitchen and aimed a pinch at my crotch. "Honest prayer is always answered, Josie," she said. "Now I know I'll learn about my

Manny. Patience," she said and sighed. "It takes patience, and sometimes that's hard, but just look what prayer can do!"

Sheika was sure that our days were filled with good signs, but she didn't live under our roof. She couldn't feel that all our calm was brittle and dangerous.

It was a false quiet, and it was broken by a swarm of hornets.

The seven days of Ernestina's prediction had passed and Uncle Paddy sat in his usual place by the radio in the backyard. He had the earphones on and he whistled a dance tune to himself in late afternoon sunshine. John Joseph was off to the East End with his women, and my mother was in her bedroom with the door closed, a way she spent much of her time now. I sat on the woodhouse steps, just back from sneaking another day of diving with my friends. I let the sun bake the chill out of me, for even though it was high summer, we had been having a cold current, and an afternoon in the water could purple your lips and set your flesh up cold for hours afterward.

Great Aunt Theophila was outside too, brooming off the back doorstep, since my mother would not come out and do it herself. My great aunt finished the doorstep and then moved to the small section of the walk that led to the side stairs. I watched her without paying much attention as she swept the lower steps and then went around the corner of the house, still brooming. There I saw her stop, and I saw the broom handle poke back and forth as she busied herself with something she had found under the steps. I heard an indistinct word, then an oath, then a shout, and then she threw the broom down and came tearing around the corner cursing in the old speech and flailing the air around her head. I jumped to my feet, but Uncle Paddy, who was closer, put his hand on the spigot and turned on the hose. That's when I saw the hornets. Great Aunt Theophila kept batting at her face and slapping her arms, and Uncle Paddy played the hose over her. He kept spraying, and finally the spray worked. The hornets thinned out and withdrew behind the steps and left my great aunt shaking on the sidewalk, her soaked dress pressed to her body and showing her surprising gauntness, her ribs and pelvic bones, and her small, fallen breasts. Her hair had been knocked from its pug, and it streamed down over her hunched shoulders. She looked like a drowned woman risen to come and curse us in broad daylight—and she did curse, breathtaking strings of oaths in the old speech, all punctuated by howls of pain.

Uncle Paddy moved her into the house and called my mother, who began daubing each sting with baking soda. "Get Ernestina," she told me, and once again I ran off up the long hill. By the time I got back with Ernestina, my mother and Uncle Paddy had taken off my great aunt's clothes and laid her beneath a sheet on the bed. Ernestina calmed my aunt with a dose of one of her teas, and then she daubed the stings again, this time with a brindled paste made of herbs and what I thought I recognized as duckshit, but I kept my mouth shut as Ernestina plastered the horrible stuff on Great Aunt Theophila's arms and face, seventeen welts by my mother's count. Ernestina dotted her as though she was being painted for some strange party or parade. My great aunt complained of dizziness, but Ernestina's paste made the pain go away, and my aunt cleared us from the bedroom so she could rest.

Ernestina stayed with us a while and then Sheika dropped by, followed by Fanny Neves who brought a box of day-old loaves of bread from the Bluefish Inn. She divided them up among the households and then there was a short discussion about whether bee stings were worse than hornet stings. Finally the women left us to ourselves. My mother sat at the kitchen table and went into a reverie, gazing off into space as if she were very, very far away, looking both sad and detached at the same time, and no one bothered her until a knock came at the door. It was Carmine.

Maybe my mother understood that he had come now to seal our bundled fates. Maybe she had been off to glimpse some far workplace where the saints had been milling our fortunes. "Oh," she said, as if she had conjured him, "you're here."

"This week's *Post* for Paddy," Carmine said, holding up the bright cover of the magazine. "Paddy's snoozing out on the swing and I didn't want to wake him, hey." He smiled at my mother.

Then my great aunt spoke from the bedroom. "Rosa, I want some more of that tea that Ernestina brought."

"Just a minute," my mother said. But she didn't move. She sat looking at Carmine. She looked like she was studying him or trying to figure out the answer to a difficult problem.

Great Aunt Theophila spoke again. "Rosa!"

"Just a *minute*," my mother said. But by now Great Aunt Theophila had come to the bedroom doorway and stood looking into the kitchen, her faded wine-colored robe wrapped around her body.

"Hettie!" said Carmine. He looked at my aunt, her stringy hair, the lumps, the thick paste covering them, and something moved over his face. It was just some bare impulse pulling up at the corners of his mouth and eyes. Great Aunt Theophila caught it just as I did. It was the start of a smile, the kind that grows into a laugh. Carmine checked himself quickly, but there was too much between them now.

"Hettie was stung by hornets," my mother said.

"Do you think this is funny?" my aunt asked, looking at Carmine.

"Not on your life, ma'am."

"Then what are you laughing at?"

"I wasn't laughing, Hettie."

"You are a liar, *senhor*," my great aunt said, glaring now. In her tone she carried the accusation to mean his entire character. That must have been how he heard it, too. Otherwise he would have just shrugged or smiled as he always did with my aunt. But there was a strain on him, too. Maybe he just didn't wait long enough before he opened his mouth.

"You know, you push everyone too hard, Hettie."

"I don't like your tone, sir," said my aunt.

"It's the only tone I've got right now."

"You do not speak to me that way in my house!"

"Well, now," Carmine said, motioning to the backyard where my great uncle still napped, "it's still old Paddy's house isn't it? He's not dead *yet*."

He may as well have slapped my aunt in the face. She drew herself up in a pure rage, all the more frightening because she looked so foolish dotted with paste. "Get out of here, you miserable *Lisbon* drifter! At least the ones across the fence can stay in one place!"

"What the hell's the matter with you two?" my mother shouted.

"Be quiet," said Great Aunt Theophila. "And you, sir," she said to Carmine, "get out now or I'll call the police!"

"You can't say that," my mother said. "If he goes, I go too. Remember, we're engaged!"

"Go." Great Aunt Theophila was ashen. "That's just what you're good for. Go! Go on, and good riddance!"

"Let's go, then," said Carmine. He was trembling with anger. He turned and put his hand on my mother's shoulder.

Then my moment came. "Josie," my mother said. It was her command to me. I looked at her and then at Carmine. I couldn't read what they expected me to do. But whatever circle they had drawn around themselves, it was something I couldn't enter. It was theirs, not mine.

"Impossible!" my great aunt said. And I found that she was right. I drew in a breath, and I thought I might rise from where I was sitting, but I couldn't. A look of despair crossed my mother's face. She could not haggle with me now and weaken herself and Carmine. He turned her around, and they walked out the back door, leaving the house to tilt in a muddy haze.

Carmine and my mother left town very early the next morning. We got the news from Sheika Nunes, who got it from Old Man Coelho, who was up feeding his dogs when my mother passed his house shortly after first light, carrying a shopping bag and her brown, scuffed suitcase. I hadn't heard her sneak back into the house to pack, which was strange, because I think I was awake most of that night myself. I had been too riled to sleep, and I kept going over in my head the three tests of goodness that I had learned in my catechism lessons with Sheika Nunes. I tried to apply them to my petitions to my saint, for if heaven really listened, then something clearly had not gone right.

First I considered *object*. What could be more *good* than petitioning for a father from the Patron of Fathers? How could I have offended anyone of the Blessed with that? Second, there were *circumstances*. My circumstances seemed in accord with doctrine. I didn't have a father. My mother didn't have a husband. The family needed saving. I should be clear on circumstances. I had petitioned in good faith. But third there was *purpose*. Here I wasn't on firm ground. Sheika had warned me about petitioning in a frivolous way, and of course my petitions were part test, because I wasn't sure if I really believed in them or not. As the night passed I made up tribunals in my head, ridiculous cartoons I got from reading the lives of saints and martyrs, where I was cross-examined.

—*Did you ever petition a heavenly saint for money or material gain?*

—No, Your Excellency

—*For earthly happiness?*

—To this I must say yes, Your Excellency.

—*You are not patient enough to wait for heaven?*

—Happiness in the family would bring it closer to God.

—*Hmm. The boy has a point. Go on.*

—Perhaps Aunt Theophila would have returned to the Mass. It would have pleased Father Santos.

—*Yes, we know of him. A good man. So you considered these ends in your petitions?*

—I did, Your Excellency.

—*But you are guilty of other offenses.*

—I sneak around and misrepresent the truth. I stole Carmine's jacket to get him to come back and see my mother.

—*You broke commandments.*

—I do penance.

—*We do not think you always repent.*

—This is true, Your Excellency, but I have always been straightforward with my name saint.

—*Have you not considered that these other transgressions, which you deem so small, might have influenced your saint in the way he decided to grant your petition?*

—I had considered it, Your Excellency, but I remembered being taught that our rewards and punishments are dealt to us in the Other World. Otherwise we would be able to judge sinners by the difficulties that they bear in this life, and that is not the case, for the righteous often suffer.

—*Astonishing! The boy has an amazing grasp of Church doctrine.*

—I owe it all to my teachers, Your Excellency.

—*Ah, and modest, too. Yet there are serious difficulties. Your mother and Carmine and their . . . ah . . . their transgressions.*

—But if he were really sent by my name saint . . .

—*We never said as much.*

—Then I must speak to Saint Joachim, personally.

—*Of course, my son. Speak away. Speak freely.*

—So he can answer my questions.

—*Don't be ridiculous. The saints do not speak. They only send signs, which you must interpret.*

—Then how do I know they're even really there?

—*Be patient, my son.*

—Am I absolved then?

> *—First we must consider the tests of goodness. Let us consider Objects, Circumstances, and Purposes . . .*

And so it went, no matter how I played it out, and I played it out over and over, like a wheel grinding against something, until I must have fallen into a short, black, and dreamless sleep.

10

Some days passed. I don't know how many. Sheika Nunes and Great Aunt Theophila sat at the kitchen table every day and talked about how my mother and Carmine had left. I don't think either of them could really believe it any more than I could. Maybe they thought that things would blow over and they'd come back. But they didn't. As for me, I was invisible. I came and went and no one seemed to notice. I felt like I was floating out of my body, and this made everything around me seem more dense, more dangerous. Everything in my reach, the planks along the fence, the cracked cement of the walk, the duckpen, the woodhouse, all looked as though they belonged to a different order of things. I no longer seemed to belong in the world. I hadn't become pure spirit; I had become closer to nothing. I forgot to eat. I refused to petition the Blessed. I tore the icon of Saint Joachim the Patriarch into little pieces and rolled the pieces into sweaty paper balls in my hand. Then I flushed them in the toilet. I gathered my presents from Carmine—even the wonderful flashlight—and I walked the long, gull-spattered catwalk on the Cold Storage Wharf out to the end where the fish hoist and gear shed sat in a ghostly morning fog, and I threw everything into the sea.

If there was word from my mother, no one told me anything, and I saw how distinctly that fit with how we always treated everything else. Nothing but silence and mystery. I didn't need the saints for that. That's what I had under our own roof. Great Aunt Theophila prayed furiously at the bedroom shrine, the candles flaming and the incense smoking. She talked to the saints, but whatever else needed saying to me, she held back.

It was Sheika Nunes who pulled me back among the visible. She came and sat in the parlor one afternoon and called me to her. "Josie Carvalho, you come here and sit next to me!" Her voice sent a strange trilling through me, and suddenly there I was sitting next to her on the sofa. The long hollow that she made in the cushions pulled me toward her like curved space, and I could smell her toilet water and a faint scent of cloves or spice on her flowing shift, which covered her to her ankles but left her great dimpled arms bare and dark in the parlor's sunlight. "You don't look so well," she said. "And Hettie tells me you haven't been eating. So listen, I'm going to pitch in here and take care of things. Not that Hettie and Paddy can't manage. Now John Joseph is a wonderful man. A beautiful man. But don't expect much from him. It's summer, you know. And you know how *that* goes. But here *I* am, so don't you worry about a thing."

"Do you have any news?" I asked.

"News? I should say not." Then she stroked my leg and patted me, and uttered three names that made me cringe. Now I knew that we were going to have some kind of moral lesson beginning with *Teresa, Sanchia,* and *Elisabetta,* the three most exemplary women saints from Portugal. What was the point? That my mother wasn't a saint? I couldn't follow any of this, so I settled back and just listened to the tone of her voice, bossy, sweet, hopeful. She lectured me, and then she fed me a supper of kale soup and bread and pinched my cheeks to bring the color back. Later, when Fanny Neves and Liliana Mendes dropped in, I escaped them all by pointing out that the duckpen needed cleaning. I got no arguments. We still hadn't gotten rid of the ducks. *That* trouble seemed small and foolish now.

I walked out into the yard and worked around the pen. The ducks quacked and waddled in excitement as I shoveled and raked. I looked over the ruined fence at Madeleine Sylvia's house. Her yard was clean, without clutter, and her garden grew flowers, yellow and pink and white nodding blossoms, and there was a lilac tree and an apple tree. It was a nice yard. But our yard was a nice yard, too. I thought about my great aunt's anger at Madeleine for trying to boss us. I didn't care about that. But she should have just left us alone. When I saw that Madeleine was nowhere to be seen, I lifted out the pan of black water that was the duck pond and dumped it over her side of the fence. I washed the pan with the hose and I filled it up again with clean water, which the ducks immediately plopped in and began preening and shaking themselves.

I went back into the woodhouse to put away the shovel and rake. The light was angling in the door at just the right slant so I could see among old saws and axes all the way to my corner by the coal bin. I decided to check my stash of coins from diving at the wharf, and I knelt on the dark floor and counted out my fortune. Then I noticed the old knife and the strange ball that Johnny Squash had given me on the night of the clambake, the night I pinched Carmine's jacket. I had not paid much attention to them since then, and now, with nothing better to do, I took up the ball in my hands. It was heavy, but not as heavy as lead or iron. I took it back out to the walk and dropped it on the cement. It hit the ground with a dull *bok* and rebounded into my hands. I held it higher above my head and let it go. It whacked against the walk and bounced back higher. I heaved it with both hands and it bounced higher still. It didn't look like it should bounce at all. I decided I would go up to the roof and drop it off, just to see what it would do.

Getting up to the roof was no problem. I only had to climb the outside stairs up to Lew's and Roger's little landing, step over the railing, lean out and grab the eave, and swing around to the flat part of the parlor's roof. From there I could reach all the peaks and gables of the rest of the roof, including the south-facing slope of the kitchen, where Uncle Paddy and Elvio the Shoemaker had mounted the rusting bedspring on a pair of two-by-fours. I realized as I stepped on the landing that I wasn't going to be able to use both my hands to swing out to the eave because of the weight of the ball. I solved this by taking off my shirt and wrapping the ball in it. Then I slung it over to the parlor roof. It landed with a thud, but Roger and Lew were not home, and I roused nobody from below. I waited a bit to make sure I wasn't discovered, and then I swung over to the flat roof and took up my shirt and the ball.

My plan was to crawl up to the peak of the main roof and lob the ball down toward the front street. I knew that the ball might shatter, and the thought of breaking something felt good to me. But just as I inched my way up to the roof's peak I slipped. It was not much of a slip, but it startled me and I grabbed at the roof with both my hands. When I let go of the ball, it rolled behind me down the wrong side of the roof and into our backyard. I heard it hit the sidewalk, and looking down over my shoulder, I saw it bounce high and then disappear into the ivy on the side of the woodhouse. There came a loud crash and then the tinkle of broken glass.

I expected someone inside to come running out of the house, but no one did. I lay against the roof for a while, not moving. The mossy shingles had kept the day's heat in them, and with my cheek lying against the wood, I eyed all the small humps, the erratic mortar between the old chimney bricks, the clever way that Elvio had hung the bedspring so that the two-by-fours made a hanger from the crest of the roof, with no nails or screws piercing the shingles. It took no

strength to hold myself there. I stayed until I was sure no one below me had been roused to come and see what all the noise was about.

I made my way down to the flat roof and over to the porch again and then down into the backyard. I looked up at the ivy on the side of

the woodhouse. There was still no way to tell that there was a window up there behind that thick tangle of green. Even in winter it had been hidden by the twisted runners. I studied the old stairs that led to the upper door. The inside frame of the stairway was still attached to the little building, but above, the outer section of the landing sagged dangerously away from it. Some of the boards had actually fallen through and rested on the scrap woodpile under the stairs. The stairs themselves were not much more than a ladder with a railing. Everything leaned toward the duckhouse at a small angle. I killed a little more time while I waited for dusk, and then I took my chance.

I saw that I could walk on the very inner edges of the steps, where the frame was attached to the woodhouse. If I kept my weight against the building, I could make it up to the landing. If I was wrong, I might bring the whole rotten staircase crashing down on the woodpile, but I didn't think I was heavy enough to do that. Someone—I supposed it was the last person to have climbed those stairs long ago—had taken the knob off the door so no one would be tempted to go up there, but I knew I could twist the bare spindle and probably get the latch to work.

The steps were stronger than they looked. I went up without a give or a creak. The doorknob spindle was stubborn with disuse, but I twisted with both hands on it, and it finally gave. I pushed open the door and entered.

The room was lighter than I expected it to be. Maybe I had thought it would be dark and dingy simply because the downstairs of the shed was like that. But here there were no coal bins and no corners full of rusty tools, and the grainy light of dusk poured into the west-facing window. The bare boards and beams were dry and dusty, but not covered with the smudge of coal dust. On the unpainted floor in front lay the shards of the ivy-tangled side window that my heavy ball had broken, and the ball itself rested against the base of a small stone and brick chimney that rose through the rafters and then through the planks of the roof. Three or four pieces of timber were stacked up in the rafters, along with an oar that was as gray and dry as a piece of driftwood. A workbench stretched across the end of the room that held the street-facing window, and on it were some old tools, a vise, a stack of big scallop shells, and some boxes, all covered with a light, fine dust. There was no furniture of any kind in the room, but a long cupboard ran along each side wall, and three trunks sat along the north wall, the wall that faced the house. I closed the door behind me and breathed the smell of the place, dry wood and old air that had not been disturbed for years.

I opened the first cupboard and found it empty except for some heavy lead sinkers, a few small stubs of candle, and a mason jar about half full of wooden sulfur matches. Spiders had spun webs in a corner along some of the shelves, and their dried bodies now hung on the dusty threads along with the mummified husks of a number of flies. The other cupboard was filled with liquor bottles, each one corked and filled with a thick, dark orange liquid. I picked up one of the bottles and tilted it to the remaining light. The stuff oozed slowly, like honey, a large bubble moving to the uptilted end. I didn't have to open the bottle. I had seen this stuff before. It was blackfish oil. I remembered John Joseph using it on the wheels or gears of some contraption years before. I remembered its rancid smell. I put the bottle back and turned to the trunks.

The first was a steamer trunk with brass handles and a brass hasp, all heavily tarnished. It was lined with fine light wood, and except for two tattered gray woolen navy blankets, it was empty. The next trunk was just a hulking blue wooden box with a hinged top. Inside there were several lance heads for spearing big fish, a heavy grappling hook, two thick coils of twine that had dried out beyond any use, some lead mackerel jigs, several lumps of blue carpenter's chalk, what looked like a small lamp of some kind, a black rubber sou'wester that had hardened into the shape of its folds, and a cracked leather packet. The packet crumbled a bit when I opened it, and I took out several old charts of the harbor, faded and marked over with dark pencil. The last thing I took out of the trunk was a small brass box compass set off in redwood, the rose decorated with intricate red and blue scrollwork. I turned it to the four directions and watched the compass card dip and spin. I knew this was a wonderful prize. I couldn't believe that Uncle Paddy or my grandfather would have left such a thing to be forgotten up here. Even in terms of its salvage value at Juney's Tap, it was great find. I sat on the floor with it, and I opened one of the charts and lined the compass up with the declension mark at the bottom, the way Uncle Paddy had once shown me. The chart showed features that weren't part of the town anymore. Where a vacant lot now stood against a seawall in the West End, the chart showed a fishery. And some of the wharves that I knew as short and stubby were here on the chart as long lines extending past the low-water mark. There were more weirs shown in the harbor, and there were courses traced in pencil along channels and around bars, and someone had made notations of small wrecks in a broad, heavy hand. The chart showed all the buildings along the water, their lots, the towers of the town, everything in block outline, so that a sailor on the water might be able to take a bearing off any feature he could make out ashore and find his position.

I fell into a kind of trance as I sat over the chart, and I must have sat there for a long time before I realized that night had fallen. The lone streetlight out on the corner caught enough of the west window to cast faint shadows in the room, and I was staring at the stained paper barely making out anything at all. I walked over the to the ivy-hidden window and I gently poked a finger through the broken pane and held a penny-sized spot of the ivy open for me to sight through. I could see the yard, the front door, the little light above it. Elvio and Uncle Paddy sat at the ell table playing with the big radio. It was odd to look down on my great uncle from this perspective. I could see Elvio leaning into the radio and turning the dial the way a safecracker might delicately nudge a combination lock. He cocked his head from time to time and listened in the earphones. But Uncle Paddy sat staring off into some distance, quiet and still. His spell had left some mark on him, and I didn't like thinking about that.

I couldn't tell if any of the women were in the yard, but even if they weren't, I would have to wait up here until everyone had gone inside before I could climb down those steps again. I went to the first cupboard and took out a candle stub and set it in a scallop shell. I opened the mason jar and shook out a sulfur match and pulled it across the rough brick of the chimney. The pointed tip of the match smoked and went out. I tried another, and the tip smoked, hissed faintly and smoked some more, then slowly grew into a pale yellow flame. I lit the piece of candle and set the shell on the floor beside me.

What was it about being up in that shed, that little room hidden from the world? I should have felt safe, locked away from the world and all its uncertainties. But I felt trapped now because I could not come down the steps, and then all the troubles of summer came crashing into my head again. Now there was new scandal, something else for my great aunt to bear. I knew that even at that moment *Lisbons* and *Picos* alike were probably sitting in the PASO Hall talking about the

Carvalhos with pity and scorn in their voices. I was suddenly tired of the charts and the other papers that had been bundled in the leather folder, and I gathered them up and laid them on the top of the blue box. Then I opened the steamer trunk and took out the navy blankets. I folded one long and lay it down on the floor, and I rolled the other one for a pillow. I lay on my back on the floor looking up at the rafters. Then I began to shake. At first I wasn't even sure what was happening to me—almost as though I were fooling myself, but then, yes, I was shaking. My hands trembled, and then the trembling spread inward so that I felt like I was shaking at my very center. Then I started to cry. I didn't move. I let the hot tears run down the side of my face and around my ears. I didn't want to let myself think anymore, but I couldn't stop crying and shaking.

I don't know what happened after that. Maybe I fell asleep or maybe I just lay there as though I slept. All I remember next is opening my eyes. The candle had burned down to a puddle of wax in the hollow of the scallop shell, and the flame guttered there feebly. But I had heard a noise. I listened hard. It might have been someone in the downstairs shed getting kerosene or looking for a tool, but that was doubtful this late at night. Then I thought it might just be the little shed settling and creaking, the way the house did sometimes after dark. But then a plank groaned and the door creaked and the air changed in the room. I sat up and whirled around. A figure stood in the doorway and pointed at me. "*Be still*," came the coarse whisper. Suddenly a long, thin blade glinted in his hand. He closed the door behind him and I saw the deep shadows of his face, the outline of his beard, the floppy felt hat. "Carvalho," he said. "Jesus H. Christ!"

"*Avo!*"

"What the hell are you doing up here?"

I caught the wine-heavy exhalation. I could tell he was drunk.

"What are *you* doing up here?" I asked.

"That god-damned candle. You can see it from down in the street. Do you want the fire department up here? Or worse, Hettie calling the cops?"

My heart was banging in my chest. "You could have been a ghost," I said.

"Ghosts are dead. I'm only half-dead."

"You've been drinking." I sounded just like my mother.

"You're an expert on that subject?" He slipped the knife into his boot.

"Why aren't you off with your lady friends? Or your pals?"

"To hell with everyone," he said, waving his hand.

"Us, too?"

"What was that?"

I started to swallow my words, but then I didn't. I didn't care anymore. "Everything is a mess around here, and you don't even care. You don't even come around."

"My presence would help things?"

I didn't say anything.

He let out a sigh. "Your aunt blames me for everything. What good would I do around here?"

"She listens to you."

"Hah!"

"She does."

"Maybe. But she blames me, too. She thinks I should have come to this country and become a squire, made a fortune, installed her somewhere as a great lady. She forgets."

"What? What does she forget?"

"She forgets," he said, flourishing with his hand, "that *I* am the reason she's here at all and not in some shack back on Pico boiling soup over a cow-shit fire. *I* am the one who got us here. *I* am the one who paid the prices."

"No one ever talks about that stuff, you know. The old days. It's like everything is a big secret."

"Um."

"What? What's the big deal? Did you get in trouble for fighting with a knife? Is that it?"

"Who told you that?"

"See what I mean? Nobody talks about those things. You came in here with a knife. What was that all about?" I liked the anger now because it made me bold.

"You could have been a summer boarder. I had to be careful. Even a small man can be dangerous. You never did tell me what you were doing up here."

"I was up by the bedspring with that stone ball, and it rolled off the roof and came through the window." I pointed to the crashed pane. "I came up here after it."

"And then what?"

"I found some things. And then there were people in the yard and I didn't want to come down." I didn't tell him about crying.

"You went through the boxes?"

"Yes."

He entered the room and knelt by the trunks. "It's been years since I've been up here. Got to get ahold of old Paddy when he's feeling better and fix those damn stairs." He leaned over and picked up the box compass from where I had left it, and he fiddled with the catch and opened it. "I left this up here so nothing would happen to it." He looked at me. "Carvalho, I know all about Carmine and your ma. I heard."

"You had to hear it from somebody else, though," I said. "You didn't even hear it from one of us."

"What are you saying?"

How could I tell him that I had a hand in this? How could I say anything about the praying or the jacket? "I'm saying I'm afraid of what's going to happen next. I'm afraid of how this is going to turn out. *You* don't have to worry. You go off with your pals, or you go off down to the other end of town with your lady friends. But I'm here. I can't just go off like you do."

He looked at me for a moment. "Then we have to stick together. You and me."

"Well, you're the one that has to do the sticking."

He reached into his jacket pocket and pulled out a flat, clear, pint wine bottle. He unscrewed it and drank from it and stared into the bottle. It was about half empty. He tilted it back and drank again. "I understand your point, Carvalho, but tell me, how can I help with this? What do you think I can do?"

"It seems like you could do *some*thing."

"Yes, I suppose so," he said. He fell silent, and I kept quiet too. I was still angry at him, but I was glad he was there. I wanted a way of keeping him there. He took the knife out of his boot and began moving it around the edge of the compass, pulling the card around with its steel. "It's a beauty," he said after a while. "You know where this came from? Wreck of an old schooner. Went up on a bar out to Race Point in the middle of winter, and it got all pounded to hell, too. You can bet there would have been scavengers all over it, but the tide came up and the wind shifted and the wreck blew back off and disappeared. Damnedest thing you ever saw. And I saw it.

"It was Johnny Squash, Domingo, Petey Flores, and me. That was years ago. We walked the wagon ruts out to the coastguard station to get a look at that wreck. Well, come summer, everybody had stopped thinking about it, but I knew it had to be out there somewhere. I spent a week just trolling around with a couple of grapnels. I struck plenty of junk out along those bars. But I struck that old schooner, too. Or the best piece of her. I had to go down the line, I bet forty feet to get at the wheelhouse, and I almost drowned knocking this loose. But Carvalhos have good lungs. See. Here's where I had to break it with a pry bar."

He ran his unsteady hand along a grain in the wood. I couldn't see any scar in the bad light.

"I filled it with sawdust and glue, and dyed it with iodine and revarnished it. This is an object that is no longer made anywhere on earth." He put the compass down and took another drink from his pint. "What are we going to do with ourselves, Carvalho?"

"I don't know," I said.

He drank again, and he was silent for a long while. "The old lady's right, you know."

"What do you mean?"

"Hettie. She says all I'm good for is foolish stories. She's right."

"That wasn't a foolish story about the compass."

"But it's not what really happened. I did get it off a wreck—in a way. Domingo found it, and I bought it off him. I think that's how it went. It was a long time ago. I really _could_ dive down in those days. I found other stuff. But I just put those things together."

"Oh," I said.

"And the knife. Well, I put it in my boot, all right. I'd have used it too, if I had to. But when I saw it was you, I pulled it out anyway."

"Why?"

"To make an impression." He drank again and sighed. "You see, Carvalho, they're right. The women are right. Everything is like a story to me. I can't help it. You want me to be old and wise, but I'm not. You want me to have answers, but I don't." He coughed a little cough into his fist. "I am not apologizing for this, you understand."

He looked unhappy in the unsteady candlelight. I never thought about that before—that he might be as unhappy as anyone else. He always seemed beyond all that.

"Your aunt has her stories, too, you know," he said after a while.

"You mean the saints? The visions? You don't think that's true?"

"I think it's true. But she makes the story as she goes."

"Are the saints real?"

"They must be."

"Why?"

"Why else would we talk about them?"

"They don't answer petitions," I said.

"Maybe, maybe not. I'm not the expert."

"The ancestor's not real, right?"

"He's real."

"But he's a story."

"And I'm telling you I don't know the difference. And neither does anyone else, and if they did, they'd tell you the goddamned truth about it."

I watched him tilt the wine bottle again, and I tried to figure out his mood.

"You're feeling bad about it, too, aren't you?" I said after a while.

"About your ma leaving with Carmine? I should have seen it coming. I don't take any blame for it. But it's not a good thing. It makes us all look foolish."

"You sound like *Tia*."

"God help us."

"What if something bad happens?" I was thinking of Carmine and my mother on the bed, but that's all I said to John Joseph.

"Look, your ma's tough. She'll be back for you. She won't get hurt."

John Joseph spoke of my mother to reassure me, but something odd moved inside me. It had to do with Carmine. He had left me, too, and there was nothing even to be said about that. He was, as my aunt had said, an outlander, someone with no rights or ties. And yet here I was, hurting for him.

A car came around the corner and scatter from its headlights moved across the walls. My grandfather stood up.

"Don't go yet," I said.

"I'm not going anywhere," he said peevishly. "Relax. I know you're feeling beat-up. I'll stick around. I *said* I would." He scanned the room. We have to cover that goddamned window if we are going to sit around up here. If I spotted you, someone else will spot us. Isn't there something?"

I pointed to the navy blankets. After a few false starts, he managed to drape one over the curtain rod, blocking the pale shine of the streetlight.

"That candle's about dead." he said. I showed him the little lamp I had found. He held it in his hands. "I remember this. It's an old port running light. Runs on kerosene. Wick's pretty bad." He fumbled with it, steadied himself, smacked at it with his palm until something gave, and then opened the little brass pot at the base. "Let's try some of this stuff. Like the old days."

He went to the cupboard and reached for a bottle of the blackfish oil. "Here," he said, "open this. My hands."

He gave me the fillet knife and I pulled the cork out piece by piece. The oil's thick smell rose in the air.

John Joseph fiddled with the apparatus, dropped some small part, and cursed it until I fetched it up from the floor for him. He steadied himself again and dripped some of the heavy oil into the base of the lamp and then massaged some of the goop into the crumbling wick. When he was finished, he set it down, drew one of his wooden matches across the bricks of the chimney, and touched the lamp. The wick hissed wetly, flared, died. He swore in Portuguese and tried another match. The wick caught this time and began to burn with a dirty orange flame at its edge. He adjusted a turnscrew, and the flame shrank to a sliver. He screwed the red glass over it. "Snuff that candle, now, what's left of it," he said.

Then we sat in the strange gloom, the red light glowing. John Joseph steadied himself against one of the trunks and filled his pipe. He struck a match and puffed a cloud of Prince Albert into the scant light. "Well, here we are," he said.

"What now?"

He puffed and sighed and pulled out the wine bottle. "There's the ancestor," he said. "We'd better do that. It'll take our mind off things."

"You've told me that story. I'll hear it again, though."

"No, no. I mean right from the beginning," he said. "I mean the whole thing. I've never put together the whole story. Did he come to America? Yes. But I've never told you the beginning. There has to be a beginning."

"Then there has to be an end, too," I said. "We have to figure out how he disappeared."

"Another failure," he said, but then he laughed through his nose. "You know young Lew thinks we might have nailed him. Not *him* him, but you know—*hints* of him. Columbus had more information than he was allowed to say."

"Lew told me it was possible."

"Yes, possible. That's right. And probable. There's where you look. And if we find him, we claim him." He raised the bottle. "For the Carvalhos are a great family, and deserve a great ancestor. The hell with all our troubles." He waved the wine bottle, and it glinted like a fistful of stars in the red light. "We are the Princes of America. We descend from the great Carvalho, Navigator, Finder of the New World."

I had him going now, and I knew he'd stay. At least for a while. "You always say he sailed from our islands," I said.

"He would have to. It would have been stupid to sail from the mainland. All right, so that's where we'll start. The Azores. Pico. They didn't always belong to us."

"I know," I said. We had gotten this from Lew's books. "The Flemish."

"The Flemish. The Flemish Islands."

"But when *we* came over we named them after the hawks that flew there."

"The *Azores*," said my grandfather. "But he just didn't pop out of nowhere. I can tell you how he sailed, but where did he come from?"

"A tavern," I said.

John Joseph snorted. *Treasure Island*," he said. "What does that have to do with us?"

"A noble family," I tried again.

"Ah, I doubt it. Here. Here it is. A young boy. Maybe your age. He's brought from the mainland out to the islands to work for one of the Flemish. No mother. No father. He's a mystery." He turned to me quickly. "The islands are full of churchmen. Why?"

"The king is thinking of taking them over. The king needs to stay in good with the Pope, so everywhere the king's men or soldiers go, the priests go, too."

"Right. Exactly. We're on the same page, Carvalho. The boy, the boy, the boy. He's sent over to be a servant in a landowner's house, but the landowner—let's call him Van Horten, sends him to study with the priests. So we are on Pico, and there is a priest—no, two priests—and four lay brothers. And there's one priest I have to tell you about. His name would be Fray Costa. That's what he'd be called then. He's small and thin. He wears a brown robe and a hat with a big brim." John Joseph stopped and thought for a moment. His shape seemed to sink into the shadows that the sputtering running light cast around the room.

"I don't know why Van Horten would have sent the boy off to the priests. But maybe it had something to do with his past. Maybe there was something between Van Horten and one of his servants—a woman servant. And the boy, you know the boy could have been theirs. Maybe the boy was an embarrassment. You follow me, right? But he'd show them, though. He'd show them.

"And the priests taught him a lot of things. Why, that one priest—Fray Costa—he taught the boy to read. But the Church didn't capture him. It was the sailors that he loved. Because they were on an island, far from the coast, far from Lisbon. Anything valuable came to them by sea. So listen. Picture this boy watching along the water for the sails of the big *rondels* that would haul out the provisions and trade with the islanders. You couldn't hold onto this guy. He'd sneak away from the church brothers and go down to the wharves and talk with the sailors and watch the cargo come in. Sure. And most of that stuff was bound for Van Horten's cellars. Now some of the sea-going men had been south from the mainland to Africa. Some of them had fought in the wars there. Some of them even remembered the days of Prince Henrique. Remember, he had had a vision from heaven that sent him looking south for a way around Africa to India.

"So the boy takes it all in. He's like a piece of bread in a fish soup. He's tempted by those sailors. Hard, dark men who had been to the ends of the earth. *They* were the ones who held the keys to the world—and not the priests. The priests' lives were boring. They'd pound catechism into this guy and make him recite holy dates. They taught him how to serve Mass and how to read books, but he hated life in the cloister."

My grandfather drew on his pipe and found it dead. He scratched one of his matches against a brick in the chimney, and the match popped, flared, lit his features. He looked grim, gathered in concentration. The tiny flame inverted itself over the bowl of his pipe as he drew in air, then disappeared abruptly with a wild flourish of his hand. I listened to him puff a while. He was making things up. I knew he would go ahead now.

"The church itself. I want you to see it now. It was a small building that rose on a rocky knoll at the edge of the village. Next to it was the sacristy, and then the refectory and the dormitory. All this is bordered by low walls and then fields. They grow grapes there and olives, and there are small *campos* for the cows to graze. The kid helped with everything, and the churchmen liked that. The lowest novitiate lay brother could boss him around, and he had to do their bidding or take a hiding. But he hated it. He learned the hours. I can say them. Vigilae, Matins, Prime, Terce, Sext, Nones, Vespers, Compline. Around and around, and nothing but working and praying. Now that one priest, Fray Costa. He'd be patient with the boy. He'd drill him and teach him. He wanted the kid to make a vocation of the Church, but the boy knew it wasn't for him. In some way he was a bitter disappointment for that priest. This Fray Costa, you see, believed that the Church was the greatest power on earth. He believed that the best thing a man could do with his life was to serve the Church. The priest always called the Church *Our Holy Mother.*

"But look. The boy was quick. He learned whatever the priests showed him. That's where he learned how sooner or later everything gets connected."

"I don't get that," I said. "Connected how?"

"Like fate—*fado.* Or like in a tale. You know what I'm talking about. One thing leads to another, and once it does you look backward and see that nothing was an accident. This stone you dropped from the roof. It came up out of the ocean. See how it brought you here? And then me? That's *fado,* right? Has to be."

"You don't think it was just an accident?"

"Listen to me. You know the island of Corvo, the westernmost of our islands. You know there's *velhos* in this town who come from there, and they claim that there's a man of stone that stands in the surf and points to the west? And because of that, those people from Corvo take credit for the discovery of the New World. Well, that man is there all right. The ancestor saw him. Maybe it just looked like a pile of rocks to anyone who didn't have the sense to see it, but our old navigator saw him, Carvalho. When he was just a boy out on those lonely islands. And he knew that rock man was pointing to something. He watched the sea. He read the westerlies and the currents bearing wood from that direction. Don't ask me how, but he knew land lay to the west even before he began to learn all those things from the priests. Things from books . . ."

John Joseph stopped and took a noisy swig from his bottle and shuffled a bit in the shadow he had settled into. I prompted him. "So the priests he went to live with taught him stuff about the world."

"Yes," he said. "That's just right."

"Those old writings about land in the west."

"That's what I mean."

"Saint Brendan's Island. William of Rubrick," I said. We talked about these things with Lew.

"Yes. And you know the islands were sitting there at the very western edge of the world. The known world, I mean. All the waterfronts were buzzing with stories about the East—you know, China, India. Like that. Well everybody out there figured that you could get to the East by either going south around Africa, or by going west from the Azores. And the king wanted to get to the East, and the Pope, too. You know why, right?"

"Prester John," I said. "But he wasn't real, either."

"Wasn't, hunh? Did that make a difference?"

"Well . . ."

"The Pope thought this guy had a Christian kingdom right in the middle of the Muslims. He figured all he had to do was find him, join forces with him, and cut the Muslims in two. Do 'em in. Am I right?"

"That's what we got."

"So was he real? He was the force that kept the Church going. Kept all the kings trying to get to the East."

"But spice and that stuff."

"That, too.

"Get this. The boy is out there on the islands, and he sees those fine ships come in to replenish. The caravels and caravellas. The design was Prince Henrique's himself. Small, like daggers, with lateen sails. You could sail them right into the teeth of the wind. So here's our boy. He sees the ships and the sailors, and he knows something big is going on. He knows that someone is going to get a big piece of the world because in those days it was up for grabs, and he wants it. He wants it. But not as a priest. That's not how he wants to go out in the world. So he waits and learns and takes in what he can from the church school, and then he runs off on a ship. He leaves a short note to his teacher, Fray Costa, the gentle priest I just told you about. And he jumps a ship."

"And then what?" Another car came round the corner. One of Old Man Coelho's dogs barked across the street, and our ducks sounded off. I stiffened, as if the noise would somehow betray our presence up in the woodhouse, but a minute passed and we settled back again. "Now he sails off on a caravel," I said.

"No," said my grandfather after a while. "No, not yet. That doesn't work. A king's caravella was the most advanced machine on the earth. On the seas, I mean. So they were secret. No, he wouldn't get a caravel at the first." He shuffled and thought some more. "No, he doesn't get on a caravel. He ships out as master's boy on a lugger that hauled trade between the islands. Salt fish, chickens, cloth, tallow, hogs. The old master of that ship was named Matta. He wasn't really that old, but he was hardened by the sea. His face was lined with deep cuts and creases, like a fist of wax after you draw sealing twine through it. He chewed hemp, too, with the few teeth he had in his head, and he used to tell everyone that this helped him to predict the weather. He always over-loaded that old boat, but man, he could sail, Carvalho. He could cut half a day off the trip between Santa Maria and Pico just by swinging out into a current he'd find by watching the seaweed drift. And when we had to change sails, he'd send us all aloft, and that cloth would go up or come down like snapping a finger. Then he'd bring her around and snap wind into those rags. He should have been master of a better ship. Ah, well, one day then. But I don't want to lose my way now."

"You were saying 'we,'" I said.

"What do you mean?"

"'We.' Like we hoisted the sails."

"What's the difference? How can I do this if you plague me about stuff like that?"

"Old Man Matta, then," I said. "Go ahead."

"The kid spends two years hauling candles and salt, barrels and sacks. But he's learning all about the sea now. He's learning from Old Man Matta. Matta is the one who first takes the kid out to the reaches of Corvo, the end of the known earth. That's where the boy sees the stone man for the first time, pointing. He gets stronger and smarter, this kid. He's getting ready for something, you see."

A car passed by in the street then, and the sudden sound of its engine, the swish of its tires in the outside air, broke the spell of my grandfather's voice. He stood up suddenly. The floorboards creaked under his weight.

"What is it, *Avo*?"

"Just a minute," he said sharply. He picked up the running light and held it in his hand, using it to peer around the room. He had to hold the lamp very close to things in order to see them. He peered at the bottles of blackfish oil, then moved to the workbench and passed his hands over some tools. He poked at the charts and papers I'd found, and put the pack of them into his coat.

"You can't be finished," I said, thinking he was getting ready to go.

"I'm not finished, god damn it. Let me think. Why do you have to pester me?"

"You looked like you were going to take off," I said.

He shook his head, sighed, paced a little, as much as the little room would allow him. "Power," he said finally. "He has to cross with some real power, or none of this works." He handed me the running light. "Put this thing out, for all I care."

I didn't put the light out, but I placed it in the narrow space behind the trunk, and the room faded into a lush darkness. John Joseph settled into his place against the wall, and he began to speak again.

"He meets Alvaro Simoes on a ship at a quay at the bottom of some cliffs. It was in a place we called the Big River, on the island of *Sao Miguel*. Matta had gone there to take on a load of beets and flax. Alongside the little wharf there was a huge three-master, one of the big ships that ran to the mainland and back. Now Saint Michael was the most settled of the islands. There were more people there and big houses and plantations. More than on the smaller islands. And so there was a sharp trade between Saint Michael and Lisbon. Matta called at *Sao Miguel* pretty often, and from time to time they'd see those slow, grand ships from Lisbon.

"Rondels," I said.

"Exactly. So this time Matta tied up alongside the big ship, offshore of her, like they did in those days—well, like you see right now at our own wharf. You know what I mean. They had been there a day, and the kid talked to a mate from that big ship—the *Feliz Maria*, she was called. She was bound for Lisbon in three days, and of course the boy had heard so much talk about Lisbon and all its wonders. Lisbon was the capital of the world at that time. It was the frontier. Well, that boy knew he'd go there sooner or later, whenever the time was right. He believed in his *fado*, you see. He believed he would make a great mark in the world. But how do you know when the time is right?"

He paused, and I kept silent.

"By the outward signs!" he said suddenly, answering himself. "Fate or accident. Listen, Carvalho. He talks with this mate of the *Feliz Maria* for no more than an hour, when a man aboard gets run down by a hogshead rolling off a plank. It breaks the bone in his leg. They have to haul him off to the local priest, who takes him by cart to the church on the other side of the island where a brother can set his bone, and lay him to heal. And the kid, seizing his time, signs aboard to take this man's place, and he asks for no wage except for the passage to Lisbon. You see, he'd read the outward signs, and he believed the time was right for him to make this move."

John Joseph stopped talking suddenly, and I heard the bottle come out of his jacket, saw the dim glint of light on its edge. He took a swig and shook it. Empty. When he went for several more minutes without speaking, I began to worry that he might go off for another bottle. I pushed him a little. "And so this Simoes, he was the captain of this ship, right?"

"He was the *owner* of that ship," he said quietly. "That ship and others. This will be Alvaro Simoes, secret financier of the king's explorations, and our ancestor meets him in a most remarkable way." My grandfather waited for me to ask.

"How?" I said.

"Simoes calls him into his cabin to accuse the ancestor of murder."

"Whoa," I said. "Wait a minute."

"With a knife."

"Oh, brother," I said. "Oh, boy."

11

My grandfather shifted slightly and the room began to creak again. In the quiet that followed, one of Old Man Coelho's hounds bayed at something, and the ducks quacked again in their pen. Voices, nearly smothered, rose from the sidewalk below, and then footsteps made their way up the side stairs to the main house. Roger and Lew returning from a night downtown. The hour would be late. We waited for a while until the sounds of our own breathing and the low susurration of the oil lamp took us back to where a story might unfold. "I want to tell you some things about Alvaro Simoes," came my grandfather's voice from the shadow by the chimney.

"He had come out to the islands on one of his ships for God knows what. You never knew what to believe. He had vast holdings in the south of the country, though. And the king had granted him more land on *Sao Jorge* and *Santa Maria*. So it made sense that he had come to inspect his holdings, never mind the fact that some minion could have done the same thing. Of course, he might have been out there for other reasons. We'll come to that soon enough. But think of our ancestor—the kid, the young man. His head is boiling with self-importance. In one swift move he's left Old Man Matta's smack. Now, the old man isn't happy about seeing him go. He's left short-handed. He even throws a pair of the boy's pants overboard, and he refuses to pay him for his last trip. 'The sharks on that big ship will make short work of you!' he screams at our boy. But the ancestor doesn't haggle. He knows he's making a move that will change his whole future. He knows great things are in the wind. Remember, he's studied with the priests, and he's hung around the waterfront. He knows the king is on the verge of some great discovery. Somebody will make it, and he thinks that it may as well be him. But he's ignorant still. He's just an islander, and he doesn't know anything about politics or power. He still has to get to Lisbon.

"Lisbon, though, was not going to be reached without some trouble. First there were the strong easterlies. They couldn't get too close to the wind in that big lugger, so they had to pound their way toward the coast in tack after tack, with changes of sail every few hours on the glass. This is the month of October. They'd say it like this—'close to the feast of Saint Evaristus.' There was already a trace of cold iron in the wind. Truth be told, Old Man Matta, if he was the master of that ship, would have found a better route. He would have used longer tacks, or at least two longer legs giving some days on a broad reach, but this captain didn't think that way. The weather wasn't good, either. Always threatening with the wind coming off the land, and high clouds so you couldn't see the stars at night. The course was held by dead-reckoning.

"And then, on one of those black nights a seaman disappeared. It's terrible, Carvalho, to be washed over to your death out at sea. You never lie in your grave. You are eaten by fishes. But that's what happened. This man was found missing when his watch was called up to change sail, and he was still missing when the crew was mustered at daylight. The captain called for a search of the ship, and when he wasn't turned out, they were all mustered again, on deck, forward of the poop. The master called out to them and said that if any of the sailors had seen or heard anything in the night that might shed light on this tragedy, they should come forth. But no one had. Then this Senhor Simoes appeared at the poop. Now the ancestor would only have seen glimpses of him topside where Simoes came a couple of times a day for a walk around the deck. He would always be with the master or one of the mates. But now Simoes does something extraordinary, Carvalho. He tells the captain to come off his tack and make a broad circle to see if they can find this man, or at least his body, so they can bring it back for decent burial. The captain didn't want to do this. He wasn't making good way as it was, and he didn't know his position in relation to Lisbon. Yet the order had been given in front of the mustered crew, and it became clear that Simoes was a man whose orders were followed. They spent several hours of the glass in expanding circles with men on the spars and on the bowsprit and along the poop as lookouts, but they turned up nothing and eventually they went back to their beat to windward.

"Simoes is a singular man. The ancestor has never felt the presence of anyone like him. Not the priests, not even old Van Horten, who was like a duke back on Pico. No, the ancestor sensed right away how small his world had been back on that little island. He saw Simoes for what he was, a big, big fish. Ha. But even then he didn't know how big. You'll see what I mean. I have it figured.

"Simoes called the ancestor into his cabin after nightfall. He had called some other crewmembers in there also. His cabin lay in the most comfortable part of the ship, beneath the poop, a place where no common seaman ever went. But this Simoes wouldn't let go of the fact that a man was lost from his ship. He sensed something was wrong. Men like Simoes have the knack of sensing what's going on around them. I've seen this many times, Carvalho, and that's what separates the great from the rest of us. The ancestor was like this too, though. I'll see if I can't make this plain to you.

"Simoes's cabin was a marvel to the kid. He didn't even think such a place was possible on a ship. It was small, but there was a table, a chair, a fine bunk, some candles set in holders, and they made a warm light on the low overhead and close bulkheads. Now on the port bulkhead you had a shelf of books. That was something rare on a ship in those days! And a stave ran along their spines so that when the ship heeled to starboard the books wouldn't spill out on the deck. There were two small ports in the aft bulkhead of the cabin. They were closed, but you could feel a small draft of the cold night coming through. Simoes sat on the bunk and held a woolen blanket over his shoulders. He didn't say a word when the ancestor walked into the cabin. He only watched him. The ancestor couldn't tell much about Simoes from looking at him in the candlelight, but he saw the shape of his face, like an oval, but with too much flesh on it. Yes, that's it. He carried the extra weight of a rich man, but there was something in his features. High-toned. You know what I mean. The kid was unsure of himself. His eyes moved around the cabin, and they came to rest on Simoes's hat, upside down on the small table. It was a beautiful hat, Carvalho, made of some bright skin, and brushed and polished so that it shone in the candlelight. Inside on the sweatband there was a label with writing on it. The ancestor was uncomfortable, and so he tried to read it instead of looking at Simoes.

" 'What do you see in my *carapuca*?' Simoes says to him. Maybe he's trying to catch him off guard. He used the word for a fisherman's floppy cap, like this fine hat was just a scrap of old clothing to him. Maybe it was.

"The kid looks him in the eye and says, 'Sewn for Dom Alvaro Vaco Simoes, by one Franciso Gomes, Milliner, Lisbon.'

" 'You read,' says Simoes.

"'I do,' says the ancestor.

"' Strange for a common seaman,' says Simoes.

"Well, the ancestor could go into a story about the priests and all of that, but he doesn't. He doesn't say a word. He just waits.

"'You weren't on watch when this man Carvalho went over the side?'"

John Joseph's voice took on a tone when he spoke for Simoes. But I thought I misheard something. "*Avo*, you said a Carvalho fell overboard."

"I did. Well, listen then. Listen to this little bit. You have to figure it all out. I said that the ancestor was raised in Van Horten's household and then sent to the priests. Well, what would his name be? It wouldn't be Van Horten now, would it? Now Fray Costa, the priest, would have called him *de Jesus*—maybe as a joke, but as far as anybody on that ship knew, he was Francisco Matta. Ha. You see? Matta wouldn't pay him the money he owed him because he jumped ship, so the old boy took his name!"

"Why does he become Carvalho, then? What gives?"

"Use your head. We're making a story here."

I thought for a while, but I wanted him to tell me.

"Well," said my grandfather, "Simoes was convinced of foul play. He said as much to the kid. 'You're the new man, aren't you? The Islander?'

"'Yes,' he says.

"'There's something about you, Islander. You know that our man Carvalho met with a murderer on my ship?'

"Simoes bores into him with his eyes—green eyes. He must have accused all the others, too. To see how they'd react. 'Tell me,' he says, 'Why you murdered him.'

"Well, the ancestor reads the thoughts in Simoes's face, and he tries to figure out what to say here. They watch each other for a while, and then our boy takes his chance. You see, he did kill that sailor, and he knew that Simoes could read it in him, so he told him as much, straight out."

"But why?"

"Why do you think?"

"It would have to be something big."

"Well, remember, our ancestor has big ideas about his destiny. That sailor, the man named Carvalho, tried to interfere with him. You see, he wanted the kid to be like a slave to him. First night on, he stole his boots and sold them to someone else, and our boy had to fight to get them back. Then he says, 'Matta—meet me on deck tonight after the watch is set.' Remember, he's still Matta. So what does the ancestor think? Remember what the old man yelled at him. 'Those sharks will make hash of you,' or something like that. This was the situation. This tough was going to ruin the boy, and the kid knew it. So he goes to meet him. There's nothing else to be done. Sure enough, this huge lout of a man came after him, and he made it clear that the kid was to be his to do with what he pleased. He tries to put hands on him, Carvalho. You know what I mean? But he didn't figure something. He didn't figure that the kid had big ideas and couldn't let himself be ruined like that. So like a flash he pulls a fish knife from his sleeve and he catches that sailor once in the belly. Just enough to stop him, but he just stands there looking at the kid, and the kid knows he's in for it, now. Maybe he just meant to cut that sailor, show him he wasn't afraid to do it. But now he sees that this guy will just as soon kill him as spit. So it's once again across the throat, in a flash, and he goes down. He goes down against the rail, Carvalho, still alive maybe, but the ancestor can't stop now. He puts a foot on him and it's over the side for that fool. Thank God the ancestor couldn't see the man's face in the dark. But it was over the side for him.

"All this happened in the hearing of the watches, but they knew that Carvalho would go after the boy, and they weren't going to get in the middle. What could they have thought when the kid came sneaking by with a bucket and rag to clean up some mess on the foredeck? But on the next morning, when there was no more Carvalho, whoever those men on watch were, they thought differently. One even came and offered the kid his biscuits to get on his good side. They realized that our boy was not to be fooled with.

"Simoes just watched the kid as he told the story—in more detail than I'm telling you. But the ancestor had read him right. You see, in those days, it was a man's right to kill if he was being interfered with. So the boy tells him everything, and then do you know what's the first thing Simoes says to him? 'My eyes burn from too much study by candlelight, and my manservant doesn't know letters. Take up that book and read it to me.'

"And what do you think he had him read in that tiny cabin? The ancestor had confessed a killing and told this man of criminal vices aboard his ship, and what do you think was on Simoes's mind? Get this. It was, you know, Marco Polo's book, about traveling for years in the land of the Khans. You see? Simoes was interested in the East, and yet he had come out west to our islands! Don't think that our ancestor didn't catch on about what he was up to."

"But what's the deal with that man Carvalho? He kills him and then takes his name?" I could hear the tone in my voice. Here was John Joseph telling me about the ancestor, and sure enough he had gone and made him a murderer.

"Well," John Joseph said, "he was truly repentant for killing him. But he was a boy and half-crazy over the prospects of his life. Maybe he misjudged how far he had to go. But he was raised in part by priests, you know. So he consecrates his life to his victim. When they reached Lisbon, he went straight-away to the big cathedral and begged heaven for forgiveness. It came into his head to carry his name forever with him, because now his dreams were worth a life. In a strange way, killing that man made the fire in him burn that much harder. See?"

"And Alvaro Simoes didn't say anything?"

"Simoes had his own uses for the ancestor. From now on, we call *him* Carvalho, see? He sent him on a voyage to Africa as a spy."

"Against who?"

"Against *whom*. Against his own men, and so would you have. That was a time of great intrigue."

"Then what?"

"Columbus. Vasco da Gama!"

"Oh," I said.

"But I don't have it all yet." A silence fell over the room for a long time, and then my grandfather stood abruptly. "Enough," he said. "Pretty good, though, hah?"

"Yeah, good," I said. I wanted more, but I remembered that the wine bottle was empty, and we had been there a long time. The story faded, and the ugly world came back. Below us was the house, my room. Carmine and my mother were gone. The family was mired in tribulation. "You going back down to the East End now?" I asked.

He stretched. "No, no," he said. "Tonight I go back to the house with you. I sleep in my own cot tonight. I'm remembering our deal. We stick together."

This almost worked. I watched him move to extinguish the light, and I wanted to touch him, just put my hand on him and feel him there, or maybe bury my head in the florid odors of his shirt and breathe him into me. But then it struck me. "*Avo*," I said, "the reason you're here tonight—why you're staying here. That woman down to the East End. You had a fight or something, right? She throw you out?" He turned and eyed me up and down and coughed into his fist. "See how much you learn from being around me?" he said.

I felt myself flush with anger again, but before I could think of anything to say, he was already tiptoeing for the stairs.

12

"*Florida*?" I hated the crack in my voice when I repeated the word.

"Hettie didn't want me to say anything to you about it, but she's wrong to think that way. Don't tell her I told you."

"Of course I won't, *Avo*." It was late morning and John Joseph sat on the Cold Storage seawall working an eye-splice into a bright new length of line that had come into his possession without costing him a cent, as he told me. He looked shaky, with a dark flush and a puffiness in his cheeks, but his hands were steady now. He kept his eyes on his work while he spoke, but he moved his jaw as though he were chewing. I knew he was turning something around in his mind.

"I think I made a big mistake," I said.

"Because you didn't leave with them? You were smart not to go. There's something between them that's complicated, Carvalho. And it's your mother's thing. You're better off not being there. You'll get some news."

"How do you know?"

"I don't know. But that's what I'm saying anyway."

"I could take a bus to Florida too. I have enough diving money put away."

John Joseph spit. "I suppose so."

We were quiet for a while. "Great Aunt Theophila is mad," I said finally. My grandfather pursed his lips and concentrated on another turn in the splice. I didn't know how much more to tell him, because what I had to say involved him. I had heard yet another fight in our little house when I had walked back into the yard from the beach earlier that morning. I stopped on the back steps as the rise and fall of pitched voices had come straining through the doorscreen. "You act like nothing at all has happened," I heard my great aunt say. "You go about your business—whatever *that* is—and you don't do a blessed thing!"

"Hettie!" My grandfather was using his most reasonable voice on her. "Hettie, there is wisdom in knowing when not to interfere."

"Is that why you run off with these women when our family is in ruin? What happened to your ambition? Your pride? Since . . . the trouble. . . . Since Rosa's mother went back to the old country, you've been good for nothing!"

"That's a long time ago, Hettie. Let it lie."

"You don't let it lie, yourself. You don't let anything go. You just push it on down inside, like I don't know. You carry everything around on your back. That's what all this drinking is about."

"That's enough."

"You think I wanted a calamity? Let me tell you, I prayed that that . . . that *sneak* might be a good man. I had hoped, *Joao Jose,* despite what you think. But I can't do it any longer. I can't direct this family."

"That might not be a bad thing," my grandfather observed in a neutral voice.

"And what will become of us?"

"We're strong . . . we're . . ."

"Don't start with that great family stuff. Your drunk stories. We all thought something good would come to us. *You* thought so. You were ambitious."

"Now I consider ambition a vice," said my grandfather. "My life is more pleasant without it."

"And so you go with whores."

"Hettie, you're being unreasonable."

"Go," said my great aunt. "Abandon me. Leave us alone. Go to your women. You are worse than nothing. You undo everything I've ever worked for."

"I'll go, Hettie. But I'll be back when you've calmed down. You'll see it's best not to pressure."

"Go away," seethed my great aunt. "I don't care if you never set foot in front of me again."

I could tell that my grandfather was about to come through the door, so I slipped around the side of the house so he could not have seen me listening. Now when I gave him an opportunity to tell me about the fight, he let it slip by. "Your Aunt Theophila's nature is to be mad," was all he said. "A lot of this is her fault, you know, but I don't want you throwing that up to her."

"It could be my fault, too."

"Don't be a damned fool. You listen to Hettie and Rosa and you'll be blaming yourself for everything."

"I meant about praying and . . ."

"Enough!" he said sharply. Then he shook his head and spit off at the beach. Out on the bar, by where the *Caravella* was anchored, a man and a woman—summer people—with their pants rolled up to their calves and their sailor hats pulled down over their ears—poked about and dug some quahogs with their fingers. John Joseph watched them as he worked the wooden fid in between a strand of line. The woman collected the clams in a big handkerchief. My grandfather, in his protectiveness of the sandbars—his poaching grounds—would sometimes watch summer people dig their small catch, and he would walk out to them, introduce himself as the shellfish warden, and confiscate their dig. Then he would bring the quahogs home and eat them. I watched him for a sign of this now, but he was in a different mood, and when the couple had filled their handkerchief, he just sat and watched them walk away. "You slept in pretty late this morning," he said, as the summer people passed off to the west, out of sight. "Are you okay?"

"I'm all right," I said.

"Lew stopped me on the sidewalk. He's got some more of those books for us. I took a couple. He has some for you."

"Oh."

"He thinks we're right."

"What?"

"The ancestor. The islander."

"Oh," I said. "Sure."

"What's the matter?"

"Nothing."

He stopped handling the line, pulled his pipe out of his pocket, and packed it with Prince Albert. "We've got to go for a sail, don't you think? We have to deliver that propeller back to those summer boarders, if nothing else. Juney says he wants to buy some more mackerel, too."

This sounded hopeful to me. "When do we go, *Avo?*"

He thought for a minute. "Day after tomorrow is good. I have to take care of some things. We'll have to leave before dawn to catch the tide and still have the whole day. What do you think?"

"I'll load the *Caravella* the night before," I said.

"We have a deal, then. Let's put this line on her right now, though. I want to watch you finish the splice."

I worked the splice well enough, although I could tell that my fingers simply weren't as strong as my grandfather's. He pulled on his pipe and brooded and spat as he watched me work the line. He had not spoken of our meeting up in the woodhouse. It was almost like it never happened. With John Joseph sober, and by daylight, I felt like I was with someone else—not my grandfather of the night before. I was still angry at him. "Are you really going to stick around the house more?" I asked him. "Are you ever going to finish that story?"

"Don't pester me," he said. And then, "If I can make it all hang together, I'll be proving something. Do you follow?"

I didn't, but I said, "Prove to who?"

"To *whom*," he said. Then he switched subjects again. "Look, you don't have a thing to worry about. Your ma, I mean. She's a Carvalho. She'll be back. She'll be okay."

"I know that," I said. But there wasn't any way for me to tell him that it wasn't so much my mother that I was worried about. It was Carmine who was on my mind. If I had conjured him, he should have demanded that I leave with them. But I was nothing to him. I knew it was crazy, but it was Carmine who had broken my heart.

Sheika Nunes saw only the outward signs of my misery, and so she kept up a campaign to cure me by feeding me.

"You need iron," she told me when I had come back to the house, and she set a plate of black molasses in front me and gave me an end of hard-crusted bread to sop it up with. "Eat, eat," she said, aiming a pinch at the center of my lap. I ate, and presently my great aunt came and sat at the table and had some tea with Sheika. They talked with me about prayers and about how everything always worked out for the best. They said nothing to me about Carmine and my mother going to Florida. I was chilled by how totally and completely they hid the truth from me by simple silence. When Ernestina the Shoemaker's Wife came banging on the door, the conversation shifted at once. "She's up to no good, that one," Ernestina said, nodding her head in the direction of Madeleine Sylvia's yard.

"Don't we know that?" said Sheika. "It's always the same."

"No, no. I mean I have news. That Arthur Enos was up to my Elvio's shop to get back a pair of shoes, and he got to talking. They are going to serve another paper. They can't make you build anything, but they can make you tear down the old outhouse and they can take the ducks away themselves."

"To where?" I said.

"To the dump, you poor thing," said Ernestina. "They'll just wring their necks."

"Good riddance," said Great Aunt Theophila. "But if they go to the dump, it's because I say so, not her or any of those *Lisbons* down at Town Hall. I don't care a pin about Arthur Enos."

"What's this about the outhouse?" said Sheika.

"They're against the health code," said Ernestina. "That's what Arthur Enos told my Elvio."

"We don't use the outhouse," I said. "It's just there."

"I only know what I know," Ernestina said.

"That snake was going to put up the new fence before he went and ran off with Rosa. If he had, that *Lisbon* would have pulled back," said my great aunt. Then she glanced at me and silenced herself.

"Maybe *Avo* can talk to her," I said stupidly. My great aunt simply crossed herself and shook her head. I was saved by Uncle Paddy walking in the door.

"Paddy Dunne, you look like a million dollars," said Ernestina.

"All green and wrinkled," said my great uncle. Ernestina glanced at the leather thong around his neck. He still wore the *taleiga* she had given him. He came over to the table, and I got up and gave him my chair. Sooner or later, they would get around to talking about Carmine and my mother. I made for the door, and no one made any move to keep me from leaving.

The house settled into its sleep late that night, and I lay and ticked away each waking minute in some part of my brain. But I did not look at a clock as I slipped out of the back room door on my way to the dilapidated stairs, so I had no guess of what time it was when I finally entered that woodhouse room. I could tell as soon as I cracked the door that my grandfather was already there. He had draped the blanket over the curtain rod again, and the red running light was burning behind the trunk. "Quiet," he said, though I had not made a sound. I closed the door gently behind me and tiptoed to the box where I had sat the night before. The room was already heavy with the smells of blackfish oil and tobacco smoke, and I picked up the odor of tonight's wine—port. My grandfather had set a quart bottle of it on the floor by his knee.

"I *wondered* if you were ever going to come," he said sarcastically.

"Well, it's not like I absolutely knew *you'd* be here either," I said.

"Fair enough," he said. "Look, I've been looking through Lew's books and I've done some figuring. If I can fill in all the holes, I've nailed him."

"But how do you prove he's *our* ancestor? Can you prove he came to our town? And what difference does it make?" I knew that my best chance of keeping him around was to get him into telling his story, but I was let down that he had nothing more for me about my mother or Carmine. He hadn't even asked me how I was feeling.

"Difference?" he said. "Just to me, maybe. No, I can't prove it like you mean. But if it was possible, then I'm right. He was there ahead of everybody. It wasn't just a joke." He was keyed up. He took a heavy slug from the wine bottle before he sighed and settled back in the shadow of the chimney. "Look, where did we leave him?"

"He killed somebody on his trip to the mainland. And that guy was using him as a spy."

"Alvaro Simoes." My grandfather let out a long breath that blossomed with acrid sweetness. "You have to think about what the islander must have seen on that trip to Lisbon! I mean, he was just a boy. Think of it. Cathedrals and grand houses, palaces, ships at the docks. All that brick and stone. But you've never seen a city, Carvalho, so how can you know?"

"Well, I've read books, too, *Avo*," I said. "I know how to picture things."

"All right," he said. "Okay. But look. It's complicated. I've been thinking about it here. Here's how it would have to go. Now Alvaro Simoes was one of the most powerful men in this city. That means the world. Portugal was the greatest, most advanced nation in those days. Did I say that Simoes had the ear of the king? The truth of the matter was that he had the king in his pocket. Simoes financed most of the Crown's exploration. You've never known anyone like Alvaro Simoes, though you might some day. He was powerful and rich and had everything a person could want. He would have been curious about the islander, don't you think? He could have had him hanged at any time. But Simoes could afford to toy with people. He might have misjudged that ancestor of ours, though. Right? Because you can bet your ass that if Simoes was watching him, he was watching Simoes!"

My grandfather suddenly raised his arm and swung the fillet knife in the air above his head. I pushed my back into the wall and drew my head in. "You bet he watched him. And would he be afraid to speak to him? Impossible! Be bold! Be bold, Carvalho, and the world is yours!" He sensed his own drunken extravagance and pulled back some, toned himself down.

"So," he said, taking a breath. "He talked with Simoes. They talked about the East and of going west to get there. And how important the Azores would be if that was the route. And how did Simoes respond? What did he say?"

John Joseph moved in the shadows and drank again from the long bottle before going on. "This Simoes pulled a small lace handkerchief out of his sleeve and dabbed at his nose. 'You seem to have given this a lot of thought,' he said. 'But what if the western route isn't possible?'

"A good question, Carvalho. The ancestor never considered it not to be possible. He told Simoes that. And do you know what?"

"What?"

"Simoes laughed at him. He said, 'You can say those things because you only dream. You don't have any ships, any money, no men, no power to risk. Another man might be a little more prudent!'

"Tell me, Carvalho," said my grandfather, "with all the knowledge from the old books floating around, why don't you think anybody had sailed around the world yet?"

"People were afraid of the danger," I said.

"Maybe. But there were problems. There was that other exploration going on. You know what I mean. To the south."

"Africa."

"Africa was a problem. It tempted the king. How far around? How soon would they find a passage? How far did China lie on the other side?"

John Joseph's voice trailed off here, and he was still for a while before I saw him move in silhouette, heard the shuffle of his clothing and smelled the Prince Albert. He relit his pipe with a match that flared to the edges of the room and showed a flush on his face. When the darkness collapsed around us, he remained quiet, the orange coal in his pipe breathing into a glow and then dying back as he drew in smoke and thought about something.

"*Avo?*" I said finally.

"Quiet!"

We sat for a while longer, and then he said, "I've lost my way just now, but I see in order to get back, we have to follow Simoes for a bit."

He pulled on his pipe, and I saw the glint of the wine bottle as he took a pull on that, too. "Simoes," he said, "was outfitting a ship—a caravel—that was going to push south, to see how far south he could go on the African coast. He was afraid of something. Maybe he was afraid of the Spanish, but he might have been worried about the Church.

"Remember that the Church was in the middle of everything, and the Pope, even though he didn't have any army or navy, had control of the Christian world, and he could play one country against another. Simoes figured that he would do this with Spain and Portugal once Spain had gotten rid of the Moors. Well, our ancestor had no allegiances, so he was a new, clean choice for Simoes and his plans. And of course there was the matter of the killing. Simoes would hint at it every once in a while to keep our man off balance.

"He loved control, this Simoes. He began to make the ancestor over completely, and he wanted it completely. You see, Simoes didn't need an ordinary sailor from the Azores to do his work. He needed a gentleman, someone who could take a high position on one of his vessels."

My grandfather's pipe had gone out again and he paused to light it. In the flare of the match I took another look at his face. It was dark now, like the shadows he sat in. He had made a good dent in the bottle of wine. "So listen." He drew out his words carefully. "Simoes teaches him manners and teaches him how to dress. He takes him to gatherings in the evenings, and he introduces him as Francisco Joao Matta de Jesus Carvalho, a young lieutenant of one of the Azorean captains. The Lisbons liked to hear stories about the Azores because those islands were out at the edge of the world, so Francisco Carvalho told them stories, and he watched the Lisbons and learned their ways.

"There was a lot he had to learn, too. He was going to be the officer of lading, the lowest of the ship's officers, but still he reported directly to the master. Now the master of that ship—the *Maricico*, let's call her —had already been chosen. He was coming north from the city of Sines where he had been visiting his father . . ."

"Oh, yeah, it's *him*," I said. "Vasco da Gama. I know what comes next."

"Let me talk! Now all this preparation went on in secret. There were spies everywhere. Simoes invented a cover story. The *Maricico* would be sailing to Ceuta with instructions for trade. Their real mission was to push south, well beyond that city and see if there was a way around Africa to China. But with the cover story, anything they found would be protected. They kept all that secret.

"Simoes installed the ancestor in his household and lied to everyone about his true identity—including his own family—for him, that was just his older sister and his niece. Simoes doted on the niece. Her name was Maria, and it didn't take our ancestor long to understand that she was the Maria of the *Feliz Maria*, Simoes's flagship. Now this older sister, the Dona Isabella, looked out at the world as if each man and woman were responsible for the killing of Christ. She looked at you like she was calculating the reasons why you had brought such a crime about. She talked all the time about the saints and about sin, but Maria never seemed to pay much attention to any of this.

"This girl was slender, with small shoulders, and her hair was long and black and caught the light and held it around her pretty face. Her eyes shone with that same coppery color as her uncle's, and her lips were full and always with a smile or laugh on them. Well, Francisco was struck by her right away, and that wasn't good, because she was a high-born Lisbon and only showed him how much he lacked in everything that was important in her world.

"She thought he was a young lieutenant, remember, but often in his company at table—of course, Dona Isabella was always there, too—he would find himself making some mistake in his manners, or he would make her laugh by some awkwardness of his speech. At first these things made him angry, but he knew that he had to learn everything—how to talk and choose his words, how to behave in polite company. Maybe Simoes had an idea that letting him be around this young girl would point up the ancestor's weaknesses. Remember, he was supposed to be an officer, and their cover depended in part on his being able to act like a gentleman. But then Francisco came to understand that he had feelings for this Maria. And you know what I'm talking about, Carvalho. You know what I mean."

"So what's going to happen, then?" I asked. I felt myself growing cranky.

"Does he steal her? Run away?"

"What's this all about?" I said. "Where are you going with this?"

"Where it has to go. So? He has to get together with the woman, Carvalho. But does he betray Simoes to get her?"

"I'm not sure," I said. "Would he dare?"

"Maybe he'd dare. But the question is, would he survive?"

"I don't know."

"What about da Gama and Columbus?"

"I know—you put them all together. Put them all on the same ship!"

"Right, Carvalho, yes, good. That's right where I'm going. It makes sense, doesn't it? The three greatest sailors in the world? Their paths have to cross. I'll give Columbus his due, he could sail. He always survived. About da Gama I won't say anything good.

"Vasco da Gama had voyaged south before, but never as master of his own ship. The ancestor hated him on sight."

"Why? What did he do to him?"

"Nothing, Carvalho. Not then. It was the look of him. He wanted to become a saint, you know."

"I never heard of that before."

"Of course, you have never heard that. I'm going to tell you a lot of things you never heard! Gama was a pompous, stuffed up little bird with the eyes of a pig. I'm speaking about him as a young man, naturally. He hadn't grown that ridiculous beard of his yet, but he looked down on everything and everybody, Carvalho! Full of pronouncements. But he was smooth, and his clothes were bright and fine, and at table—yes, that's it—Simoes installed him in the household, too—at the supper table he would mention, Dom so-and-so, a friend of his father's, or the lovely Dona such-and-such who received him in her house with pleasure. Oh, he knew all the right names and the proper things to say, just the way to turn to someone and take a piece of cheese and strike up a conversation. Our young Francisco watched him and hated him. He was jealous, see? There he was not older than Francisco was but with all the connections, all the learning, all the polish—and he was to be master of a caravel! How could Francisco, an islander, ever compete in such a world? His own envy was poisoning him. It was as though he held a lump of lead under his tongue. The Senhorita Maria thought da Gama was ridiculous, too, though, and this brought them closer together. They would exchange secret glances at one another when da Gama was puffing himself up, and they would laugh together silently.

"Yes, but the Dona Isabella took to him. All his foolish notions of becoming a saint, you see. She took to it, all right, and was forever bringing Maria into his company to listen to him. As a joke to annoy Francisco, or maybe to ease her own time with it, Maria would say, 'Oh, but Senhor Carvalho must come, too. He thinks the world of Senhor Vasco's ideas and he finds them instructive!' Gama never understood that those two made fun of him, though the old woman knew it."

"You are hard on Vasco da Gama," I said to my grandfather's shadow.

"Be quiet now, Carvalho. Let me go on. You'll have your turn. Now listen. Vasco da Gama believed that if the southern voyages worked out, then the vaults of Portugal would swell with wealth—stones, and ivory and gold and spice and cloth—and this interested him as it did all the rich Lisbons. But he insisted that the real reason for pushing south was to bring souls into the Church. Francisco would interrupt him from time to time in his islander way of talking. 'Senhor Gama,' he would say, 'Can we hope to convert the infidels?'

"'No,' he'd say, 'We have to slay them.'

"The Senhorita Maria covered her reaction to this by holding a fan over her pretty mouth.

"'We as Christians are superior to all races on earth and have the right to all their lands and goods by virtue of their sin and error. We shall prevail on the earth and the kingdom of Christ shall reign. I intend to bring this about.'

"He was serious, Carvalho. 'And the church would be quick to canonize me, don't you think?' Here he took his thumb and etched the sign of the cross on his forehead, lips, and heart, and Dona Isabella did the same.

"Francisco took a sip of wine from his cup and looked at Maria and rolled his eyes. Maria didn't dislike Gama the way he did. Maybe it was because he knew that they would be great rivals. But she was more amused by him, I think. And the old woman often kept at Gama with talk about the saints and the workings of the Church—you would have thought that Gama was the Pope himself, the way he carried on—and this gave Maria a chance to slip out of the room for a few minutes, and Francisco would follow her and steal time with her, thanks to da Gama sucking up to the old lady.

"Da Gama was a dangerous fool. He had power, you see. But he thought in short little steps, one step at a time, one direction at a time. He never seemed to have big ideas. He was the devil to work for, and Francisco hated him even more when he had to talk to him about the lading of the *Maricico*, the design of the load, the nature of supplies, and so forth. Francisco knew a lot about settling loads from his days with Matta, and even though he had never outfitted a caravel there were things he saw that would improve their system. Water storage and cask size, changing the racks that held the barrels, things like this. Every point had to be won with Gama. He never got an idea all at once. He had to be walked through everything step by step. He demanded to be addressed as 'My Captain' or 'Commander,' and he would make the ancestor stand before him unless he invited him to sit, which he would or would not do according to his moods."

"And yet he sailed with him," I said, after John Joseph paused. I had to keep him going. I didn't want to lose him if he lost the thread of the story.

"Yes, he sailed with him. The voyage took over a year."

"And Simoes sent the ancestor to spy on da Gama."

"Everyone was watched some way or another."

"Then he must have figured out that Francisco and his niece were becoming ... were falling in love."

"Falling in love? So that's it, then?"

"Isn't it?"

John Joseph sighed. "Yes, we'll have to get to that. But it never crossed Simoes's mind that Maria would take the ancestor seriously. It never crossed his mind to take our Francisco seriously enough in anything at first. But I don't want to tell about that now."

My grandfather shifted to drink from his bottle again, and I saw him gesture toward the covered window. "The morning that they slipped from the wharf was as dark as this. It was the feast of Saint Felicitas . . ."

"Savaged by wild beasts and beheaded," I said.

"*Silencio, favor!* They had the bishop of the city himself come to bless them, and at the same time he delivered the four churchmen they were supposed to carry with them to spread the faith. They were far up the Tagus River, at a private place owned by Simoes, and they came slowly down on the tide past the other quays, the outline of the city all in the darkness, here and there a few lights, the sound of a fisherman in his dory . . .

"Their charter was to get further south than Diogo Cao, who had reached the Congo River the year before. He had sailed for the king under another private financier, Fernao Gomes, a great rival of Simoes, and Simoes's chief competition for trading rights in that part of the world. Cao had believed that the river itself was the passage through the continent that everyone had been hoping for for so long, but of course he was wrong. Simoes had learned that the passage around could not be much farther south, but he couldn't rely on it. The crew didn't know anything about this, naturally. The common seamen couldn't be trusted. Da Gama discussed this with the deck officers and the boatswain, who would have his mates keep the men in tow, especially after they passed south of Ceuta, which is where they thought they were going. I don't need to tell you who this officer was."

"Columbus, himself," I said.

John Joseph cleared his throat. "In those days he wasn't as sour in the face as he would become later, but he was pale and thin. He was loud and he bragged a lot, but nothing much about him was remarkable. Now our Francisco worried about da Gama and the others of his high birth, because they seemed to block his destiny, but who could have seen any such thing in this Columbus?

"Yet he had a way with his deck gangs. He would bully and joke and clown with the men, and they responded well to this and didn't give any trouble when their course began to point away from the east. In the early voyages sailors hugged the coast, and the wind and water there were treacherous. But to turn away and take to the open sea put you out in the strong steady winds, air that you could bite your cloth into and lean your ship against.

"So they left the coast and swung west, then south southwest. Each night Francisco kept secret logs of courses and tracks, weather and events, all for his report to Simoes. At first the journey went fine. There was so much prayer and petition on board because of the priests, you see, and the weather held, fresh and clean. But one night—they were well south of Ceuta by then, south of the line of Cape Bojador, too—one of the seamen, a Lisbon man named Alves, saw a star fall in some strange way, and he told others in the crew that this was the sign of Our Lady weeping for the loss of their ship. Da Gama flew into a rage when he heard about this, and he had the man flogged as though that might put an end to it. But in two days' time they began to buck a huge, oily swell from the south, and the wind came around and forced them into a line of long tacks which kept the men up on the decks at all hours.

"Then the sky began to show some high scud, purple and blue at sundown, and in the night the stars disappeared. By morning, the seas were so huge that they were skidding and breaking on themselves, and da Gama had to order all the cloth off the spars except for the main, where he kept a small rag, close-reefed to give them steerage.

"Francisco said they should come about and run before this storm, which any fool could see was not really on them yet, but it was coming fast. Da Gama wouldn't listen, though. At first the ancestor thought da Gama was afraid of being pooped by the huge following seas if they turned and pointed north, but later he realized da Gama simply did not want to give up ground. He underestimated this gale, Carvalho. The priests didn't know what to make of it, but they prayed to Saint Christopher and this upset the seamen so much that Columbus had the churchmen silenced.

"The ancestor took a mate and some seamen below decks to make sure nothing would break loose as they pitched and rolled. He also wanted to lighten ship as much as he could by jettisoning anything that they could do without. Within an hour of the glass, without a choice, they were running before the wind with bare poles, and every man topside was lashed to something for the sake of his life.

"Francisco had never seen a storm like this, Carvalho, not in all his years in the Azores, even. The sky blackened and rain began to fall so hard that it seemed it would stave in the decks. A sea would catch them from behind and lift them, and you'd feel the decks shudder and they would slide, as if you were going down the edge of a cliff. Everybody screamed. Each time they reached the trough of those seas, they would lose the fo'c'sle under green water, and the sea would weigh the vessel under until every board shivered and groaned, and yet that ship, that beautiful caravel, would grind its way back through that water and right herself.

"The decks were a mess, men begging God to forgive them of their crimes, lines snapping, the mizzen and all its rigging carried away along with two men who had the bad luck to have lashed themselves to it.

"The ancestor had spent the early part of the storm below the decks, keeping the battens secure on the hatches, wedging the loads to make sure that no barrels would get loose and batter a hole in the ship from the inside. They had a gang at the pumps, but the holds were awash to their waists. It was too late to wrestle anything heavy up to the decks to jettison, but Francisco thought they might get some of their trading store over the side—nothing but small chests of baubles and junk. He had made his way to the poop and lashed himself next to da Gama, who stood there hunched against the rain. He had to scream into da Gama's ear. He agreed to let these small stores be thrown over, but now that Francisco was above decks, he changed his mind. Nothing so small would have made a difference in that storm. He would not risk the men, nor open the hatches.

"He stayed at the poop, and he saw the mizzen get carried over, but the big lateen boom did not clear the deck. It became fouled there by a strong line, and it rolled and crashed like a battering ram every time they took a sea. They would all have perished if our boatswain hadn't cut himself loose, made his way to the boom, and slashed it free just as a wave crashed over them. That Columbus could pull a dagger from his boot or sleeve like a magician. The wave carried the loose boom over, but Columbus went over with it. Francisco saw him go as plain as I see you here, and even in that howling wind, you could hear him scream. There was no help for him. But Columbus was blessed. God damn, the luck that man had! Two big seas later and he was washed back aboard, and he came over the side in that wash of green water, his chin up and his arms and legs working as though he was at a dead run. The wave thumped him down on the deck like a fish, and he thrashed his way to a hatch cover. Something seized the ancestor here, something he couldn't control, and he untied the bowline around his waist, and as the ship shuddered its way up the shoulder of another sea, he ran down and grabbed the boatswain and together they stumbled back up the ladder to the poop. They put good knots around themselves in a heartbeat—and just in time—for more green water broke on them and brought them all to their knees.

"What do you think, Carvalho? Had the ancestor let him go without tying him, he would have been washed over again without a doubt. And then what would have been our Francisco's place in the world? What came over him? Was it meant to be that he would save the man who would be credited for what he, the islander, did? But he had no idea then that Columbus would be his rival, too. You see, he was only thinking about Vasco da Gama.

"Yes, Christopher Columbus was a strange man, but Francisco had already chosen Vasco da Gama as his enemy.

"Da Gama stood there at the binnacle with a look of complete rage upon his face. See, da Gama understood that something great would be his, and he hated that storm for threatening it. Why had something been promised to him and not to our islander? Was his *fado* stronger?

"Right then a wall of water broke over them. The ancestor got knocked off his feet. He couldn't get his head above water. He was going to drown. But for him to die and have da Gama survive him was more than he could stand. So he lifted himself enough to take a breath. He fell again and he lifted himself again. The design of the caravel saved them. The *Maricico* groaned herself upright, and Francisco spit up blood."

I saw my grandfather's head move, and I caught just a glimpse of his features in the red glow of the running light as he shifted his weight. A floorboard croaked sharply beneath him, and he settled back into the chimney nook. I leaned back again and shifted myself, and I breathed deeply the smells of the lamp oil and the old wood and my grandfather, and then I closed my eyes.

I prompted him. "They all survived that storm," I said.

John Joseph did not have an answer for me right away. I saw him reach for his pipe, tap it clean against the chimney, and lean from the shadows into the wan light to begin filling the bowl with fresh tobacco. "Well?" he asked. "The ship was a mess. They lost two men and a priest. What next?"

I thought for a moment and answered carefully. "Mutiny," I said.

"Hah. Mutiny." He considered it.

"Why not? Exactly that. Precisely that." He lit another match, cupped the flame, and then leaned back into his corner. "All right," he said. "A mutiny is just what comes," and he was silent for several minutes before he began again.

"Alves, the man who had seen the omen, was one of the men swept over the side, but his words hung in everybody's head as they tried to piece the *Maricico* back together. After a day, the sea eased up. They could by now come together on the deck, and da Gama called his officers together for a report. Some things were obvious. Two masts were gone, and the remaining mast with its lateen boom and sail needed repair. Most of the stores came through all right because of the ancestor's careful lading and choice of casks and containers, but the crew's spirit had been broken, and they talked about turning back.

"Da Gama wouldn't hear it. He knew that a failure would finish him. He needed this voyage and more like it and, of course, souls. He needed souls for his sainthood! Even two of the officers, two dandy Lisbons named Dirsa and Viera, argued for turning back. Francisco kept his mouth shut. Columbus pointed out that they had no idea where they were and they wouldn't know their position until they could see the sky again, which was still gray and full of clouds. Columbus thought that they had probably been blown north and that they might be able to hit Madeira, where they might outfit themselves.

"Da Gama was against this. He thought they might not be able to hit that island. Francisco listened carefully. Remember, he was supposed to report everything to Simoes. Now he guessed that Gama would not go back into Portuguese territory for fear that news of his disaster would reach the wrong ears. Gama proposed making for the African mainland and outfitting there. Viera was scared by this. They would be landing God knows where, and they were in a weakened state. He had heard of cannibals, you see, and other dangers which he didn't feel strong enough to face. 'You, Carvalho, what do you say?' da Gama said.

"Our islander took a long time to speak. Wasn't it also in his interest to have the voyage a success? 'Africa,' he said, 'and there is the good chance that we will encounter one of our own settlements.'

"It wasn't so simple as that, though. The crew had met in the fo'c'sle and sent a delegation to Columbus. 'Turn back,' they said. 'The voyage is cursed, the ship is damaged, and we have sailed under false orders.' Columbus brought this up now. 'You tell the crew, Senhor,' said Vasco da Gama to Christopher Columbus, 'that I will flog and hang any man who speaks again of turning back.'

"Well, you can imagine the effect this had on Dirsa and Viera, who had just been arguing that very thing. They darkened and left the poop.

"The ancestor knew there would be trouble. That storm had opened more than their small seams. On the first hour of the afternoon watch, Viera caught Francisco below decks where he had a mate and his gang clearing water and debris. He called Francisco aside. 'Will you stand with us against that fool?' he asked.

"'I can't,' says the ancestor, 'That's not the way to approach him.'

"But da Gama must have caught wind of Viera's movements because he called a muster of the crew on the foredeck. He stood at the forward rail of the poop. 'I have prayed for guidance,' he yelled over the wind, 'and I am reassured that all will be well with our voyage. We will make straightaway for Africa, where we have nothing to gain but souls for Christ and treasure for our pockets.'

"Pretty good speech, no?" said my grandfather. "But this is what happened. They were holding on a course with the wind behind them. They had to make for land soon. At nightfall, da Gama called Dirsa, Viera, and the head priest into his cabin and there they stayed for a long time. Columbus and Francisco huddled around some candles in the boatswain's locker and waited.

"At daybreak Viera himself mustered the crew again. He and Dirsa could not convince da Gama to give up, so in the night they had talked the crew into going over to them. He now asked for a vote as to what their course should be, and a couple of the mates called out, 'Back to Lisbon, back to the homeland.'

"This was grave business, Carvalho. Both Dirsa and Viera wore their swords buckled on, and someone had gone into the armory and given weapons to the mates. This was stupid, arming these men. At least the seamen were not given weapons. The mob raised a clamor, and finally Gama appeared from his cabin with his own sword in his hand, and he ordered a dismissal. No one moved.

"There they were, Carvalho, their ship in tatters, the sky still like lead above them, and a huge swell lifting them, dropping them. Da Gama was white with rage. And where was Francisco in all this? Moving! He edged his way aft to the armory hatch and drew out a crossbow. He kept to the edge of the muster.

"'Disperse your men,' da Gama says to Viera, 'and follow me to my cabin.'

"Viera wavered, but Dirsa stepped in. 'My Captain,' he said, 'I invoke you in the name of God to accept our vote.'

"Gama glared at him and said nothing.

"'Will you agree sir?' Dirsa says.

"'Dismiss these men,' says Gama. 'I won't give that order again.'

"Well, this was a fix, Carvalho. Da Gama was standing them down, and I don't think that these Lisbon dandies expected this. They were weak in their position. Neither one of them had unsheathed a sword, and yet Gama stood with his iron fully drawn. You see the picture. Gama was a small man and not graceful, but he would be able to strike at least one of them down before their swords cleared leather. So they stood there. It was one of the crew who started the fight, though. There was a mate among them, a Lisbon guy named Passarinho because he had a nose like the beak of a shore bird. He believed the bad omens. The islander saw him move, and when he turned his head he saw Passarinho's crossbow raised. He was taking aim at da Gama. He would have shot him dead, Carvalho. Passarinho cried, 'Ave Maria, forgive us all!' but in the moment that it took him to say this, the ancestor whirled and fired his own dart, which caught him deep in his shoulder. Passarinho's weapon fired, but the dart carried crazily over the rail. Viera turned and saw the blood, his man on his knees, and he drew his sword. Francisco drew his, too.

"Now listen to me, Carvalho. The ancestor still didn't have a side in this matter. Really, Columbus's idea of going back to Madeira made the best sense. Francisco had no loyalty to da Gama, but he disliked the Lisbon officers Dirsa and Viera just as much. He only shot Passarinho because he wanted to head off a huge bloodletting. To his thinking, they couldn't afford to fight one another. They needed crew and officers intact if they were going to survive.

"Dirsa saw the ancestor's shot and turned on him. Not one of Gama's men moved. None of the crew, either. No one in their condition was eager for a fight, but Columbus rushed to the ancestor's side. Francisco held up his sword and parried Dirsa's slash. But Columbus slipped beneath his arm and around him, grabbed his neck, and held a dagger -there—Christ, that man could make a stiletto come out of the air! Dirsa yielded on the spot. Da Gama took the moment and advanced upon Viera, who fumbled with his sword but couldn't bring it up before da Gama's blade was on his throat.

"'Dismiss these men!' da Gama yelled, and, of course, the day was won. Viera called for the crew to disperse, and they did, seeing their leaders brought low and one man on the deck with the ancestor's dart in him.

"The skirmish seemed to break some spell. That night the clouds broke and they were able to chart their course by familiar stars. Why, Carvalho, they had been carried south! Oh, da Gama was happy. What an argument against any return to the north! He called Francisco and Columbus into his cabin and had them kneel and say a rosary there on the boards. Then he offered them a cup of wine. 'They are both agents, of this I am certain,' he said of Viera and Dirsa.

"'Of whom, my captain?' says the ancestor.

"Da Gama looks at him. 'There are those who would have us fail. I thought it might be either of you. Spies everywhere! I shall reward you by making you my lieutenants when we raise the coast.'

"Well," said my grandfather, "what do you think?"

"Great," I said, "but what about the mutineers?"

"Oh. Well. Da Gama would have hanged them."

"And the ship?"

"Rebuilt it on the beach."

"And then what?"

"Carvalho, ease off. Enough for now."

"But . . ."

"Look," John Joseph said, "I can't keep going. Not tonight. I don't know where this is going. This is hard, Carvalho. I'm tired of talking, and my back aches. My legs ache, too. I didn't think it would be this hard to fill in all the holes. Look, he hasn't even left for the New World yet. What if I can't do it?"

"What's the big deal?" I said. "You talk about the ancestor all the time."

"But not to make it all work out," he said. "Not to get it to hang together so it's possible."

I had never heard a tone like this from him. He sounded bewildered. He was angry, too. Like he was blaming me for his own hard time.

"Look," I said, "I don't care how it comes out."

He blew out some air. "Okay, Carvalho. I am making too big a deal out of this. I know what I told you—about you and me, and Rosa being gone and all that. But I'm going to take off for a while tonight."

Welching already. I was mad, but I knew better than to cross him right now.

"I'm coming back. Don't sweat it. But I've got to think."

"Think here," I said.

"No, that's not what I want to do." He stood up. "Hey," he said, changing his tone, "not so bad, maybe. I mean we saved da Gama and Columbus, right?"

"Right," I said, but I didn't have any enthusiasm in my voice.

13

"You know, no one in this family ever tells anybody anything," I said. Uncle Paddy looked at me with his gray eyes, gave my great aunt a glance, and looked back at me. It was a signal to me to be quiet.

"Some things aren't meant to be talked about," said my great aunt. She didn't look up from her bowl. We were eating kale soup at the kitchen table, a little past noon.

"What about *Avo*? In the old country. He was going to be a priest once, right?"

"Where did you get *that*?" said my great aunt.

"I thought I heard him say that once."

"You can't believe anything he says. When he was small he went to school with some priests at the church back on Pico. He was very bright. Nothing ever came of it."

"Then you all came here."

"He came first. You know that."

"He was a sailor for a while."

"He fished. He was a ship's boy. He turned tough on us. He went everywhere on boats when he was just a boy. He came here because of the work fishing. Him and Domingo Costa. Neither one of them ever did much after that. Of course, poor Domingo."

"Then *Avo* got in trouble somewhere?"

My aunt narrowed her eyes and looked at Uncle Paddy, then back at me. "Who's telling you stories?"

"No one," I said. "That's the problem. Everything is a secret around here."

"For good reasons," she said. "Are you saying your prayers? Are you lighting candles to the saints?"

"Sure." But of course I wasn't.

So there it all was. Not much about my grandfather. And she was not going to volunteer *anything* about my mother and Carmine. Not a word. And I was not going to ask her. It would sound too much like begging. And also it might sound to her like I wasn't on their side. I didn't know if I was or not, but I knew I was not on Great Aunt Theophila's. I was not going to give her the chance to make me an ally. There was only one person in the family that I would let myself hold onto now, and I didn't know from one minute to the next if he'd even show up.

And if he did show up, it would be for his own reasons.

Maria Simoes sat in moonlight on an iron bench behind the great wall of a dense, ill-kept garden. Her face was illuminated in a silver light that seemed to slide from the deep sheen of her hair, which she wore pulled back at the sides, held by a pair of small tortoise combs. The ancestor sat next to her, his cloak wrapped about them both, and he was no longer the old mysterious figure that haunted the dooryard conversations. He was young, roughly handsome, something of John Joseph, of even Carmine, in his features. The light glinted sharply off his own face.

"Oh, you mustn't," Maria said, her body drawing up from his touch beneath the cloak, but she sighed then and leaned her head to him. He kissed her on the lips. He whispered something to her. "No," she said, "it would be impossible . . . the Dona Isabella, and then my uncle's position."

"It would be only temporary," said the ancestor, speaking in whispers that carried to where I stood, beneath a sweetly fragrant apple tree, feeling a small chill move over the shrubs and flowers. I drew up my own cloak. He touched her again, and a small, familiar cry issued from her, and they drew together under his wrap. A wind came up then, softly at first, making a sound as it approached, and then it was upon the garden, and the trees all shook and leaned with it. I turned my head and looked away from them. Suddenly I wasn't in the garden any longer but stood instead upon some black rocky ledge, a great height.

I felt the wry, sharp air on my face and smelled the sea. Far below us stretched a line of rocky beach, and beyond that, across a gloss of deep gray water, another line of rocky shore.

"He came back to Pico, then? After all."

"Had to. That works it out for us. He was deeded land on the island of Pico, you see. Almost, Carvalho—almost—the seat of an empire. He must have thought that, anyway. He returned from Africa a rich, rich man. Ivory, stones, information, stature. He had been granted this Azorean land and his own caravel by the king himself. But his eyes had been opened. He saw terrible things. He did terrible things."

Suddenly my grandfather was on his feet, pacing the little room. His quick movement jarred me out of the story. I squeezed against the chest where I had leaned and nodded and followed his narration and his voices, and I pulled my feet in close to me as he thumped back and forth on the bare floorboards.

There was a nervous energy all around him, and he seemed impatient about something. The despair and self-pity of the night before were gone now—or were replaced with something else. He seemed to vibrate. He stood at the window now in the dim, red shadow-light just as a ghost might stand, some menace in him, some sorrow bigger than any of mine. He pulled the corner of the blanket aside and peeked down into the street. "It all came down to me," he said. "All the hundreds of years of our family. And then I was it, the inheritor of all that. I was the forefront." He turned. "And now it's you. Do you know what that means?"

"No," I said.

He laughed sharply. "Well, I don't have a goddamned idea, myself. This is a rough old story, isn't it?"

"Sometimes," I said.

"I have it worked out. I have it figured, in the big ways."

"I'm ready," I said.

"Hey, how's the dory, by the way? We need to catch us some cash fish."

"Loaded. Ready to sail. Fishing gear, everything but bait."

He cleared his throat. "I have some business down to the east'ard. I'll be going down there before I leave."

"*Avo* . . ." I started to protest, but I knew I would sound like everyone else, chiding him about his women. Really I didn't care what he did.

"I've worked things out. Why don't I meet you? I'll pick you up in the boat after sun-up. Can you sneak away that early?"

"Of course. They all . . . I don't know what. They hardly see me anymore."

"End of Cold Storage Wharf, then. About a half-hour after light."

"I'll be there," I said.

"Well, we have the dope on Columbus and da Gama, I'd say."

"I guess so."

"And that voyage the three of them went on was a great success. Nowhere to go from here if it wasn't."

"No."

"That's when da Gama's true colors came out. He believed himself to be so right, you know. He knew that God and the Church were on his side. So Portugal was the anointed country, and da Gama was its anointed hero. All of this was in da Gama's mind, I mean to say.

"He saw that his accord with God and country gave him the right to slaughter the natives along the coast, if they didn't happen to please him or serve him. He argued that they had no souls!"

John Joseph turned to the wall and settled again in his dark nook, took out his pipe and began to fill it.

"Now Columbus, for all his faults, was a compassionate man, and he tried to talk da Gama into a more gentle sort of Christianity. It wasn't any good." A billow of sweet smoke filled the room as my grandfather lit his pipe. "Now where would our Captain Francisco stand in all this, Carvalho? With Columbus, of course. But he didn't stand all that strong. He hated da Gama for what he was and for what he did—executions, ambushes, betrayals, theft—it's all in the books, right?—but he saw also how much ivory they carried away, he knew the worth of the precious stones that he was able to get his hands on. Now they were supposed to bring back a profit for Simoes, and there was a system of shares among the officers and crew—with a share for the owner, and—"

"Like our fishing boats."

"Right. That's it. And Simoes and the king would get the lion's share. But they all kept something back in secret, and these gemstones that I am talking about were small and could be hidden in a bunch of different ways. He liked this easy wealth, Carvalho. And he needed it if he was to carry out his own *fado*. So you see that da Gama's policies, his cruelty and stupidity, helped our islander to make his own fortune out of that coast as they pushed south. No use in pretending that our Francisco was innocent about anything. That ship was so heavy with loot, they were worried about making it home.

"And right after that trip, Columbus connived an audience with the king. That would be King Joao. Columbus wanted to give up Africa and go west. He wanted to use the Azores for a base. Now Columbus even wrote about this himself. I checked Lew's stuff. But the king, King Joao, didn't trust this sailor from Genoa—remember, I told you that

Columbus could be loud and boastful. Maybe that's what turned the king against him. Maybe Simoes was behind it. At any rate, Dom Joao sent Columbus away, and later Simoes told Francisco privately that he himself might finance the voyage west when the time was right, and that Francisco would be his man! He was pleased, you see, with Francisco's secret reports of Vasco da Gama's trip."

"Did he catch da Gama doing anything?"

"You bet. He kept back profits from Simoes, and he falsified his log. He didn't say anything about the mutiny. He reported that Viera and Dirsa were killed by cannibals, and he bribed the crew to be quiet about it. He even said that they got farther south than they did, and he reported that they had talked with a king who told them about a passage to the East. Wow!"

"Yeah. So what did Simoes do to Gama for all these lies?"

"For the love of Christ, Carvalho, the islander didn't tell Simoes any of that! Use your head. Simoes wanted to know that he had picked the right person for his enterprise, so that's what he let him believe. This is what he did. Francisco met with da Gama as soon as they reached Lisbon and told him who he was and that he was a spy. Hah! Vasco da Gama turned green! He drew his sword on the islander, Carvalho! As though he were going to have at him."

I saw my grandfather move in the darkness, and I caught the glint of running-light on the narrow blade of his fillet knife, which he held murderously in front of him as he spoke. I saw in that moment the young John Joseph, brash, dangerous—yes, maybe someone to be reckoned with on those dangerous wharves of New Bedford. I thought too, in an instant, how no one is ever just what he seems to be, how you never know what's inside anybody until it comes out.

"'Come ahead, you son of a bitch,' says the ancestor, 'and die trying!' Vasco da Gama wasn't so brave when he wasn't firing ten-pounders into native villages, or cutting the throats of hostages. He didn't like the look of the ancestor's sword, and Columbus had taught Francisco a thing or two about handling a blade. So he gets the little peacock in a standoff. It was too early for him to die. How would he ever become a saint, with so few souls on his ledger? Well, finally they connived, and they each made their own pacts with their own devil. They would lie. They made sure that they would give the same reports, the same charts and logs. Yes, and da Gama would get Africa again, and it was what he wanted, but that would leave the West for Captain Francisco Carvalho, our man, our great ancestor."

My grandfather paused here and drank from a bottle that he pulled from somewhere in his clothing. He leaned back into the shadow then, but I didn't mistake the smell of the cheap muscatel that soured its way across the dark room when he began speaking again.

"He betrayed Simoes, and he ran off with the Senhorita Maria to his granted land on the island of Pico. They left in secret early in the morning, and they made their way down the Tagus on his ship—*his* ship, Carvalho, the *Five Wounds*, and before Simoes could catch them, they were already married. Fray Costa, our old mentor, was only too happy to perform the ceremony for them, in private, within the little stone cloister on *Sao Jorge*. Directly after, Francisco talked him into coming to Pico with them. Fray Costa was afraid of getting in trouble with his bishop, but Francisco told tales of what he'd seen and where he'd been, and he showed him that he could muster influence if it was needed. Pico needed priests, after all!

"The priest was really disappointed in Francisco when Simoes arrived weeks later, all in a snit, a contingent of men-at-arms on his ship. Francisco hadn't told the priest that they'd eloped, you see."

"Eloped," I said. The word sounded so odd to me. "People always get married when they elope, right?" I said.

"I suppose so," John Joseph said. "But don't go off on that subject. I know what you're jumping to. I wouldn't count on anything one way or another. I'm just putting things together here. You follow me?"

What was I supposed to say to him? But his story seemed like two stories. Or three. How did you keep everything from happening all at once in your head? I said something to him just because I knew that's what he was waiting for. "You mean Simoes came out to the islands to take Maria back?"

"What was Simoes going to do? Have him killed? Destroy the father of Maria's child? Don't look so dumb, Carvalho. What did you think? That marriage was an urgent thing, and once Simoes understood the weather, he changed his tune soon enough."

"You mean a baby?"

"Soon enough."

I felt sick. "Why did you put that in? You didn't need to put that in!"

"Hold your voice down. What do you think? Besides, he was our ancestor—he had to have kids for us to be here, you dope. This story has nothing to do with you."

"I don't believe that," I said.

"Believe it or not, it's all the same to me," said my grandfather. He leaned forward and took a swig from his muscatel. I wouldn't answer him now, and he stopped speaking, and I don't know how we would have resolved that silence if right then a drunken voice hadn't risen in song up from the street, an indistinct but somehow familiar melody that I recognized, as it came closer, to be a *fado*, sung in a lilting, careless way in the old speech. It sounded like Petey Flores coming from Juney's Tap—unless it was too late for Juney's, and then he would be coming from one of his drinking places down along the water. I knew of two of these places, one a rusted-out fish hopper, bigger than a shed, which lay on its side behind one of the Cold Storage's outbuildings, and the other an overhang on the old stub of a fueling wharf just farther to the east. I had discovered his caches of pint bottles of port and muscatel in each of these places, and once, out of the same sort of boredom that would have me roll a stone ball from our roof, I smashed a half dozen of these bottles with a piece of tide-smoothed brick.

The singing grew closer, passed down the sidewalk opposite our covered window, and faded off toward the beach. But it didn't fade entirely. It seemed to linger in the little room, sink into the wood and shadows and rise out of them again. And then I realized that my grandfather, sunk now into the darkness of the chimney nook, had picked up the old sad tune and was humming it in a low voice. I listened silently. When he stopped, he said, "Stories are never simple, Carvalho."

There was something conciliatory in this, and so I answered him. "I know that."

"You don't know it, but maybe you're learning it. At any rate, there's nothing we can do. We can't go back and undo something. I say we push on."

"From Simoes and Maria?"

"What would you suggest?"

"Go on," I said. "It's what you want."

"All right. I said that Simoes came to the islands to fetch Maria. But that wasn't the whole truth. He got to other important things pretty quickly. 'Vasco da Gama is for the East,' he says. 'Even as we speak, Bartholomew Dias takes a fleet to the south to better your last mark. If he succeeds, da Gama will take the following expedition. It has been decided.'

"'You know what I think,' says the ancestor. 'Out here on these islands, we are probably closer to the East than any rounding of Africa. I know that Christopher Columbus made his proposal to the king. He took my ideas.'

"Simoes gives him a look. 'Or *my* ideas,' he says. Suddenly it comes into Francisco's head that just as he had sailed with da Gama as a secret agent, so might have Christopher Columbus. Could he have been so thick not to consider this?

"'Tell me about Columbus,' he says.

"'It isn't necessary. Understand that he has slipped away and carries secrets to other governments. He has even gone to the miserable French.'

"'They sail like farmers,' says our man.

"'They can do us damage,' says Simoes.

"It was true that the French had raided some of the king's shipping. 'Would they try the West?'

"'My sources say otherwise. But I am afraid of the Spanish.'

"Fray Costa coughed nervously. They had left him once the conversation had turned from the proprieties of marriage and family to the politics of voyaging. As a churchman he wouldn't have been so strongly against other Christian kingdoms. Frenchman, Spaniard, Genoese. They were all under the rule of Pope. Simoes dropped the subject, but he came back later, followed by two men-at-arms who bore a small chest.

"Simoes wanted Francisco to meet with him in private, so he left Maria in the cottage where they were staying while their big house was being built, and he went with Simoes to the sacristy of the little stone church that had been built by outlanders some years before. It was empty, and they struck up a bunch of tallow candles, which lit up the damp stone room. Simoes posted the men outside and opened the chest. 'Some things of interest,' he said. He folded open a heavy parchment letter and spread it on the stones of the floor. 'Read here where I have marked.' He pointed and Francisco read. It went something like this. *I send to His Majesty a chart, made by my hands, wherein your shores are shown, and the islands from which you may begin to make a voyage continually westward, and the places whereunto you ought to come and through how many leagues you ought to arrive at the places most fertile in all spices and gems.*

"'Look at the signature,' says Simoes.

"It was signed in a heavy hand. Paolo dal Pozzo Toscanelli."

"Toscanelli's Chart," I said. "I knew that was coming." I wrapped my arms around myself and leaned forward.

"Uh huh. You know as much as I do that it was the first really useful map to show the round world. Nobody alive today has seen a copy.

Only stories of it have been passed down in books. Listen. Simoes folded the letter back up and reached into the chest and pulled out a dried-up leather packet. He took the chart out of that packet. This Toscanelli was a Florentine, a doctor, and he had sent this item to the king—not Dom Joao, but the old king, Dom Alphonso, who did not act upon this information. He could have sent a voyage west ten years earlier, if he had wanted to.

"'How did you come by this?' Francisco asks. He saw that these papers had been sent to the old Crown.

"'None of your business,' says Simoes. 'What do you think?'

"The chart showed Lisbon and our Islands and Madeira and the Canaries, and to the west beyond them the land of Antillia, and farther west, Japan. Quinsay, China, lay at the western edge of the chart. Toscanelli had divided the sea distance into twenty-six equal spaces of eighty leagues apiece, or twenty-one hundred leagues in total. I worked this all out. I checked it out.

"'See how our Islands guard the route,' says the old captain.

"'I am aware of this,' says Simoes. 'If ever the time comes, Pico would be very important to us.'

"'It is important to build here.'

"'Which is why you came,' he says.

"'And why *you* came?' says Francisco right back to him.

"I mean, Carvalho, think about this man who comes after his niece's honor and brings such a chest of documents with him. And the men-at-arms that he brought? They were to be the start of a private garrison there on the island. They were placed under Francisco's command."

"But Simoes could have left them just to watch the old captain," I said.

"Right you are, Carvalho. Yes, no one was to be trusted. No one. Remember that. And so why should our captain be trusted? Hah! Why, indeed. After all, he wanted to build a presence in the Islands, and he wanted the western route to the Indies. He would be the grandest duke in all the Christian kingdoms. Duke? Did I say duke? Wouldn't the Islands with their strategic position and great wealth from the western route become a kingdom in their own right, as powerful as any on the mainland of Europe? All he needed was a navy. You might think this sounds foolish, but in those days it was possible. Think about what England would do."

John Joseph was interrupted just then by Old Man Coelho's hounds, which raised a racket from their pen across the street. I heard the slam of a car door and voices, too, and in spite of myself I thought, It's *them* —they've come back. But as I strained to listen, I heard only the voices of some men, summer boarders, whose words I couldn't make out, but who walked off toward the hill, leaving the dogs to howl after them. This set the ducks off, and the neighborhood seemed to erupt until, some long minutes later, like a hand passing over us, quiet fell again. The outburst shook me up a bit. There was always the risk that my great aunt might wake up and find me gone from my bed. I listened hard for any sign that the ruckus had awakened the house, but none came. "Tell some more," I said after a while, settling back against the sea chest.

My grandfather coughed a wet cough and swigged some wine. "All the intrigues," he said. "The chart. Like that old map in *Treasure Island*, right?"

"Yes. But you know, you don't say much about Maria. Is she somebody from your own life?"

"What do you know about it?" he said peevishly.

"I don't know anything about it," I said. "That's why I'm asking."

"It's all a story, Carvalho. In the end that's all there is—stories. It would have been Maria that got him through that first voyage, though," he added.

"I don't follow," I said.

"Listen. The ancestor—think of how he would have come back from that trip. Scarred from wounds and badly knit bones, his teeth loose from scurvy, and his flesh barely hanging on his ribs. His sleep ruined with dreams of the skirmishes, the sounds of guns going off in the night. He had done real evil. He had gone to a place beyond any of the rules of the world that we know. He had gone so far away that nothing mattered. When he got back to Lisbon, he went to the church to make a confession, and all the while he talked to the priest, all he could think of was that the priest had never left civilization as he had, and so he couldn't have any idea of what was inside him. Priests couldn't heal our captain."

"But Maria could?"

"He thought she could."

"And what happened then?"

"Why don't *you* say what happened? Let's see how well you do with it."

I had hit another nerve. I thought hard but I came up with nothing.

"Well, Simoes's daughter became his ally."

"You mean niece," I interrupted.

He sighed, drank again from the bottle, and set it on the floorboards, empty by the sound of its clink. "What did I say?"

"You said Simoes's *daughter.*"

"That's what I meant."

"Why?"

"Ha, well, it was all a masquerade, this niece-uncle business. He was her father, you see. And the mother was . . . never married to him. But he wanted the daughter. He wanted some good for her in this life. He wanted to give her the New World, and he saw the ancestor as his instrument."

"But he wanted the New World for himself," I said.

"What does it matter? Listen, I'm not kidding, we'll lose our way with this. This won't get us to the rest of the story. If I can't show what happened to him, then we lose him. We lose the possibility of him. There are great voyages to talk about. We shouldn't get stuck here. I am not the man to talk about daughters and wives."

"I won't interrupt," I said.

"That's what you say." He lifted the wine bottle again, as if to check to see if it were really empty, then he replaced it on the floor and began to fuss with his pipe. I saw this all as movements of a shadow against a wall of shadow. He struck a match and burst into fierce relief for a second, his face drawn, not looking good in the orange flare. Then the room collapsed around him again, and we were off.

I didn't know what I was looking for in Maria's story, but he was not going to give me anything. I could see that. Instead, he drew out Fray Costa for me again as a narrow-faced man with a high brow and sober jaw, slightly snaggle-toothed, and he told me how the priest and Simoes sat for long hours in one another's company. Simoes, as I saw him, was portly, always in his shiny hat and with a lace handkerchief tucked partway into his sleeve.

"Maria, you see grew heavier each week with the baby. Simoes himself stayed for a season with them, lending his crew to the building of the fortress, and laying plans. Francisco would still read to him at night. Sometimes Maria and Fray Costa would join them. And privately, he would still remind the captain that he had once killed a man on his ship.

"Well, all this went on for a spell, you know, the waiting and so forth, and then it was time for Simoes to go back to the mainland where he could place himself in the middle of all the schemes and conniving among the Lisbons. But before he left he gave Francisco a gift. He gave him a hand-copied edition of Marco Polo's book. 'This is identical in every way to the one we first sailed with on that, ah, eventful voyage of the *Feliz Maria,*' he said. 'Keep it safe. It is a treasure.' And it was, you see. Books in those days, Carvalho, were handmade one at a time. . . . But let me tell you the plan before I lose track here!

"The ancestor was to continue to organize the island and to prepare his caravel for the voyage. Simoes would send word as soon as he could get wind of the results of Dias's voyage. He would tell Francisco what he wanted him to do. 'I need a messenger that I can trust, an agent no one will suspect,' he said, and he took Fray Costa with him.

"Three—no—four months passed. Finally, a fast caravel arrived from Lisbon filled with supplies, bombards and powder, bright cloth and fineries for the great house they now lived in, and, a welcome sight, Fray Costa himself, who carried a cipher from Simoes, a sealed parchment containing only columns of numbers separated by dashes, and the words *From our shipmate.* Maria and Francisco and Fray Costa opened the cipher and studied it. But what was the key? Fray Costa had not been given it in order to protect him as well as the message. Simoes seemed to think they would know it."

"I know it," I said.

"Oh, you think so, do you?" said my grandfather.

"The book. 'Our shipmate' is Marco Polo, the Guinea Francisco first sailed together with. The key is the book. I know that kind of cipher. I know how it works."

"Indeed," he said.

I enjoyed the nettle in his voice. I pushed ahead. The cipher was from a secret code book that Lew had given me. "The first number of every pair was a page number, and the second number was the number of a letter on that page. Since one book had been copied out identical to the other, there was a perfect cipher."

"Maybe I should turn this story over to you," my grandfather said grumpily.

"And since there were only two books, even if someone guessed the key, it wouldn't matter. Only the two people with the books could work the cipher." I waited for him to pick up the story again, but he was quiet except for a ticking I heard from his shadowy corner, a finger tapping something. "*Avo?*"

"Go on," he said. "You know so much, what did it say?"

"News of Dias."

"Of course. Precisely that." He fell quiet again.

"*Avo*," I said, "I want you to finish." He would make me beg for the rest of the story if he had a mind to.

"You might not do so badly with it on your own," he said.

"*Avo*, come on!"

"Well, listen then. Yes, the cipher was about Bartholomew Dias. He was the real hero. He was the one who finally rounded Africa. God damn, he was a sailor! The cipher came out like this. *Dias has found passage. Seventeen hundred leagues. Forced to turn back. Gama will build fleet. East is his. Proceed West with fair wind and weather. All in secrecy. Remember the first Carvalho.*

John Joseph was really into the story now. He was pushing toward something he had worked out. He shaped the old priest's high voice in careful tones.

"'You are to leave for the West, then?' Fray Costa asked.

"And then the ancestor's voice again: 'I am,' he says.

"'Then there are more ciphers for you,' the priest said. 'Dom Alphonso told me to give them to you only after I heard that from you.'

"Ciphers, Carvalho! There were pages and pages of them, all sealed up in oiled leather packets. Fray Costa unwrapped them. They worked on them all night. In these messages Simoes laid out plans, gave the latest information about the political situation in Lisbon, and offered all kinds of logistical ideas for the voyage. The caravel he had just sent would be the second ship for the voyage, and Fray Costa would be the priest. He had sent the extra guns to help with the fortification of Pico, but the *Cinco Feridas* and the new ship, the *Ceo Silencio,* would each carry ten cannons, but mounted so as to fire at water level. This method of mounting the guns had been an idea of the king himself, and you know that a caravel armed like this, and with its great speed and maneuverability, could shoot a bigger ship to pieces.

"The old captain had kept his ship in readiness—her bottom was scaled and tarred, her boards were tight—it needed only supplying, which would take a matter of weeks. But there was so much to take. Casks of wine, water, pork, rice, vinegar, olive oil, biscuits, beans, onions. They had to load the heavy stone *padroes*, too, which would mark claims on any new lands, and they needed to take some treasures too, so that when they arrived in Quinsay, China, they could represent the kingdom of Portugal properly as the most powerful nation on the face of the earth.

"They also carried the usual swords and daggers and handmirrors

and bowls, all decorated so they could give them to kings and trades-
men alike—and glass beads and cheap cloth to trade. They began all

this work right away. They moved in a fever, Carvalho. Remember,
Columbus had defected and was now trying to sell their ideas to any

king in Europe who would listen, and da Gama was building and planning for that big voyage south. Not a minute passed that our captain
didn't think about the pressure from those two rivals of his.

"Simoes had thought through the voyage pretty well. But remember that our captain had spied for Simoes, so he figured that he couldn't
trust the other captain and crew of this new ship. Surely there were
spies aboard, and probably not only spies for Dom Alphonso Simoes,
but for worse. But who would they be? Well, Francisco could never
guess, but he decided to remove the captain, a smooth *Lisbon* with
high speech, and with him he took away fifteen members of the crew.
These men he installed in the garrison, and he put the ship's crew to
work with his own men on the island.

"Then there was only one man he wanted in charge of that new
ship, and now he had to send a smack out to find him. They caught him
on *Sao Jorge*, and lugged him to Pico, kicking and screaming. Well?"

I didn't have to think too hard. "Old Matta," I said.

"Old Matta, is right." My grandfather's voice was strong with momentum now. "The best sailor Francisco ever knew. He took some per-
suading, but when he came aboard that caravel, and he saw the wonder
of it, and learned he would be captain, he gave in.

"So, Carvalho, they got ready and spread the word that they had been
ordered to the Cape Verde islands on a mission for the king. Maria by
this time was going to have another baby, but what could be done? The
ancestor had to leave. They were close to the Feast of Saint Cyril, and
by Matta's reckoning, the currents and winds would be right at such a
time in March, and the hard weather was easing. Maria cried each
night, but during the day she took charge of things. She would turn
out to be the real power on Pico. They were ready, Carvalho!

"So in the dark hours of the night, on the Feast of the Annunci-
ation, a fresh breeze came out of the northeast. The senior churchman
on the island, a Fray Segura, came down to the quay with Maria and
their little son, Manuel, all looking grim and tired—and Maria suffer-
ing from the morning sickness. A handful of houseservants and soldiers joined them there, and the priest blessed their ships and they
slipped off into the currents of the Atlantic Ocean."

14

The dim running light sputtered in its place behind the trunk, and then in a thick exhalation of blackfish oil, it ebbed and died away. Neither of us moved to refill it.

"Well," my grandfather said slowly, "I thought that this first crossing of the Atlantic was the big adventure—the big story. But I can see now that's not it. I've learned different. All the real stuff is in the politics, the backstabbing and double-crossing. You know how it is. But after that trip to Africa with da Gama, coming west would be easy. Our old captain had prepared and studied and picked all the right men. They were Portagees, remember, so no one cried because he was out of sight of land for so long. Nobody whined about turning back."

I heard him shuffle a bit in the darkness. He broke wind loudly, and then he was quiet for a while before he picked up a thread of the story.

"Thirty days after leaving Pico they made landfall. It wasn't Japan or China, though. They knew that right away. They didn't find any great kingdoms or riches. Here it is. The landed on a beautiful white beach, but when they tramped inland, all they saw were swamps and snakes and mosquitoes—and giant alligators that could eat a man whole."

"Alligators. Florida."

"Yes, that's it. Florida. Can't you see it? But they were supposed to be somewhere in the Orient. Get it? So they sailed on north, because, you know, they would have figured they were south of Quinsay. Quinsay! So for three or four months they sailed north along that coast, marking progress with the stone *padroes* that they carried. They talked to natives. No one knew a thing about great cities and great khans. Fray Costa saw a lot of souls to be won for the Church, though. The old captain should have taken more notice of this, but he was busy with a thousand things. The crews were nervous and wanted the big cities of the East, and he had a charge from Simoes to find them. So he pushed on. They bartered for vegetables and fruit with those strange people along the shore. The woods were full of deer and rabbits, and the fish in the water just about jumped into your boat.

"And Carvalho, he was like a madman at his charts and logs. He sailed north, and he knew that this was no island. It wasn't China, either. They sailed four hundred leagues, explored harbors and bays and rivers, but never a city, never more than small native villages. It crept up on him slowly, Carvalho. They were walking upon a new world.

"That's when he came here. But you see there wasn't any town. There was nothing here at all. But there was this harbor, as perfect a harbor as he'd ever seen, and they pulled their ships around the point and anchored and went ashore. He put his last stone *padroa* on the highest hill over the water and claimed all these lands, from the coast of snakes and mosquitoes to the hook of this cape for the King of Portugal. And for himself, too.

"So, you see, he *was* here. They overhauled the bottoms of their ships here. They fished here and built weirs and a small settlement of huts on the shore. But it was now in the month of September, and they knew that they couldn't winter here. The crews were restless for home, and so was he. Had he failed, or had he come upon something even bigger than what he had come looking for? He would have to re-enter the world to tell.

"So they sailed back. They raised the Azores in thirty-two days."

"No storm? No shipwreck?"

"Nope. Fine weather all the way."

"But..."

"But what happened? Why did he disappear? What became of all his claims on the new land? This is where we have to be careful. Don't you see that if he was just sunk in a storm, we haven't proved anything? He disappeared from history for a reason. We have to show cause and effect. If everything doesn't connect, we don't have a story. We can't make a history. It's the only way we can mean something."

"Go on, then. Don't stop." I could tell the weather was shifting outside our little room. I felt a damp chill creeping in among the bare boards. I wrapped my arms around myself.

"When he reached Pico, he was greeted not only by Maria and Manuel, but by a new son, Joao. Two sons, Carvalho, and he should have had the sense to become a happy man. But Simoes was there, too. He had been keeping vigil there for the past months. No one knew whether the ancestor would return, you see. Simoes was disappointed that they hadn't raised the East, and he was puzzled by what they had found.

"But he was amazed at their logs and their specimens. 'You must say nothing of this,' Simoes said when he heard their stories. He dabbed at his forehead with his lace handkerchief. 'This is for the king's ears alone,' he said. 'We can do nothing until he considers this information.'

"It was this secrecy that would undo our captain. Secrecy and stupidity and treachery. Consider it, Carvalho. He had been to a new world, and he could tell no one."

My grandfather made a strange noise—not a sigh, not a cough, but something between the two.

"And so he was betrayed," I said, just to hear him answer.

"That's exactly what happened," he said. "It's indisputable. I will tell you about the Borgia Pope!"

"It wasn't Simoes who betrayed him?" I said.

"Simoes, you say. Well, listen. It's true that Alvaro Simoes was not pleased Yet he couldn't count the trip a failure, after all. He expected Francisco to return—if at all—with news of the East. But what had he brought him? News of a wild land, primitive. Uncivilized. *Did* he count this as a failure? There was no way Captain Francisco could have known, because Simoes didn't give him any clues before he left so quickly for Lisbon and the king.

"Maria, for her part, showed as much wear from the journey as the ones who had actually sailed. Her sons, Manuel and John, kept her busy from morning to night. She had servants, mind you, but she would never let the boys out of her own sight or care for very long.

"Late one night Maria confided to Francisco that she had dreamed his death, and that once that had come into her head, she couldn't shake it away. She had believed them lost all those final months when her uncle—her *father*—had come and kept watch with her on Pico."

The chill still wafted its way through the room, and I thought I heard the fog bell on the tip of the point clang across its mile of water. Behind my eyes rode that film, like a layer of ash, that comes with heavy tiredness, but behind that something like an engine of my own worked.

"All his plans . . . lost. All his desires . . . undone."

"What?" I said.

"All his stuff, Carvalho. All his charts, his logs, his samples of plants and skins, his journals—everything! Everything was delivered to the hands of his enemies."

"I don't think it makes sense. Why would Simoes double-cross himself?"

"Well, wait a minute and maybe I can make things work out. You know the story from here, Carvalho. Everybody does. You know that Christopher Columbus came upon those charts and duplicated Francisco's voyage—or nearly did—for the new Spanish king, Ferdinand, and his wife, Isabella. The Spaniards. But look harder, Carvalho. Tell me, what happened in that year?"

"I can't think," I said. It was true. I couldn't *think*. All I could do was push forward in a sea of images.

"The Church is the key. It was the key to everything. It was what would undo Simoes in the end. And the ancestor. These Spaniards, Ferdinand and Isabella, drove out the last of the Moors from the mainland of Europe and reclaimed the whole of Spain for Christendom. It was one of the greatest victories in the world for the Church, and that year also came a new Pope—"

"The Borgia Pope!" I said, grasping now what he had said before.

"A man from a family of murderers and poisoners. This is how I understand it, Carvalho. The Spaniards were given Francisco's materials as a reward for throwing out the Moors. The Pope would have engineered this, and then his charts and logs were passed to Columbus when he proposed such a voyage. *It was a gift to Spain from the Pope!* Even though Portugal had already been there, you see. Columbus's voyage was set up only to legitimize this theft!"

"It doesn't seem possible," I said. "Are you sure?"

"Of course. Use your head. This Pope, this Alexander VI—what was his true name? I looked it up. It's all right there—it's been there all along. How could we have kept missing it? Roderigo Borgia of *Aragon*! An Aragonese, for Christ's sake. And what had Ferdinand been king of? *Aragon*, for Christ's sake! Yeah, and Ferdinand was owed some favors, you can be sure, and the Borgia Pope paid them.

"I read the books, Carvalho. Didn't he issue Papal bulls in favor of Spain keeping all the lands discovered in the west and the south? Documents that undermined sixty years of Portuguese exploration! And didn't he falsify the dates of those papers to make them appear to have been drawn up before Francisco's voyage? These are the facts. Check Lew's books. Check any books."

He breathed heavily in his excitement. It took him a while to fix himself on the story again.

"Simoes doesn't return to Pico until early in fourteen hundred and ninety-three. He corresponds in coded messages, but Franciso learns that all of them don't get through. Something was terribly wrong. Simoes had told them to fortify the garrison and stay put until they hear otherwise. You see, King Joao wanted a war with the Spaniards, but you can bet that many rich Lisbons feared too much for what they might lose if that happened, and so they undermined the king's will. Spain was afraid of Portugal. The navy at that time would have reduced their shipping to splinters. But when Ferdinand offered to negotiate, the king's counsel urged Joao to accept. You can imagine that our Simoes was in the middle of all of this, looking for a place to land safely. Did he still think that the Azores would be the gateway to the western route? Hard to say. He wanted China, Japan, and Captain Francisco told him about a new, dark continent. Did he betray our islander? Yep, in a way. He had agreed to keep Carvalho's voyage secret. Columbus followed the islander's track across the ocean. And the Church had chosen Spain to inherit the world.

"This voyage of Christopher Columbus had Simoes upset. He had sent the old captain a coded message as soon as he learned that Columbus was headed out with his three pitiful ships, and Matta and Francisco were to swoop down on them in the *Cinco Ferridas* and the *Ceo Silencio*. Man, Carvalho, there would have been a sea battle for you to imagine! But remember, Columbus was lucky. This coded message was one of the messages that Francisco never received. He only learned of it after Simoes himself came back to Pico. By then Columbus and the Spanish king had spread word of the discovery all over Europe.

"I know what you're thinking. It's possible that Simoes never sent that message and just told the ancestor that he did. It's possible, too, that Columbus was not as stupid as he looked when he insisted that he had landed on islands off the China coast. He may have been smart enough to lie. You see, there was plenty of money in Europe to find a western passage to India and China, and that's what Columbus told them he was on the verge of finding. Would he have gotten the money for more voyages if he had come back with news of an empty land? It's hard to tell. But he kept saying he had reached the Indies when all the evidence pointed otherwise. An island, Carvalho. Columbus hit only a dumb little island, and he returned a hero!

"So you see he had to go back. The ancestor had to make another voyage. They had kept their discoveries secret and it cost them. Now they had to go back and plant more *padroes* to make good their claims. When Simoes came back from the mainland he gave orders to do that, but he warned Francisco Carvalho there were traitors among them.

"So right away the islander sets to watching the men, the captains, the lieutenants. Who could they be? Escolar? Cabral? Farroba? He goes through the lists, but it's useless. Finally, he just leaves. He leaves Pico for the last time in the gloom of night, with his two ships. He knew it was his *fado* never to see anyone there again.

"A battle, then," I said. "Not a storm, not an accident. A battle. That's how it has to be. *Captain Blood.*"

"Three sails dogged them almost from the beginning. Think of it. They were Spanish ships, but how did they know Captain Francisco was sailing and, worse, how did they come upon him so fast? The only answer was that they had lain-to in the islands somewhere, in secret, with confederates, and waited for a signal."

"Nah—the islander would have heard. His own spies . . ."

"No. Listen. He has to deal with the Spanish fleet."

"Okay. He blows them to smithereens."

"No. That would have risked the expedition. He outfoxes them, comes around them in the night and sails away from them, east. They thought that he had left them behind, and they sailed off ahead on the last line he let them track on, a course carrying them slightly to the south of the one he intended to sail."

"He would have to come *here* again. Something would have to happen at our town," I said, suddenly understanding where he was going with this.

"Well, you'll see. After the old captain fuddled the Spanish ships and left them on the wrong course, he hails the *Ceo Silencio* and they lay-to alongside one another. They were twelve days out of Pico, and they were outfitted for the second voyage. The ancestor was in good spirits because they had slipped away from the enemy. He hadn't counted on mutiny."

"Another one?"

"Well, nothing like the uprising aboard the *Maricico* when da Gama and Columbus and the ancestor sailed on her. Now the Lisbon confederates among them rose up and demanded to turn back. They wanted to scuttle the voyage, have Francisco give up the West. That meant the money was on Africa again. Vasco da Gama's hand was behind this too, believe me. Here is how it happened.

"They doubled back on those Spanish ships, Francisco hailed the *Ceo Silencio,* and they put their bows into the wind and came alongside one another. They were able to tie up and go dead in the water, and this is what the ancestor wanted. It would let the Spaniards slip more ahead and to the south, and he wanted to go aboard the *Ceo* and talk with Matta, who was in command over there. They had intended to follow their last route on a line with the Madeiras, but they knew the Spanish ships had knowledge of that line now, and our islander would have to keep further north. It worked out fine.

"They decided that it would be best to take up where they left off, here at our town—the end of our cape, I mean, to replenish and push farther north to see if there was passage through this land mass. At any rate, they'd keep laying down *padroes* to maintain their claims in this New World. Matta told him also that he smelled a great storm coming from the south, and indeed there were signs—high scud in the air, and a growing sea from that direction. 'We've seen the last of those Spanish ships, unless I miss my guess,' Matta says. 'They go off into the teeth of a gale. God help them.'

"'The devil take them,' says Francisco. They were in Lopes's cabin, just off the poop, and they were sitting over cups of wine just as they'd finished their planning. Suddenly there comes a banging at the door. Lopes opened it, and there stood his mate, a dark, chunky man named Souza, with his sword in his hand. 'Come out on deck, Captains,' he says.

"There was no mistaking this man's intent. 'Put away that damn sword,' says our captain.

"'I take my orders from a higher source,' says this fool, Souza. He laid the flat of his blade on Matta's back and shoved him out of the cabin door. But Captain Carvalho doesn't move. So Souza turns and gives him a little prod, too. It was the second of time that Francisco needed. You know that Columbus himself taught our old captain the art of drawing a dagger from his sleeve. The ancestor's blade caught Souza through his windpipe. He died in his own blood. Man, the ancestor was in a rage, Carvalho. He flew out on deck with his sword drawn, ready to strike down the next traitor, but too late. A party of Lisbon-bought mutineers had finally showed its colors. Old Matta was on the quarterdeck, held by two of them, their crossbows drawn. Francisco looks around quickly. He counts not more than ten of the traitors, but when he looks over at the *Cinco Ferridas*, he sees that they've been seized, too. Another ten men had surprised the crew there, and while no arms had clashed yet, the mutineers had everybody at a disadvantage by seizing both decks with a show of weapons.

"What would happen? They would kill the ancestor. That much was clear. He was too dangerous to be left alive. But they would have to avoid a full skirmish. They would have to force or convince the crews to sail back if they wanted to keep the safety of both ships. But maybe they intended to burn one? Francisco couldn't stop to figure it all out. He had to act.

"He ran back into the cabin and locked the door! Now he heard the sword-hilts battering the doorboards, and those men would have beaten their way in if he had been a minute longer at his work. Finally, it was Francisco himself who threw open the door. And when he does, he throws the bloodied head of Souza, which he's cut off and used as a missile. 'So die, traitors!' he yells.

"Souza's head knocked the crossbow from the first sailor's hands, and the ancestor splits him to his eyes with a blow of his sword."

"Split him to the *chines* is what they say in *Treasure Island.*"

My grandfather passed on this. He was nearly breathless. There was no stopping him.

"Another man drew his sword but the captain struck at his wrist and knocked his sword down, hand and all. He could have finished him, but he did more good screaming and bleeding where he was. If the simpering Lisbons expected a bloodless takeover with dainty executions later, they would have to think again. In for a penny, in for a pound! They would have to wade through blood, and remember, our captain was the only one who had drawn any.

"He picks up the bloody head by its hair and throws it again, like a shot, down onto the quarterdeck. One of the crossbowmen stepped backward to dodge it, and Old Matta got a hand under the weapon and caused it to shoot in the air. Matta and the sailor rolled around on the deck, and I don't think Matta could have got the better of him. Francisco was ready to cut his way to him, when suddenly a dart flew from the rail of the other ship and struck down another bowman. They all looked over at the rail, and there was Fray Costa. He had armed himself somehow, and he was shouting, waving his hands in the air. 'In the name of Christ, stop! I beg you—everyone—lay down your arms.'

"Of course, Francisco wasn't going to put his blade down, but he watched everyone carefully. Someone might strike at him, but who would strike at a priest? So much fighting is like this, right? One or two bold moves, and then everyone is willing to back off. But no one moved. Fray Costa shouted once again, 'In the name of our Holy Mother Church, desist!'

"Well, he had everyone off balance. No one knew what to do. The ancestor took advantage of this. 'Arturo Cabral lies here dying in his own blood,' he yells, and points to the man whose hand he had struck off. 'Shall we staunch his wound, or shall I take another head?' As he says this, he raises his sword and walks toward another one of the mutineers.

"It was Fray Costa who carried the day, though. 'I beg you all,' he shouted, and the man that Francisco had advanced on kneeled and lay his sword down. The man wanted to lay it down anyway. He saw that that the ancestor was coming to kill him. But if the priest had not spoken and given him some halfway honorable excuse to pull back, he would have had to fight. It was a wise move. And once he laid his weapon down, everybody else did the same.

"Except the ancestor. And this where he makes a mistake. He's got all the mutineers bound, twenty-three of them. He should have hanged them all.

"Well, the truth was that he considered that. He called a counsel with Fray Costa and Matta and their two seconds in command, Sylvester Escolar and Manolo Farroba. Hanging was one solution. Another was to put them on the other ship and send them back. Captain Francisco didn't like this idea, but Fray Costa pointed out that they shouldn't put themselves in any position where heaven might curse them. Being merciful might bless the voyage. Well, this argument carried weight with Matta, who was not a man for blood or revenge. The ancestor was still for killing them all, but then he considered the practical side of things. If they hanged all twenty-three, they would have to sail their two ships shorthanded. Or he could hang them and burn one ship.

"Well, in the end here's what they decided. Strip the *Ceo Silencio* of all but enough provisions to reach the mainland. Jettison her guns and give her to the Lisbon confederates to sail home. Now a young lieutenant, Manuel Pavao, was turned out as the leader of these traitors, and when Francisco announced what he would do, he begged the captain to let him keep the guns because he was afraid of running into a Spanish patrol. Our captain didn't care a hang about them or their safety, but it made some sense to let them have a few guns and some shot. That way if the Spanish found them, it would be better that they could offer resistance. A skirmish would divert any ships looking for the ancestor, and he bet that he could trust them not to go over to the Spanish without a fight. Let them run interference then. He had the priest make the mutineers swear a pledge not to bother the expedition any further, and they all took it as they sat there on the deck. Then they began the transfer of supplies.

"The islander let Escolar supervise the off-loading, and he took Matta with him. Francisco and Lopes put down the long boat and went over the side. Dusk was coming on. They would shine no lamps or torches after dark with the enemy in their waters. They worked fast. They sculled the boat alongside the *Ceo Silencio*, and they fendered her back to the rudder. Lopes held the boat steady while Francisco worked on the *Ceo*'s rudder pins with an iron saw and pincers. It was hard going, but finally he got them loose, top pin then bottom pin, and they hauled that big rudder off. It crashed to its side in the water, and they put a line around it, and they ran the line back to the *Cinco Ferridas*.

"When the mutineers saw that Francisco had stolen their rudder, they gave up a great wail, and they begged him not to leave them adrift this far out at sea with no means to sail home. Our islander let them beg and grovel, but he wasn't going to leave them without a rudder. He would cast it loose after he pulled away from them, and he would let them worry about getting it back into working order again. That would be his real assurance against being interfered with.

"But like I said, this was all a mistake. In four days' time, Francisco spied their sail, dogging them, staying back, trying to dip over and back of the horizon to hide their position. Think of it. What could it mean?"

"They fixed the rudder pretty fast."

"Come on. And what else?"

"They must have thought they would have a chance against the ancestor. They must have thought they could engage him and win."

"Yes, precisely that. But how? How could they think that, after he had left them the way he did, short of supply, a minimum of charge for their guns?"

He went on to answer his own question this time. *"Because they knew that there were still some traitors aboard the ancestor's ship, and they expected help from them when they engaged him."*

"A final battle, then!"

"Yep, but not tonight. What the hell time can it be? I can't go on anymore."

I saw his figure stretch in the darkness, strike a match, and peer around. My grandfather stared out at me and at the room from behind the flame of his match, and he looked wrecked, hungover. The empty quart wine bottle lay by his knees, and he picked it up, shook it wistfully, then dropped the match with a sudden oath as it reached his fingers. He struck another match. "Jesus H. Christ," he said. "It must be halfway to morning. I have to be somewhere."

"No," I said.

"We'll finish this another time," he said, suddenly impatient. "And remember to meet me so we can sail in the *Caravella* after dawn."

He dropped his match, lighted another, and moved to the window, where he loosened the old blanket and let it drop to the floor. The scatter from the streetlight fell upon the window, and the room blossomed into dusky detail—cupboards, trunks, workbench, eaves, chimney. John Joseph stood at the window, boldly, though at this hour no town person would be abroad to see him. The pale light silhouetted him, and I looked at him carefully, at the hang of his clothes, the way his pants fell in uneven rolls into the cuffs of his boots, the angle of his shoulders.

"Just finish it," I said. "You're close enough."

"Don't pester me now, Carvalho. I am all in. I've given this everything I have tonight. Be satisfied. Okay?"

"Okay, *Avo*." I let it go. I was tired myself. I felt like had just walked out into the sunlight after sitting in the movie house for an afternoon.

"Good. And now we must be like stealth itself," said John Joseph, dramatically. He crept toward the door.

I followed him down the stairs, stepping carefully on the safe spots. The bad wood croaked under our weight. The sky had wheeled around and constellations shone now in unfamiliar aspects. A deep, humid weight hung in the cool air. We roused the ducks as we passed the pen, and they charged against the wire fence, looking for a handout, quacking softly. My grandfather waved his hat at them as if to shoo them away, and this roused them more, until he placed his hat back on his head and loped down the sidewalk, nearly at a run, leaving me to deal with the ducks and the problem of sneaking back into the house again.

But I didn't go back to the house. It stood before me like a hulk, dressed out in shadows, silent and cold. I turned and crept back up the stairs to the top of the woodhouse, and I entered that room once again. I could still smell John Joseph there—or at least his effusions, sweet wine and Prince Albert. I sat down, in his place this time, where the chimney and the wall made a corner, and I pulled the old dry blanket around my shoulders, a small comfort in what had become the damp chill of the early morning.

15

An enormous *bang* clapped to the earth and bolted me from my sleep. It might have been a cannon shot, but we had left the ancestor's story far behind. It was full morning now. I saw the dirty light of a squall pressing on the woodhouse window. A sullen rain left tracks on the uneven glass. The sky broke open again and another flash of lightning railed over the West End. A fraction of a second later, thunder once again shook the frame of the little building. I tried to collect myself. I knew that I had been asleep for too long. Something was wrong, but I couldn't put my finger on it. I moved to the door and looked down into the yard. Roger and Lew stood there in the rain, along with Uncle Paddy and my Great Aunt Theophila. They were all staring up at the roof. I had no time to think. I eased out the door and half slid down the leaning stairs before anyone could see me. Little fingers of smoke curled lazily up from our roof, and what had once been the bedspring antenna of my Uncle Paddy's radio lay in tangled, smoking pieces all over Madeleine Sylvia's yard and even on the roof of her own house. Madeleine herself was on her back porch in a yellow slicker, and she was screaming something at my great aunt.

I backed my way down the walk and then entered the yard as if I had just come in from the beach, but that wasn't necessary. No one was about to pay me any attention. There was another blare of lightning and thunder, and then the siren on the Cold Storage began to wail in a string of long, single, modulated blasts. It was the signal for fire in the first district, the West End.

"It's okay," Lew said. "It's okay." He was talking to Uncle Paddy, I think, or just talking out loud, but Uncle Paddy answered him.

"I'm going to go up and look around, just the same," he said.

"Let me go up and look at the inside again," said Lew. "You go out to the street and see what's going on with the roof."

I ran ahead of Uncle Paddy, up the walk again and out to the street. Our roof still smoked, but there were no flames that I could see. The two-by-fours that had cradled the bedspring lay against the roof, scorched and splintered. Some neighbors had come out of their houses and stood in the rain looking up, their arms folded. Old Man Coelho, in a work cap and foul-weather gear, stood by his front hedge and shook his head. I was in the street for only a minute or so before the big red LaFrance fire engine rumbled around the corner from the firehouse and rolled to a stop by our front yard. Louis Avila was driving, and Skinny Henrique, Manny Buckets, and Freddy Pessoa jumped from the running boards and ran down our walk, rolling out flakes of big canvas hose.

By the time I got back into the yard, the men had all gathered at the foot of Roger and Lew's stairs. Uncle Paddy was telling them, "No harm done, nothing's afire. We just got a mess to clean up."

Skinny Henrique came out of the upstairs door. "All clear up here," he called. "Damn lucky, too, if you ask me. What the hell was all that business up on the roof?"

"Antenna," said Paddy. "Jesus H., look at my beautiful radio." No one had noticed it, but now we all looked and saw that the big short-wave's chassis was buckled, just like someone had taken and bent it across his knee, if such a thing were humanly possible.

"Lemee foot this ladder up to the roof and see what she did to your shingles," said Skinny. The men had brought in a long sliding ladder, and Freddy Pessoa started to angle it against the side of the house. That's when I saw it. It was just a wisp at first, and I didn't move or say anything because the men were busy footing the ladder. It was a hole in the window of one of Madeleine Sylvia's dormers, and a scant stream of smoke now curled from it. Even as I watched, it grew darker and thicker, and soon a vapor was starting to roll from the thick shingles. Then I don't know who yelled out first, but a couple of men jumped the ruined fence into her yard, dragging the canvas hose. Madeleine had stepped off her porch now, along with four or five of her summer boarders. "My flowers," she yelled. "Stay the hell off of my flowers!" She came toward the fence far enough for her to be able to see the dormer, and then she yelled again, something shrill from the old language. I couldn't understand it.

Skinny and Freddy ran the ladder over to her house, and in seconds someone in a black fire hat was shouldering a hose through the broken window. I couldn't tell what was up in that room, but before they knocked the fire out, I saw flame, and the smoke turned black and greasy before it died.

Maybe everything was over in minutes. I couldn't tell. But both yards were a mess. Our little garden had been trampled, and kale and turnips lay crushed on the wet ground. The ducks kept up a frantic quacking that was almost like a shriek, and some sort of fight had broken out between Madeleine Sylvia and two of her boarders, and they stood on her porch and yelled at one another, Madeleine pointing toward our yard and shaking a finger. The men from the fire truck hunched against the house to stay out of the rain as much as they could. They smoked cigarettes and from time to time stepped out and looked at the roofs. Every once in a while the radio on the fire truck would break into static and then a loud electric voice would garble something.

But the fire was out, and finally Skinny and Freddy gathered up the ladder and the rest of them started rolling up the hose. The sky had darkened again, almost like true night coming on, and then the wind came around again and drove a hard, slanting rain under the overhang of the houses, dispersing everyone. I waited in the yard and watched Madeleine. Whatever the fight over there was about, it didn't seem to get resolved. Her two borders stalked off down her walk and left her on the porch alone. Her yard had gotten the worst of it. Her flower beds were completely trammeled, and there were little pieces of bedspring everywhere. A big scorchmark smeared upward on the white clapboards of her dormer. The window was now broken out completely. The inside must have been a mess. She surveyed all this too, as I watched her, her arms folded on her chest, her shoulders slumped.

The wind seemed to be blowing from all directions at once. Thunder boomed again, moving to the east, but the rain turned violent. I backed against the door and finally went inside. Great Aunt Theophila had already begun praying at her bedroom shrine, and the house smelled of frankincense and sandalwood. Paddy sat at the table with a box of papers in front him, shuffling through them. I undressed and toweled off and put on some dry clothes. Before long, Ernestina and Elvio the Shoemaker banged on the door. "What confusion," said Ernestina smiling.

"No harm done," said Paddy. "At least not here."

"Jeeze, that bedspring," said Elvio. "We got to clean it up."

"I'll help," I said. "Madeleine Sylvia is really mad."

"Can't be helped," said Paddy. "Act of God."

"Act of God, my foot," said Great Aunt Theophila, stepping out of the bedroom. "You two and that foolish radio. A bedspring!"

"Ah, well, Hettie," said Elvio.

"That'll do," said Paddy, and Great Aunt Theophila suddenly pulled back.

"I'm just afraid of that *Lisbon*," she said. "Things were bad enough already."

"Act of God," said Paddy.

"Elvio is going to help you fix your roof," said Ernestina.

"Nothing to fix, really," said Paddy. "But maybe we'll take a look at her when the weather's good."

"No roof," said Great Aunt Theophila very quietly. "I don't want you up on the roof."

Ernestina laughed and shook her head. "What men," she said. "Trying to talk to the old country on all those wires."

"Offer Ernestina and Elvio some tea, nice boy," my aunt said. I got down cups for everybody.

"Josie, what's the matter with you? You look terrible."

"I'm all right," I said.

"You shouldn't contradict Ernestina," said my aunt. As she spoke, I became aware of an emptiness in the house. My aunt's eyes were dark and swollen, and small dark pouches sagged under them. She made a small, quick gesture with her hand, pointing to me and then vaguely to someplace away. It made me think of Carmine and my mother. She may as well have spoken. I poured some tea into Elvio's cup and put the teapot back down on the table.

"I heard your grandfather clomping around this morning," Aunt Theophila said. "Getting ready to go off fishing, I think. As if there's nothing to do around *here*."

A stone dropped on me. I had missed my rendezvous with him. I had forgotten our plans.

"Well," she said, when I did not reply, "I'm glad to see he didn't pull you off with him. I don't want you in that old boat, anyway."

"Are you sure he went out? He wouldn't go out in this weather."

Uncle Paddy put in, "Wasn't storming till a few hours ago."

"Where are you going?" Aunt Theophila asked, as I put down my teacup and left the parlor.

"Just down to the seawall. I'm going to see if the *Caravella* is there."

"Sit down," she said, "We have company."

"I'll be right back."

"Take your slicker," said Uncle Paddy, before she could speak again. The heart of the storm had moved past our town, but the rain still fell in fine, steady sheets. Standing on the soaked timber of the seawall, I could see that indeed the *Caravella* was not at her mooring, and as I peered through the rain at the outer harbor, I saw nothing that looked like my grandfather's ragged sail. From moment to moment a small wind would rough the surface of the water, but there wasn't a bad swell running—just a bumpy, ragged chop pocked by the rain. I walked along the top of the seawall and over to the Cold Storage's long back stairway and climbed to the first landing. The height did not help me to see much through the rain. I had wanted to see over to the cove on Long Point. I knew that that was where John Joseph would be anchored if he had been anywhere westerly when the squall came up. He would be tied off to one of the old hulks that lay abandoned in that shallow finger of the harbor, a graveyard for old boats. I remembered an old scow there, and a down-easter with no engine under its deck. He would be huddled out of the rain, smoking his pipe, and if I were there, he would be showing me some knot or splice to pass the time. But I hadn't been on hand to go with him, and I couldn't see as far as the cove. There was nothing to do but wait for him to get back.

Rather than go directly back to the house, I wandered east, over through the boatyard. Two draggers lay hauled up in the big wooden cradles on the railway, and as I walked I hugged the shelter of their hulls, and I breathed the barbed smells of red lead and deck enamel, blunted now by the weather. The place seemed deserted, but the intermittent sound of a buzz saw told me that the men were working inside the cinder-block building. Rain dripped from everything, the cradles, the planking on the scaffolds, the eaves of the workshop. Old paintpots lay around, some of them upright with rainwater brimming in them. Paint-splattered canvas hung from the crosspieces of the cradles, wet and heavy. I didn't want to go back home, but I knew if I hung around the boatyard, sooner or later Freddy Pessoa or Skinny Henrique would walk through the big double door and chase me away. I hunched myself down in my slicker and walked off toward the house.

"How's the dory?" asked Great Uncle Paddy when I had finished hanging up my oilclothes in the back room.

"Not there," I said.

"Off to the East End with one of his women," my great aunt sniffed quietly. She and Ernestina and Elvio and Uncle Paddy still sat at the kitchen table, a new pot of tea on the trivet between them.

"Or anchored in the cove," I said. My great aunt raised her teacup to her lips and ignored me. Ernestina smiled and watched the rain through the parlor window.

I slept that night in my own bed, listening at first to the storm as it waned, the rain easing away to silence in the street. I was tired. I moved off through the warm, dark water of sleep until a quiet tapping came at the back door. I also heard a stirring off in the other side of the house —Great Aunt Theophila or Uncle Paddy shifting in their big springy bed. I got out of my own bed quickly and pulled something on and went to the back room before either of them could get up. I opened the back door silently. It was Captain Raul. "Where's John Joseph?" he said.

Out of some reflex I looked over at my grandfather's cot, but of course it was empty. "What's wrong?" I asked.

"Better get your Uncle Paddy, Pard."

I didn't have to. Uncle Paddy appeared at my side. He had pulled his pants on, and they sagged around his belly. His suspenders hung down at his knees. On top he wore a sleeveless undershirt. His eyes were still clouded with sleep and his hair was mussed, but his voice was alert now and clear. "Hey, Raul, come in, come in."

I stepped back from the doorway and let Captain Raul into the back room. He still had his oilclothes on, and I could tell it must be very early morning, that he had just come from the boat. "We got John Joseph's dory behind the *Tarcado*. I found it out the traps."

Uncle Paddy grunted, rubbed his face. "You want some coffee?" he said to Raul.

"No thanks, Pard."

"He never came in yesterday," said my Great Uncle. "That squall."

"We emptied the trap," Raul said. "Never found nothing. Damn thing is, that wasn't any blow to speak of yesterday. John Joseph has been in a damn sight worse than that."

"He probably tied off the dory out to the cove and it just got away from him," I said. "That's where he'd go if he was to the westward."

"What's all the commotion?" my great aunt called from the other room. She sounded peeved.

"Go back to bed, Hettie," my uncle said. It was a command.

Her tone slackened suddenly. "What is it?"

"I have to go help Raul Mendes with something."

He pulled on a wool overshirt and took his straw hat from a peg in the back room and sat on the cot to put on a pair of workshoes. I ran to my room and put on my shoes and grabbed a jacket. "You better stay here with your aunt," Uncle Paddy said when I came back dressed to leave with him.

I took a breath. "I won't do that, *Tio.*"

Captain Raul looked at me. "Let him come, Paddy. It probably don't mean anything." When we were in the yard, Captain Raul said, "You want to come and check the boat?"

"I got another notion," Paddy said. "You go on, Raul. Go on to the wharf and do what you need to. I'm going to check that place down to the East End and then I'll meet you."

I got into the *Pulga* and settled into its torn leather seat. Uncle Paddy worked on the starter pedal like he were stomping a rat, and the engine finally sputtered and caught, backfiring a small barrage of flashes out of the tailpipe. When we pulled away from the side of the house I looked behind us again, and I caught the outline of my great aunt's face watching us from the bedroom window, motionless, a shadow within a shadow.

We rounded the bend in the front street, and our headlights shone into the bleary half-darkness. I had not looked at a clock before we left, but the small light, now the color of pond water pooling in the sky, showed that dawn was not far off. We turned up one of the narrow side streets, a lane hemmed closely by high hedges gone slightly wild and the big dark trunks of elms and chestnut trees. We crossed to the back street and turned east, and the street rolled out before us like a dark empty river. We chugged past the center of the town, the town hall, the monument, DeAvila's Garage, all in silence, my great uncle driving with a concentration that pushed his breath from him every now and then, his nostrils widening, his lips pursing. When we had nearly reached the easternmost edge of our town, a place where the front and back streets moved out of parallel and met at the state road, we turned down a small lane, and came out on the front street, the harbor side of town, opposite a long, white picket fence. We crept along for another minute or two, my uncle driving very slowly. He looked hard at the houses along the water—neat, prim Yankee and *Lisbon* houses with freshly painted clapboards and shutters and trimmed bushes along the straight walks. Finally, we rolled to a stop against the sidewalk. Uncle Paddy cut the engine. "Stay here and watch out for the car," he said. "I'll be right back."

He opened a gate and headed toward a small cottage down in back stay ashore and take care of the dory, Pard. You can do that better than we can. Paddy, you ought to stay around home in case somebody has to get ahold of you."

I took off my shoes and left them on the wharf and went down the ladder to the *Tarcado*. Squid Dutra tossed me a bailer and I pulled the dory alongside and stepped in. Squid and Raul had bailed her enough to tow her, but the cold water in her came up almost to my shins, and the old *Caravella* settled lower, with an uneasy lurch, as I gave her my weight. "Can you handle this all right, Pard?" Captain Raul asked me. I didn't look at him. "I need a sponge," I said.

Squid Dutra tossed me a sponge and untied the *Caravella*'s line from the cleat on the trapboat and transferred it to a crossboard on the wharf's ladder. I bailed while they fired up the *Tarcado*'s engine, and I kept bailing as they pulled away. After they had left, I looked up once at the wharf and saw my great uncle, one leg up on the timber that ran along the wharf's edge, both arms crossed on the knee of that leg, his hat too low, resting almost on his ears, and his gray eyes looking down at me. When I looked up again, he was gone.

I bailed and sponged until the *Caravella* was dry, and I shook out her anchor line and coiled it. One of the oars was missing, and all the gear stowed under the seat was gone, but the gear in the small forward locker was there, jumbled together. I took it out and spread it on the floorboards: a small blue Edgeworth tobacco can full of fishhooks, a larger, red round Prince Albert can, empty, a wet dropline with a fluke rig on it, a bottle of Coca Cola, and a tin of sardines.

The tide was coming in. I sat on the center thwart of the dory and watched the water darken the edges of the pilings and the uprights of the ladder. The heavy weed that grows on the barnacle-eaten wood spread upward as the water reached it, and it undulated silently. A cramped school of oilsmelts wiggled just below the surface. From time to time I heard the slog of hip boots and the whisk of oilclothes up on the planks of the old wharf, but I didn't look up. I watched the water come up a few more inches, maybe a half a foot, and soon the sun had climbed high enough to begin to dry the sail and to warm my back through the thin cloth of my shirt.

There had been almost no breeze in the time that I spent in the dory —enough motion in the air to draw the *Caravella* eastward on its line, away from the wharf, with the harbor glassed off, like a smooth fleck on the belly of some smoother stone. But now the wind came up a little, a mild shift, and the dory's line slackened and then the gunwale of a long, high, dormer-roofed house. He was gone for several minutes and then came back up the walk with a woman who had a long, brightly patchworked quilt wrapped around her like a sarong. I could tell by her face that she had been sleeping, and even without the broad straw hat and with her hair in a muss, I recognized John Joseph's friend Cynthia. Great Uncle Paddy was quiet when he climbed back into the *Pulga*. "*Avo*'s lady friend," I said.

"Yes," said my great uncle, "but he hasn't been there."

It took us only a few minutes to get back to the West End. We drove in silence, and my uncle, rather than parking the car in front of our house again, pulled alongside the back loading dock of the Cold Storage building. Dawn was spreading over the Truro hills when we stepped out onto the wharf. Captain Raul was waiting for us. "Wasn't at the woman's house," said Uncle Paddy.

Captain Raul scratched his chin and tugged at the visor of his cap, then turned abruptly down the wharf.

We followed him out to the ladder where the *Tarcado* was tied up, a good catch of herring brimming silver in its hold, and there behind her, a foot of water still sloshing over its floorboards, wallowed my grandfather's dory. The sail was up, soaked and sagging, the boom lashed to the tiller. "She was up against the trap, capsized," Captain Raul said. "We looked for John Joseph, but we couldn't find anything."

"It wasn't light enough," I said. "We should go looking now tha there's better light."

"Okay, Pard," said Raul. "We will. I called the harbormaster and h got ahold of the coastguard. They'll do whatever they can."

I looked at my great uncle's face. There was nothing in his expre sion to make me hopeful of the coastguard. "Sail was up when yc found her?" he asked.

"Yep," said Raul. "If she broke her mooring, she wouldn't have h sail up. No, I think he lost her."

"Think of this," I said. "He could have been holed up somewhe like the cove, and he could have had the sail up to dry and the b could have got away."

"Possible," said Raul.

My uncle looked west to breakwater, and I could have guessed thoughts.

"Are you going back out now?" I asked Raul.

"Pretty quick. I'm going to let Squid take care of the offload, I'm going back out in the skiff." He didn't wait for me to ask him. "

bumped gently against the poles of the wharf. There was enough breeze to give some way. I untied the painter and shoved with the oar to get us clear, and the wind pushed lightly on the sail. I angled to windward slightly to get away from the wharf, and then I took the dory around the end and back to shore on the other side, where I pulled her bow up on the sand as far as I could and ran the danforth up into the sand on a tight line. The incoming tide would float her side-to in a few minutes, but I would be back by then. I ran up through the Cold Storage yard, hopped the fence and got some gear out of the woodhouse, and ran back to the dory.

The wind showed some signs of freshening, but it was still lazy, as though yesterday's squall had wrung something out of the weather. I took the breeze over the port side until I was out past the wharf again, and then I pointed down to the west, tied off the sheet, and let us run sluggishly. I watched the water, the patterns of light and dark on the surface, the boil of baitfish rising from something underneath—squid, perhaps, or mackerel. To the south a line of lobsterpot buoys spread in the distance, their colors pale in the shine of the harbor. Somewhere off my quarter I heard the thudding of a marine diesel, the whine of a small outboard. I didn't look around. I kept on going up to the west until I reached the mouth of the cove, the tide just right for taking the *Caravella* into that shallow inlet.

Gulls rose from the beachgrass and cried in fast circles as I slipped inside, and there was a scrubbed, salty smell in the air, some trace of where we stood in the season, some little difference in the climb of the sun. The water shone cold beneath us. I let the sail go slack and I poled up to the bleached husk of the down-easter that lay there, heeled slightly over in the shallows. Tidewater pooled in its bottom, and vandals had kicked holes in the side of its wheelhouse. I tied up and hopped over to her peeling deck and looked around. In a protected corner of the wheelhouse there was small pile of old human shit and ratty, soiled Kleenex. On a smooth section of the inside bulkhead someone had printed in charcoal, *Marina Lopes SUCKS boys*. There was nothing else.

I sat on her deck for a while until I saw the tide shift direction and begin to empty back into the harbor, and I untied the *Caravella* and with the help of the oar rode that little current back out. Just as we made clear of the cove, a sudden school of striped bass raged through the shallows and startled me so violently that my heart banged in my chest. The big fish swept along the shore, hundreds of them, sending schools of smaller feed into frenzies over the surface. The fish raged in and out, all around and beneath the boat, and I nearly lost my balance as I stood to watch them. They fed in this fury for three or four minutes before moving off again as quickly as they had come. It took me a while to recover myself from that sudden excitement, and the race of my pulse stayed with me as I put the dory into the wind and started beating down to the east.

I watched the water again, but this time with a special, willed keenness. The harbor was flat and plain as far as I could see. Once, something ominous floated in the distance, but as I closed on it, I saw that it was only a fishbox, weathering, half submerged. Another time, losing perspective of its size, I followed up the corpse of a big herring gull, its wings floating to either side, some tarry stain soaking the ruined feathers. The wind stayed slack and it took me hours to traverse the harbor the way I did, zigging and zagging up and down, watching the surface, following pieces of flotsam, avoiding other boats and anchorages.

I sailed full down to the east and came about and zigged and zagged in long tacks toward home, the cold gray tower of the Pilgrims looking down on me from its hill over the harbor. Finally, when I passed the town wharf and the bright steamers still tied there, I straightened my course for Captain Raul's weirs, and as I began to close on them, I watched carefully to see what would be the best place to come alongside them and where I could tie off the *Caravella* without danger of entangling us in the trap.

I circled the trap widely, well away from the guy lines and the poles, and pulled up on the lee side. I would have felt more at ease if there were some real wind, some chop on the surface to create some movement around those gnarled poles, but the small breeze did nothing but glaze the surface. The afternoon sun lay on the water in broad paths that intensified the shadows and darkness of the big trap. I skulled up to one of the poles with my single oar, and I took a few bites around it with the painter and tied us off with a half hitch. The tide had been ebbing for about three hours, and it was still not right for what I was about to do, but I couldn't wait for the water to creep lower. I couldn't count on my nerve to wait with me.

I sat on the dory's thwart, looking at the flat water that was in places a mirror, like black lacquer, and in other places simply opaque shadows that breathed in all the light and returned nothing. There were too many reasons, good reasons, for me to not go over the side here, and when I began to consider them, I understood that I was weakening myself. Even while some bright, clear voice in the choir of my head chanted that I should do otherwise, I pulled on my green goggles and let myself over the side. The water sent a quick chill over me, and I had to move to keep my warmth up. I lowered my head as I swam and looked below. The water was very deep, and lines of sunlight slanted down through it like broken columns, losing color as they descended. The bottom faded into an obscure pallor. If there had been craters down there, I might as well have hung over the surface of the moon at dusk. I kicked away from the boat and swam with my head down.

I could make out objects on the bottom, some paint pots, a little midden of shells with dark weed rising from them, the white bones of a giant fish. And off in front of me the butts of those awful poles, barnacled and weed-heavy, ascending from the desolate bottom. I could not force myself to swim up against the trap, but I began to swim around it with a good view of the distant bottom. It was a long circuit and I was shivering and feeling my wind by the time I had come around the back side and began closing on the dory again. The bottom showed only more junk, distant, flat, dead. I hadn't thought through to what I would do if it had shown otherwise.

Just as I was completing my round of the trap—I was perhaps not fifteen or twenty feet from the *Caravella*—I did spot something. There on the bottom I saw the small white shape of an outboard propeller, and it could only have been the one my grandfather and I had taken from the summer boarders, fallen from the dory when it overturned. I maneuvered to just above it, and then I tread water and breathed heavily in and out, pumping myself full of air, keeping in a last breath and then going down after the propeller. It was a deep dive, and I had to pop my ears as I descended, blowing air all the way. I was already out of breath when I reached the cold bottom. The pressure squeezed me, but I managed to swipe at the propeller and grab it. Then I turned and looked back up at the surface. It was impossible. It lay above me like the curve of the sky itself. I had come too far. I started to kick and to pull with my free hand, and each kick seemed to bring the surface only inches closer. I kept up a steady kick, swallowing against my urge to breathe, watching the veil of light above me get closer and closer until finally I burst through it, my timing off just enough for me to take in a great mouthful of seawater.

I gagged and coughed and thrashed my way over to the dory and pitched the propeller and my goggles in over the side. I could only hang there while I fought for breath, and when I could finally pull myself into the boat, I just lay on the floorboards and coughed until I gagged, and then some of the seawater came up. I retched for a long time and shivered in the chill of that deep water, and I heard myself wailing in my own ears, a sour, pathetic sound that seemed to come from somewhere else, not me.

16

My memory of those days after the squall is uneven. I am not sure how many days passed, or if what I remember happening in one day really happened across the span of a week. I know that the house would slowly fill up with people each day—*Pico* ladies from up the street and men from the wharf or the Cold Storage, and the women would gather in the parlor with my great aunt and burn incense and say rosaries and novenas and dab at their eyes with their hand-kerchiefs. The men would sit at the table with Uncle Paddy and drink ale and Fleischman's. They would intone their different ideas of what must have happened, speaking quietly to one another, their cigarette and pipe smoke hanging like sea-vapors over the oilcloth.

Sheika Nunes was with us daily from early mornings to late nights, saying prayers with my aunt, leaving often to go up to the church and light rows of tall votive candles in front of the altar of Saint Peter, patron of Fishermen. She stayed with Great Aunt Theophila during the whole vigil of waiting for the official report from the coastguard. After the first day and night there was only the hope that John Joseph's body might turn up, but it did not.

I also remember hating my great aunt, for she had willed John Joseph away just as she had forced out my mother and Carmine. But when I strode into the parlor to tell her this—to hurt her as best I could, I walked right in on Madeleine Sylvia.

I stopped short and my breath caught in my throat. I realized I had never seen her before in any place other than her yard. I had never been this close to her. She stood facing Great Aunt Theophila. She was even shorter than she looked from a distance, and her eyes were black —like little marbles set into her coppery face. I was near enough to her to see the line of dark hair on her upper lip. She frightened me, and I stepped back, but the two women had locked gazes and paid me no mind. My aunt sat in the purple wing chair, her face rigid and without expression. Madeleine held a huge bowl of rice pudding in her chunky arms. "It has to be settled, Hettie," she was saying, "but not during a time of such a big loss for you. When this grief is over. You know it's only right. I am out money. Something has to be done. That's why Arthur Enos and those papers. But I want you to know that I am not one to kick a person when she's down. That's the way I am. So that's why I came and brought this. We can talk about that other business some other time."

My great aunt did not move, and that is when Madeleine suddenly noticed me standing off to her side. She looked at my aunt and then at me. "Here, boy," she said. She passed me the bowl of pudding, rubbed her hands on the front of her apron and walked out. Great Aunt Theophila looked over at me. The parlor light caught in her spectacles like tiny stars. She made a small movement then. Her hand, crooked around her rosary beads, rose from her lap. I thought she was going to say something, but then she just let the hand drop again. I was struck with an idea that I hadn't thought of before. She suffered like I did. And then it shook me to see that her sorrow was even deeper than my own.

I put the bowl of pudding on the table, but later Great Aunt Theophila came out and poured it all into the toilet and flushed it. Then she opened the back door and dropped the bowl ceremoniously on the cement walk, where it shattered into about a dozen large pieces.

I didn't know if I should sweep the pieces of bowl up or not. But Sheika Nunes told me to sweep them up and put them in a paper bag. Sheika was busier than I had ever seen her. She took care of our house as well as her own. She fed us and our houseful of mourners. She brought us all fishcakes, balls of flipper dough, linguica sandwiches. She shooed the men away when the hour grew late and the liquor bottles had been deeply tapped. She nagged me to pray.

But I wouldn't pray. I cursed God, like in the Bible when Job was told to curse Him and die. I remember sleeping one night in one of the coal bins. I don't know why I ended up there, but that fitful night seemed like the whole summer for me, dust in my teeth, hard angles bruising my flesh.

When we were sure John Joseph was not coming back, I went down to the beach on a morning's low tide and worked on his dory. I tidied it, cleaned it, cleaned it again, hauled up the sail and made sure that it was dry, checked all the battens and batten pockets, rubbed the cleats and hardware with oil and steel wool, walked the length of mooring line and checked the buoy, the chain, the buried mooring itself. It was warm on the sandbar. There was no breeze yet, and the tide still rolled a hundred yards or so out beyond me, at its far ebb. I sat on the gunwale of the boat. I would have to take care of it all the time now.

I sat there for a long time. The tide had inched up around the dory's bottom and was almost ready to float her, when I looked up the beach and saw a figure sitting on the seawall eating something. It was Lew. I slid off the gunwale and walked up among the rills and pebbles. He waved when I was halfway to him, but I didn't respond until I reached him. "Lew," I said.

He chewed delicately, turned his head aside and spit a small seed. "Grapes," he said. "Big and sweet, from your friend Mr. Pereirra." He held a rumpled brown paper bag out to me. I did not feel like eating, but I tore a small cluster off and sat in the sand. Lew continued to eat grapes, one by one, with a look of deep concentration on his face. He chewed carefully, turning and spitting. "I don't know anything about your kind of grief," he said after a while. "I've been lucky so far, I guess. You are ahead of me on that one, my friend. I miss him, though."

"I know."

"You cry much?"

"Yep. Nothing left in me. I hurt from it."

He spit a seed, took another grape. I took one too, chewed, spit, just as he did. "We won't ever forget him, will we?"

"That doesn't help," I said.

"No. I'm not trying to help. I'm just thinking out loud."

"I don't know what's going to happen now. This wasn't right."

"It doesn't seem so."

I told Lew about our meetings up in the woodhouse, about how we had finally put the ancestor together. I told how John Joseph had drunk wine and worked out his tale.

"Yes," said Lew, "I can see it."

"It was really important to him."

"It *was*," said Lew. "But he was telling you something about his own life, too."

"Yes," I said. "I figured that out. You couldn't tell what part was him and what wasn't—except for the stuff from books."

"He lived by his own rules, I guess," said Lew

I took another grape. "I should have been with him," I said. "I was supposed to meet him and sail with him, and I fell asleep, and I missed

him. If I had been there, we would have made it through that squall.
We've done it before."

Lew bristled. "Don't be foolish, Joachim. You are puffing yourself
up at your grandfather's expense. I won't hear it." His dark eyes shifted
and pinned me. "Don't you think that John Joseph could sail his little
dory without your help? He was born on a damned island. He saw
more storms than you could ever know about. Who do you think you
are? He didn't get in trouble because *you* weren't there."

I couldn't answer him.

"Look, Joachim," he said, shifting his sharp eyes to a grape in his
fingers, inspecting it, pitching it away in irritation. "Do something useful with your grief. If you had been with him, you wouldn't have come
back either. You think the old man would have liked that? You are the
last one. If you had gone, there'd be nobody. The end of the line."

He softened, reached over and slapped me on the shoulder, a peace
offering, but I still couldn't look at him straight on. I don't know where
we would have gone from there if Roger hadn't shown up with his
sketch pad and a shoulder bag. He sat down and talked a bit and then
began sketching the dory. He used soft sticks of color which he pulled
from his bag, smudging colors together with the side of his thumb.
Lew and I watched in silence until he finished. Then the two of them
took me over to Vinny Spaghetti's Diner, where we sat for a long time
and drank Coke from white paper cones.

Later that night, after Sheika had driven the men from the drinking
table, and after my great aunt joined Uncle Paddy in the big iron bed,
I lay awake in my room. I could hear the fogbell on Long Point clang-
ing at the far edge of hearing, and closer there was a noise like breath
rising and falling, a heavy snore from the room across the house. And
there was the house itself, too, settling, its timbers groaning and whis-
pering. Every once in a while I would startle to the sound of voices out
on the sidewalk, summer people talking loudly, often merry, sometimes in odd tones of anger or despair.

Finally, it was too much for me, lying there, so I rose and dressed
and tiptoed through the rooms to the back door and sneaked outside.
There was no sky. A heavy overcast had come in with the tide, and the
wetness of the night hung over everything like a dark gauze. In the
yard now, I could hear the long sounds of the foghorns, and the siren
at Wood End. I walked slowly to the stairs of the woodhouse and began

to climb. The ducks did not rouse. I opened the door and slipped into the room.

I don't know what I expected to see. The blanket lay where I had left it, beneath the window, and the trunks were arranged in the same way —of course, nothing had been moved or touched. Even John Joseph's empty quart bottle sat on the floor by the chimney, in a glimmer of streetlight. I could still smell tobacco, and something more, something of his presence. I bent and picked up the blanket, covered the window, and lit the running light. The absence of his shadow in the chimney nook was almost more than I could stand.

I sat there with my arms around my knees and went over the ancestor's story in my mind. What had he left me? Some details to complete. The final traitors, the last battle. It would be here, of course. The battle would take place in our harbor. Not the big hulks in Sabatini or Stevenson but caravels, the *Five Wounds of Christ* pursued by the traitors on the *Silent Heaven*, small, dark, and sleek. They would sail on a broad reach for our spit of land, whitecaps rising on the open sea, an end coming soon to everything.

I was shaky. It was not hard to feel the wind cutting across our deck, not hard to see the ship that shadowed us, still hull-down, but with her sails peeking over the horizon, relentless. I tried imagine myself the ancestor in this tale, but I found that I was not the old captain. I simply seemed to stand to one side and watch him, like in a movie. Over the port bow we raised the outer arm of our peninsula, and we held our course until we were close enough to make out the long sand hills on the shore, and then the shore began to break away from us to the west. The ancestor shouted orders down to the tiller, and we came west and trimmed sail, moving through the fierce tide and race of white water that ran to our advantage as we rounded the first point of land. Now a man hurled a weighted shot and took soundings, for the caravel would be making its way through the great sandbars that stood far off shore.

The Captain ran from rail to rail watching his crew and officers. He shouted orders. He called adjustments in course. He kept a track on the *Ceo Silencio*, which dogged our course and closed on us ever so slowly.

We came south, then east, and we passed the tip of Long Point, narrow and bare and lapped by water as colorless as kerosene. Here we came about sharply and pulled inside the harbor. The hills that would be our town gleamed empty. We found deep water and lay to.

I knew that this was going all right so far, but all this was easy, and John Joseph had left me the momentum of the chase. But now there was nowhere to run, for I had brought the first ship into the harbor and the shadowing caravel would soon be upon it. It was time to get ready for the skirmish.

The crew armed itself with crossbows and grapples and short swords, and some of the men put on iron breastplates and helmets. I knew this was correct, but I could not see everything clearly. I went through the arming several times, and when it was as right as it could be, the ancestor ordered the guns made ready for firing, and men primed them and loaded stone shot down the barrels.

When the old captain had made all of the preparations for battle, he called to his priest, "A blessing!" And Fray Costa made the sign of the cross over himself, and then over the crew of the ship. "For God's will and the Glory of the Church," he cried, and the men took it up as a battle cry: *God's will and the Glory of the Church!*

Then we could see the mast tops of the *Ceo Silencio* on the other side of the low dunes as she paralleled the back of the point. Carvalho ordered his sails close-hauled now and started east, to maneuver outboard of the other ship and try to force it aground on the bar at the tip of the point. If we could ground her, then we could pick her to pieces with cannon shot. If we failed in forcing her up on the bar, we would come close aboard with grapples, fire a charge into her rigging, and put all hands over the side and onto her decks.

We would come about, hard into the wind, just as the traitors' ship came rounding the finger of sand and made for the harbor. Then we lined up on her course, keeping her inboard and ready to squeeze shoreward with the hope of running her up on the bar, but the *Ceo Silencio* did not come about, and she sailed past us and let loose a round of shot from her guns. This was a wasted volley, for by the time they fired, we had cruised to the edge of their range, and though some of the stone flew through our mizzen, most went wide and short, and one even bounced ineffectively off the hard planks of our side.

We could see disarray on her decks. Captain Carvalho ordered us around, and we closed on her once more, and before the mutineers could get wind enough to pull away, one of our men slung over a grapple, which caught fast on the other ship's rail. Then as our hulls began to come together and the crew on our decks began hurling more grapples, we let loose with a charge close aboard that brought her rigging down in splinters and tatters and sent several of her men sprawling across the deck. The air was full of fire and sulphur, and the shattering noise of our guns raised a shout from our crew. With cries of "God's will and the Glory of the Church!" the first wave of pikemen went over to the decks of the *Ceo Silencio.*

Then I stalled. I stared into the distance in front of me, and I could see the confusion of the battle, but there was something more to be done than just to play it out. I had to do more than crib from the old pirate stories. I looked over at the shadow where John Joseph had sat with his wine, telling his tale, and when I did not see him there I was scoured again with surprise. I had begun to see this was a part of the way this grief would operate for me—the recurring surprise at his absence.

But he had set something up, something obvious, and I had to work toward it. I slipped from sorrow back into the images.

Men swarmed on the decks of the two ships and swords clashed. Captain Carvalho and Matta and Sylvester Escolar stood apart, their backs against the poop, each armed with a crossbow. They watched the skirmish and shouted orders. But they also were watching for the traitors—the ones who had been left among our crew, the crew of the *Cinco Ferridas,* looking for what damage they might do. Our men were fierce fighters, all tough islanders and led by *Picos,* and they had carried the skirmish to the decks of the other ship, but two of the mutineers from the *Ceo Silencio* used the battle as cover and slipped over the side and onto our main deck. One of them made straight for the hatch and ducked below. Sylvester Escolar shouted after him and ran for the hatch, and Matta fired his dart into the leg of the other man, who fell to the deck crying for a confessor.

Fray Costa had been running madly over the decks, a sword in his hand, ministering to the wounded, regardless of whose side they were on, disregarding his own safety. He looked like a lizard or a strange shorebird in his priest's cowl, and he ran now to this stricken man who was bleeding in gushes from his leg wound. "Leave him!" shouted Captain Carvalho. "Get to shelter!" But the priest, splashed in blood, tied the wound and said a prayer. Suddenly, in the middle of all the fighting there came an enormous roar, and the decks rumbled and buckled beneath us, as though the mutineers had somehow mustered another volley from their guns and fired into our waterline. Smoke and flame blew up through the midships hatchcovers, and then we knew that the man who had slipped below had reached our powder.

Sylvester Escolar staggered from the fiery hole of one of the hatches, his face half gone, his jerkin torn from his body. He spun and dropped to the deck. Fire now sprang up on our ship, and some of the men unfastened their breastplates and jumped into the sea.

But Captain Carvalho saw what must be done. He and Matta lay down their crossbows and drew their swords and made for the lines that held us grappled to the other ship. If we stayed hooked together, both ships would perish, but if we could cut the *Cinco Ferridas* loose and turn our men to fighting the fire, we might save ourselves. Fire had spread to other ship, too, and even while some men continued fighting, others began to work with buckets, heaving water on the flames. But panic was spreading. By now, Fray Costa, who had finished prayers over the body of Sylvester Escolar, was running in circles on the deck, waving his sword and yelling, *"Agnus Dei, miserere nobis!"* He came to Matta, wild-eyed, and pushed him back from cutting loose one of the grapnels. "It's no use," he screamed. "It's no use. We will all perish!"

"Get away, you fool," Matta said, and made for the line again, and Captain Carvalho began to shout, "Back aboard, back aboard," calling to our party of skirmishers on the mutineers' decks, which were becoming more swept by the flames.

Some of the men jumped back aboard and began to turn-to on the fire, while others started to hack at the grapnel lines, seeing clearly that that was how to save the ship. But Fray Costa once again jumped in front of Matta and interfered with his work on the hawser. "No!" he screamed. "We will perish, all of us. We *must* all perish for the greater good of the Church. Martyrs, all of us!"

"You've lost your senses," Matta screamed back at him. "Let me at this line and we'll save ourselves yet."

"Never," cried the priest, "in the name of Christ!"

The timbers of the *Ceo Silencio* gave up a loud groan, and a portion of her weather deck collapsed into a bed of flames, carrying wounded and dead men with it. The flames rose again, along with the greasy, sputtering smoke from the burning of flesh, and new screams came to us as the last of the boarding party scrambled aboard the *Five Wounds* and began cutting us loose. Matta shoved Fray Costa to the deck and hacked at his line, but by now casting off the grapnels would not be enough. The mutineers' ship leaned heavily into us, her remaining rigging sagging over and tangling with ours. We were joined anew. "Aloft!" yelled Lopes. "Aloft for your lives!" But Captain Carvalho intervened. "No, we haven't time. Chop away the masts!" he cried. Once again, Fray Costa threw himself in the way. "It's not God's will that we survive!"

The ancestor strode up to him, seeing the truth finally. "It was *you*," he said. "*You* are the engineer of all this treachery."

"You are misguided, Francisco. Kneel and repent while there is still time."

But Captain Carvalho went on. "Only a priest would have had so much purchase among my men. I never would have believed it of you. You are a minion of that filthy Pope."

"He is the Vicar of Christ!"

"He would give all the Portuguese lands to the Spanish. He has given them my great enterprise. And it was *you* who intercepted my messages from Simoes. *You* passed my charts and logs to Columbus!"

"To our Holy Mother the Church," he said. "And She has the power to give them to whom She will." A strange look came into his eyes, and he moaned, "*Mea maxima culpa*," and struck the ancestor a blow to the face with the edge of his sword. It was a wild, awkward blow, but it was swift and unexpected. Captain Carvalho nearly sidestepped it, but it caught him hard and brought him to the deck. Fray Costa dropped to his knees and cradled the captain's head. It did not look as though the priest could have struck with much force, but the captain's face was laid open to the deep bone, and dark blood was spattering into puddles around him. "Repent," said the priest. "You are dying. Repent while you still can. Remember that I know all about you. You have much to repent."

The captain groaned something that no one could understand.

"We will none of us return," said the priest. "The ships are doomed, as they were from the beginning. This enterprise will vanish. It is the will of the Church. Pray with me."

I heard Captain Carvalho gurgle something, some word, and then the stiletto flashed from his sleeve and rose to Fray Costa's throat.

But the ancestor was finished. The knife grazed the old priest's neck without any force, and our captain fell dead.

There was a great crash then as one of the masts cracked and tumbled to the deck. It had crashed the wrong way and did not disentangle with the mutineers' rigging, and that ship now was consumed with fire. The fire had spread to our own sails and to our poop, and our men ran at the fires and tried to clear the debris by throwing whatever they could over the side. But there would be no saving the ships now, no saving the great Portuguese enterprise, no saving any history of the great Captain Francisco Carvalho.

There were more shouts and screams, and then an interruption, some commotion that did not come from this world inside my head, but from down in the street.

Headlights, a car door and voices, footsteps. At first I thought, It's me, I've been caught up here—or they're looking for me because I wasn't in my bed, and then I heard a voice rise up in the space where our little walk squeezed between the main house and the woodhouse. It was clear, distinct, familiar.

I jumped to my feet and ran to the door, reached out too far in my excitement and stepped on the rotten part of the landing. I felt the whole stairway buckle beneath me. I tried to spin, jump back toward the doorway, but it was too late, for in another fraction of a second the old wood gave way completely, and I fell through the planks of the landing.

17

I was dead.

I understood this without having to think. I remembered a pain stabbing up my leg when I hit the woodpile, and then something heavy struck me in the head. Sparks flew out from my eyes, and I entered a long silence. I knew then that I had passed over.

Some part of me rose and surveyed where I was. It seemed to be a long anteroom to the Other Side, a place that had been built out of light and geometry and that resembled nothing in our world, except perhaps ice. It was as though that ice had been laid out in planes as long as the sky, and some purplish celestial light had come to dwell in it. There was no distance or proportion. There was no time, either. I was aware of watching for what could have been either minutes or years before I realized that I still had some kind of a body. I moved my hand up in front of me, and the rest of me followed it, and as I looked down at myself, I saw the same purple light surrounding me in soft, moving lines.

Now all of this was heresy, or at least contrary to Canon as I had received it from Father Santos and Sheika Nunes. No orthodox view of the afterlife offered such a vision. I should have been scared, maybe, but I wasn't. I felt giddy and smug. The radiant lines of violet light wiggled around me. Somewhere near me—I could sense this in the way that in the living world I could sense heat or cold—saints were present. And so too were the resolutions to all the mysteries.

I decided that I would first seek my name saint here, and finally confront him about all the troubles of this summer. I would accuse him as the author of my grief. While I thought this, the space around me changed, and I understood that it was the edge of my thought that altered the vaults and the walls. Now shapes and shadows appeared in the near distance. These were forms that could have been anything, but I gestured toward one of them, and as before, my body followed my gesture. I couldn't tell how far I traveled, or for how long, but I sensed my motion. It was like moving toward a horizon on the water.

Other senses came to me, earthly senses, dulled or heightened—I could not tell which—but I smelled something familiar now. There were several smells. It took me a while to begin to sort them out, but after a time I recognized beeswax and incense. They seemed to fit here. I saw my progress change now, and I drifted toward one of the figures —a halo of light surrounding a shadow of light—and I recognized another smell in the ether, faint and familiar. It was perfume.

The figure before me moved, and I opened my mouth to speak. "Ah," I said. "Ah ba."

"What?"

"Bah."

"What are you, foolish? You can talk better than that!"

It was the voice that I had heard down in the walk, the voice I had run to when I fell through the woodhouse landing. I discovered that my eyes were closed, and so with considerable effort I opened them. I was lying on my back in my bed, a candle burning on my dresser, incense rising from a smoldering cone that had been set on the mermaid ashtray. Behind the ashtray a new, crisp icon card of Saint Joachim the Patriarch lay propped against a water glass. The saint stared out at me from behind his moony eyelids.

My mother sat in the chair beside me.

My head throbbed, and little sparks still moved behind my eyes. I tried to speak again, but all that came out was "Bah," and then I realized that I had crossed over to the Other Side and come back, just as Domingo the Beach Cleaner had, and now, just like him, I would never be able to communicate what I saw.

My mother scowled at me and stood up. "Stop acting foolish and talk the way you're supposed to!"

"Buh . . . Whu . . . What happened to me?"

"You cracked your head. You were fooling around on those damn woodhouse stairs."

"Oh," I said. "Yes."

She had on a strange new dress, deep blue, with flowers and birds printed all over it, and she wore earrings that were made of tiny colored shells. My head rocked. "You came back?"

"I left when I heard the news about Papa."

"Oh." Hearing this settled me deeper into the bed.

"They wanted to take you up to the hospital, but Uncle Paddy wouldn't let them. He told them that people only went there to die.

"You were out like a light. Doctor Hermann said to make sure somebody was with you for when you came to."

"Did I die?"

"What? You had a concussion."

"My head hurts."

"So I would think. You were knocked out all day yesterday and today. Doctor Hermann has been taking care of you."

"Where's Carmine?"

"He's back in Florida. He's with his brother-in-law there."

"You going back?"

"Nope. Snakes and mosquitoes. You can have them."

"Is he coming back?"

"I'll think about that. You feel good enough for a present? I'm supposed to call Dr. Hermann now."

"What's the present?"

"I brought it all the way back on the bus for you." She stooped to the floor and picked up a long cardboard box with handles on it and perforations along its top. She set it on the bed so that I could look into it when she folded back the top. A pair of beady eyes looked back at me, and then the thing opened its mouth and hissed.

"An alligator!"

"Just like Carmine said, they have them on farms down there. He picked this one out for you."

"Really?"

"Yep. This one is just a baby. Maybe he can live with the ducks."

"An alligator," I said.

"Yeah," said my mother. "What do you want to call him?"

"Alligator," I said.

"Just Alligator?"

"Alligator . . ." And then the weariness of trying to speak, the weariness of the whole strange summer, rose up like a wave, and I fell back into a long, fitful sleep.

Days passed. Things were different. I had not died, and my mother was back, and John Joseph had left us forever. I remember light flattening over the front street, the green of the hedges trembling and then lying quietly in the shortening trace of the season. The gardens showed their last blooms, and some kind of settling came over the town, as if the whole world had something to do with the fortunes of our family.

My mother seemed the most changed. Wherever she walked, the space around her seemed to crack and change, too. She had been somewhere in the large world, and it showed in her walk and bearing. She had ridden buses all the way to Florida and back, waiting in terminals full of strangers, eating in cafes full of hazards, traveling through towns and cities whose names were only words on a map to us—if we had ever heard of them at all—and nobody we knew had ever done anything like that, not even Captain Raul Mendes. The *Pico* women gave her room. And my mother took it.

She also had taken whatever I told her about my alligator's name in a very literal way, for she had built a temporary cage for him, which she made out of a fishbox from the Cold Storage, covered with window screen, and on the cage she had fixed a sign with the creature's name: *Alligator Alligator.*

Great Aunt Theophila did not like Alligator Alligator. "He reminds me of the devil, that damn thing," she would mutter when I fed him captured flies or bits of raw fish, but my mother would say, "Oh, he's only a harmless little guy." My great aunt would just raise her eyebrows and shake her head and walk out into the parlor. That was it. And that was part of the difference, part of the change that had come to our household. The bickering was gone. It was as though some new bargain had been struck between the two women.

My mother slowly took over the house from Sheika Nunes. She didn't go after the cleaning and cooking like Sheika did, but our home settled into a kind of order. My mother kept a full brew of tea going in the big pot, and she fried or baked or boiled all the varieties of fish that came to us from Johnny Squash and Captain Raul. She took charge of other matters, too.

She sat at the kitchen table for most of a day studying papers and documents. Some had to do with the serious complaints from Madeleine Sylvia and others had to do with John Joseph. She collected everything she could find from drawers, boxes, big envelopes tied with ribbons. Sheika sat with her for a while and talked about her own Manny's passing and all the papers that were involved. But later, after Sheika left, she called to my Uncle Paddy. "What's this all about?" she asked him. "What are these?"

Paddy rubbed his nose. "Old papers," he said. "What's that? A chart?"
I looked over at the table. She had found the oiled packet from the trunk. John Joseph must have stuck it in with the rest of his things in the back room. "It's some old charts of the harbor and the town," I said, even though no one asked me. "*Avo* showed them to me. He had them in the woodhouse." I left out everything about our meetings upstairs in that little building.

"Well, this is different," my mother said.
"Like how," said Paddy.
I sat down and slid a chair next to them.
"Here's the wharf, the way I see it," said my mother. "And see the Cold Storage?"
"What you are looking at there is a blacksmith shop and over here a coopery. They made their own barrels in those days," said my great uncle.
"And look," said my mother. "Here's our house. And the woodhouse and the outhouse. But what's this? It says 'barn.'"
"Could be," said my great uncle. "Horses in those days."
"But look. That means the yard is bigger. See? See the line for Madeleine's property?"
"That little black dot there," said Paddy, "That'd be the corner marker."
"A stone," I said.
"What do you know about it?" my mother said.
"Well," I said, "nothing really, except that I know *Avo* talked about the old folks leaving stones to claim land. He told me in a story, I mean."
"What do you think?" my mother asked Paddy.
"Well, you could call that Arthur Enos guy. Get somebody to survey."
"Who'd pay for *that*? What if this is all wrong?"
"Then have a look is what I say."

So they did. Or *I* did. There was no way that Madeleine Sylvia was going to let us go looking around her yard for something, so we got Roger to come downstairs and help us figure exactly where the stone would be. He looked at the chart for a while and drew some things on his pad, and then he went out into the yard. He held up a ruler, sighted along it, looked at the chart again, sketched some more. "Come here, Josie," he said, finally. I sat next to him, about halfway up his stairs. "See here? Now look. Right over by that lilac tree. Right behind it, maybe."

It was Uncle Paddy who chose me to go. "Smallest man always goes on patrol," he said. I was nearly as tall as he was, but I was much skinnier.

"My bandage," I said. "It's white. It'll show up at night."

"Watch cap," said Paddy.

"And my foot." My ankle still was sore from the fall.

"Don't whine," my mother said.

That night, at around midnight, Roger and Lew sat on their stairs keeping watch for me. Our house and yard were dark. I carried a small spade and a long steel spike. I crawled on my belly across Madeleine Sylvia's yard and reached the lilac tree. I looked back over at our house. Nothing but shadows. I looked up at Madeleine's. A light on in one window, the one below the broken dormer, now boarded up. I stuck the spike into the soft ground. It hit something, but I pushed harder and it went in. I moved it a few inches and pushed it in again. Nothing. I repeated this about a dozen times. My head itched from the black wool watch cap that I had pulled over my ears. Mosquitoes whined around me. I got to my knees and began working with the spade. It was hard to dig without leverage. I worked at a little hole and then the shovel's blade scraped against something. I dug a bit more and put my hands in the hole. Definitely stone. I felt around the edge, the top corner. I covered the hole and crawled back to our yard.

"The commando," said Lew. He talked in a normal voice now that it was over.

"*Treasure Island*," I said.

The outdoor light flicked on. My great uncle stood at the door. He touched the side of his nose. "Joachim Carvalho," he said, "what are you doing outside at this hour? Come right in here to bed!"

"We are not taking *Lisbon* money," declared my Great Aunt Theophila. This was days later. Ernestina and Sheika Nunes sat with her in the parlor. My mother was explaining the deal.

"Yes, we are," said my mother. There was no edge in her voice. This wasn't an argument. She was just explaining the deal. "First, no more bedsprings on the roof. Then we fix the woodhouse stairs and the fence. The ducks get to stay. We paint the outhouse nice. For her part, she leases the land back from us for as long as she wants."

"She pays you rent for it?" said Ernestina smiling.

"Yep," said my mother. "Every year. We got Arthur Enos to do up a paper. It's not a lot of money, but we'll use it to keep the place up. It works out."

"I don't trust the *Lisbons*," said my great aunt.

"It's all on a paper," my mother said.

Later that day I caught up with my mother by the duckpen. She was smoking a Chesterfield, looking off into Madeleine's yard. "I wonder why *Avo* never said anything about that land boundary," I said.

"He probably never cared one way or another. It probably never even hit him. He didn't think like that. He had his own way of thinking."

"A lot of what happened this summer was my doing, you know. I'm the one who stole Carmine's jacket so he'd have to come back for it."

She turned and looked me up and down. "You're foolish," she said. And then, "I don't think I would have gone away if Uncle Paddy didn't get sick the way he did. It scared me. That's what tipped it for me. I wanted to get out and do something. Somebody's got to take over here when he goes, you know. I'm going to work for Van Horten next summer. It's all settled. I talked to Fanny Neves about it."

She was in a talkative mood, so I took a chance. "Are you ever going to tell me about my father?"

"Yes," she said. "Someday."

She was quiet for a while and then she stared off very far into Madeleine's garden. When she turned to me again it was as though she had just noticed me standing there. "You know," she said, "one of your grandfather's oars is stuck up against the West End breakwater."

She turned out to be right about this. Dr. Hermann had just pulled my stitches out, and my ankle was feeling much better, so I laced up my high-top sneakers and walked along the bricks all the way to where the driftwood collected at Wood End. There among all the dead boats, the bleached gray driftwood and detritus, was the oar that had been missing from the *Caravella*. I put it over my shoulder and walked it on back to the house.

The oar caused a stir among the men. They kept coming to drink ale in the yard, just as though my grandfather were still there. They would sit and tell stories about him, or just sit and talk. I ached for John Joseph to be back with us, but I watched the men. They were tougher about it. They all worked on the water and they knew that out there anything can happen to anybody. To any one of *them*. But I could tell they missed him. Sometimes in the middle of a story the speaker would stop in mid-sentence at the sound of boots scuffing up to the gate, and everyone would turn, just as I did, just as though it might have been *him* coming back from a long drunk, or from a final prank. But each time it would only be Captain Raul or Petey Flores or one of the others, come with a bag of ale under his arm to join the talk.

The women talked about John Joseph too. The talked in the parlor over pots of tea, turning and turning the question of whether or not he died in a state of grace. All it would have taken, as we all knew, was for John Joseph to say an Act of Contrition in his final moments. So the real question was, was he the kind of man who would do that? Great Aunt Theophila pointed out his stubbornness, how he always did things his own way. Ernestina was neutral, but Sheika Nunes was his advocate. "Did you ever know a time," she would say, "when that man didn't work everything out to his own advantage? He didn't miss a trick, that one. Don't you worry."

In the end it was my great aunt who came up with the final evidence that things had gone right for him. One morning she was out prodding Dilly, Dilly, and Dilly to see which one of them might be sitting on an egg. She found her egg and when she straightened up to turn back to the house, there sat John Joseph and Manny Nunes in the old canvas swing. They were talking and laughing and carrying on with one another, although my great aunt could hear no words. They were both surrounded with that unmistakable blessed nimbus that took on the color of lemons and snow.

Great Aunt Theophila sent me to call Sheika Nunes, and Sheika was overjoyed when I told her that there was finally news about her Manny. She hugged me to her pillowy breasts, and I let myself sink into them until she stiffened and pushed me away. "Joachim Carvalho!" she exclaimed. But she wasn't really mad.

She came to the house right away, and she and my Aunt sat in the parlor and talked about the details of the vision while they waited for Father Santos to show up. He received word later in the day and came to the door toward the end of the afternoon. "Ah, Josie," he said when I let him in, "I heard about your crack on the head. Quick now, tell me— Saint Hippolytus!"

"Pierced by stilettos," I told him. "He was a schoolmaster, and his own students killed him."

"Yes," said Father Santos. "Exactly, exactly." And I led him into the parlor where Sheika and my great aunt sat with their rosaries and a pot of tea. The priest stayed with them for a long, long time and only left when my mother started frying up some whiting fillets, dragging them through beaten egg and dipping them in peppered flour. "Please stay for supper," she said. But Father Santos only looked at her deeply for a moment, some expression of infinite patience or resignation on his tired face. Then he said something to her that I could not quite hear, and he walked softly through the back door.

18

The idea for a final clambake came up one night while the men were sitting in the yard drinking ale and talking. Johnny Squash blew his nose and rubbed his one eye and said, "You know sometimes it's like John Joseph is right here in this yard, and it's like he can hear every damn word we're saying."

"Maybe in a way he is," said Petey Flores.

"Sure," said Captain Raul, who had had many ales. "I guess that's one way to look at it."

"Well, let's throw him a party, then," said Squash.

"And after the party we'll all march up to Juney's and install that oar that Joachim found. We'll stick her up on the wall."

The other men mumbled approval of this plan, although no one ever thought that I might consider the oar mine and that they should ask my opinion about it. But the idea of a party for John Joseph took hold. "After all," said Lew when I told him about it, "there was no real wake."

Great Aunt Theophila objected. "You saw what happened last time," she said. "Now we have all these papers with the *Lisbon*."

"Well," said my mother, "there's nothing in those papers that says we can't have a clambake. Besides, it's for Papa."

That was the end of it. My great aunt said nothing more except for insisting once again that the *Pico* ladies be present.

We started cooking for the clambake at about nine in the morning on that last Saturday of summer. Roger and Lew had already packed up most of their things for their trip back to the city, and they now worked around the yard, setting up chairs and hanging a festoon of old fishnet along the fence and woodhouse. Ernestina had already left us with a bushel of sweet corn from her garden. Now Fanny Neves came by with an enormous bag of onions, which she said had fallen off one of the delivery trucks down at Mister Van Horten's Bluefish Inn, and I was set to quartering them and peeling them and running them through the castiron grinder.

I worked in the kitchen along with my mother and my great aunt, and my great aunt gave me a big crust of bread to hold in my teeth so I wouldn't weep as I worked on the onions. Johnny Squash and Petey Flores would steam the bushels of quahogs later on, but my mother had decided to bake up a mess of stuffed seaclams, and for this we needed pans and pans of onions for the stuffing. We also needed dried bread, and the back room was stacked with long, unopened loaves of it, again all from the Bluefish Inn, having arrived by armloads over the past few days, all supplied by Fanny.

Aunt Theophila and my mother worked side by side. My aunt hummed some old Latin hymn as she chopped celery and green peppers on the scarred board over the sink. A good wind blew up from the beach and brought the thick, sweet smell of ocean right into the house, and the bright day passed on in a generous bustle.

I would say that the party started in earnest at about six o'clock when Petey Flores and Johnny Squash came up the walk, hauling the same kid's red wagon that they had used to cart the old salvaged gauge in. This time it was piled high with cardboard cases of Ballentine's ale. Flores pulled the wagon by its handle while Squash held on in back, steadying the stacks of cans. I had already prepared the tubs and fishboxes with ice, and the quahogs sat in wet bushel baskets by the backroom door, waiting for the steampot.

Neighbors who had not come earlier to help with the preparations now began arriving. The *Pico* ladies from up the street, Magdelena Reis and Lila Roderigues, walked through the gate, and right behind them came Elvio the Shoemaker. He was dressed in a wool cap and checkered shirt, and he wore a black string tie. He lugged with him the chassis of another old radio. Uncle Paddy met him and helped him set it by the shattered one on the ell table. "Can't do a bedspring, you know," Paddy said to him as he handed him a golden can of ale, but Elvio just shrugged and smiled. Sheika Nunes, who had been back and forth between our house and hers all day long, now returned to us dressed in a great flowing pavilion of a gown, which hung loosely about her shoulders and showed just the barest shadow of cleavage. She was still happy about my great aunt's vision. She greeted everyone with broad smiles and loud gossip. Joe Dias showed up and then Captain Raul with another burlap sack of lobsters, and I ran again over to Old Man Coelho's house and got his big lobster cooker and soon Mister Coelho himself came across the street, leaning on his knotty walking stick and squinting at the crowd as though he had just arrived in a foreign land.

Once again the women arranged themselves in a cluster of chairs against the house and the men scattered around the yard sitting, standing, squatting, and leaning. Domingo the Beach Cleaner came up the walk, and Alfie DeCosta and Liliana Mendes, and then I stopped counting as the yard filled up. With Lew's and Roger's help my mother and Johnny Squash managed to get the lobsters and quahogs steaming on the kerosene stove, and by the time everything was ready, the yard was jammed with people. Most of them were *Picos* whom we knew, but there was also a scattering of strangers. These were certainly some of John Joseph's summer boarder friends, for Amalia and Cynthia were among them.

There was too much going on for me to see what registered among the *Pico* ladies when Amalia and Cynthia showed up, but no one moved to show them unwelcome. Uncle Paddy tipped his hat to them and beckoned them toward the table, which was now heaped with steaming seafood. Petey Flores seized a moment to jump up on a chair and raise his ale can in a toast to the memory of John Joseph. "He was beautiful. He was a beautiful man," was all he could manage to say. Great Aunt Theophila and my mother began to cry quietly, but I would not let myself cry in front of all the men. Then Johnny Squash burst through the back-room door carrying an enameled basin full of sweet corn. "Hey, Flores," he yelled, "Get down off that chair, for Christ's sakes and let the people eat!"

There was some laughter then, and I think that if I had had the sense to keep Alligator Alligator locked up in the woodhouse for the night, the party would have flowed along happily from there. But earlier that week I had tried to get him to share the duckpen with Dilly, Dilly, and Dilly, and the result was nearly fatal for the little creature because the ducks did not like him floating in their washtub pond nor watching them with his beady eyes, and they quickly surrounded him and pecked at him with their bills. Alligator Alligator dodged them for a few seconds, but then one of the ducks scored a direct whack on the back of his head, and the three ducks would have pecked him to death if I had not grabbed him out of the pen. My alligator had been knocked senseless. I was about to run him up to Ernestina's house for a potion, when he revived in my hands. After an hour or so he seemed as good as new, hissing and scrambling around on the sidewalk. But I knew I needed to provide him with a better home.

So I took a bit of the duckpen for him by building a little fence of window screen that created an area for him to scuttle around in. I also divided a portion of the washtub pond for him where he could float, separated from the ducks by the sturdy screen. It worked well, and when they all weren't sunning themselves or sleeping, they would entertain each other with protracted face-offs at the dividing screen. The ducks would quack and honk at the alligator, whacking at the screen with their bills, and he would hiss back at them and lash his little tail.

The party must have had them all excited, because they started this ruckus now, and in the general low-pitched din of the eating and drinking and talking, the whole little show might have gone unnoticed. But Amalia stood near one of the tubs of iced ale next to the duckfence, and she began watching the animals. She bent at her waist and peered into the pen, then she exclaimed, "Hey, boy, there's some kind of crocodile in here!" I sensed danger, so I ran to her side.

"It's an alligator from Florida. He belongs to me," I said.

"Well, I'm fond of reptiles," she said. "Let's have a better look at him." And before I could do anything, she stooped and picked up Alligator Alligator by his tail and held him close to her face and studied him. He twisted and looked her right in the eyes with his own stare. Amalia might have been preparing to eat him for all he knew. She tilted her head back and held him up to the wan light, and her floppy straw hat—laced with sprigs of bayberry and a large cattail worn like an Indian feather in the headband—fell from her head. I quickly bent to pick it up. Now I held her hat and she held my alligator, and I offered the hat to her as if in a trade. I did not trust her with my new pet's life.

She brushed me aside, though, and said, "I'll bet you a nickel this is a girl lizard. I certainly don't seen any gear under here," and still holding the poor alligator by his tail, she waded into the middle of the *Pico* ladies saying, "Now which one of you keeps all the illegal animals up on the hill? Let's take a look at this creature—I'd like your opinion."

I caught up with her in anger. I would have my alligator back. The *Pico* ladies gasped and shuffled their chairs out of Amalia's way, and I grabbed her arm to pull her around to me so I could take the alligator from her. I can't testify exactly what happened at that moment, for I was still somewhat behind Amalia and to her right, but as I reconstruct it, she was beside Sheika Nunes, who had bent forward to grab her chair and slide it out of the way, and my tug at Amalia's arm set the alligator tumbling from her fingers and down the loose bodice of Sheika's flowing dress.

A small panic broke out, and the women cleared away from Sheika, who beat at her bosom and shrieked in the old tongue. "*Diabo, Diabo,*" my great aunt cried, and I was frozen in my shoes, for I knew that Alligator Alligator would be crushed, if not by Sheika's hands batting at her dress, then by the sheer abundance of her flesh. I could tell from the way Sheika jumped and twisted that the little creature was thrashing around for his life in there. I knew he wouldn't last long. But I couldn't take the one action that would save him. I didn't have the courage to stick my hand down between her breasts and fish for my alligator.

Squid Dutra, as drunk as he was, understood the predicament and saw what was to be done. He started for Sheika and his intent was clear. My mother, however, cut him off and saved the party from further outrage by quickly plunging her hand into Sheika's dress and pulling out my alligator, who promptly bit her finger. "Son of a bitch," she said. "Here, take this stupid thing," and she thrust him at me.

I pulled him off to the side of the yard and put him in a bucket with a board over it so he would calm down, and then I returned to help pick up the chairs and spilled plates from where all the women had been sitting. My mother and my great aunt hauled Sheika into the house and sat her on the bed and gave her some of Uncle Paddy's blood pressure medicine. Then Sheika came right back outside. "I'm here to mourn John Joseph and celebrate the good news about my Manny," she said, "and I'll be damned if anything's going to stop me. Come here, Joe Dias, and tell me about that white rat again." Joe sidled over to her, and Sheika hung her dimpled arm on him.

The commotion with the alligator must have roused Madeleine Sylvia, because I saw her standing on her back porch looking over into the yard. There was plenty going on, and I don't think she noticed me watching her. What could she have thought about us? What did she see when she looked our way?

"I invited her, you know," my mother said, suddenly standing next to me. "I invited her, but she didn't want to come." I looked over at my great aunt sitting with a plate of food in her lap. Madeleine's smashed bowl still sat in a paper bag in the woodhouse.

"I don't think it would have been a good thing if she did," I said. As if she heard us across the yards and over the noise, she disappeared through the door of her porch.

And then Squash and Flores brought more platters of food from the back room. After a while Jaime Costa got out his old guitar and sang a round of *fados*. The singing went on for a long while before winding down, and then some of the men drifted together in a circle and began telling stories. I squeezed over by them and sat on the ground by the collapsed woodhouse stairs that my mother had contracted Louis Avila and Joe Dias to rebuild. There was no moon, but the stars, in their familiar patterns, shone brightly. The heaven that they hung in was as silent to me as ever, but now it made no difference. Against this silence the men's voices rumbled away in their stories of wrecks and rescues, the great days of fishing, the shoals of cod. Already Freddie Pessoa was telling about how lightning blew the bedspring right off the roof of Paddy Dunne's house and started a fire in Madeleine Sylvia's attic. And you had to account for the fact that Ernestina the Shoemaker's Wife just might have fixed Madeleine with the evil eye, because not a damn thing happened to *Paddy's* house. Beneath Freddie's voice insects chirred off in the night, and the ducks, calm now, marched in a circle in their pen and quacked softly.

There was still sorrow in the air. There was no way to touch it. And there was the barest hint of the passing season in the harbor breeze that washed the yard. I thought of John Joseph's dory. My dory. I would have to talk Squash and Flores into helping me haul it out in a few weeks. We would tip it over in the little field above the Cold Storage seawall, and I would throw a canvas tarp over its bottom for the winter. I would gather the gear and furl the sail and store everything in the woodhouse. And I would keep the gonfalons, the insignia of Carvalho the Navigator, the narrative trappings of respectability. I thought about how John Joseph had fastened his whole life to the sinuous truths of his stories, and how he believed such truths would save us. And as I gazed around the yard, I knew that someday that's how I would look on all this, on Sheika and my Great Aunt Theophila and Johnny Squash and all the rest of us gathered here. And then it was not so much of a reach to see that this might be just the sort of peculiar and omen-filled night on which a certain captain bearing our last name could have left his safe harbor on Pico, the green jewel of the Azores, and sailed obscurely, but with great ambition, to this strange New World.

I wrote *Leaving Pico* out of a deep love I have for the town that I grew up in, love for the natural beauty of the town and for its people. Beyond that, I have always been haunted by the idea of a way of life and a generation of people passing from the earth forever. When I was young, Portuguese was spoken routinely in our homes, and the old ones lived with us, holding with them the old tales and the old ways. The rest of the country seemed to bustle through the early Cold War, but isolated at the end of our long cape, we lived in another century. The houses were filled with objects that are no longer made or no longer exist: parlor coal furnaces, kerosene cook stoves, iceboxes that actually used ice, flatirons that were heated atop the stove. The most noble and successful profession was fishing in the waters of the North Atlantic. Our men bragged and swaggered but submitted to a grim sense of fate. Our women prayed and worked and held their homes together with a variety of strengths. I knew that much had been written about my town, but nothing, to my knowledge, had been written from this rich heart of it that I—and the others like me—knew so completely. And so the book grew from all of that, but mostly it grew from the specific and singular lives of the characters of that old world. I would save them all forever if I could, but of course I can't. That is why I wrote this story.